MW00654455

PRAISE FOR *FLY, BUTTERFLY*

"Annicken R. Day has a gift for transforming bureaucracies into businesses that buzz with creativity and joy. With her debut novel, she shows that she also has a knack for crafting stories about transforming ourselves."

—**Adam Grant,** *New York Times* bestselling author of *Originals* and *Give and Take,* host of the TED podcast *WorkLife with Adam Grant*

"*Fly, Butterfly* is a page turner that draws you in and makes you nod furiously, laugh deeply, and then sob with empathy. This is a powerful novel that has the energy to inspire change."

—**Amy Brann,** author of *Engaged, Make Your Brain Work,* and *Neuroscience for Coaches*

"This is a beautiful story about life, work, love and what it means to still be human in our modern working culture. If you are a woman, you should read this book. If you are a man, you should read this book. And if you've ever aspired to be happy and free, you should definitely read this book!"

—**Meghan Fitzpatrick**, Marketing Manager

"An inspiring read about personal and professional transformation and the impact happiness really has on life—and business. To all men: You should read this book too!"

—**Thomas Erikson**, CEO, lecturer, writer, and bestselling author of *Surrounded by Idiots*

"This is such an inspiring—and important—story. To me, Maya Williams is the manifestation of what we are starting to see in today's corporate world; being brave enough to lead with heart and care for people is great for business and has the power to transform not only people's lives, but the bottom line as well!"

—**Jason Angelus**, Senior Director, Sales Engineering, Cisco

"Wow, *Fly, Butterfly* took me on an adventure! This is an authentic, bold, romantic, wise, and powerful story, which will speak to people in all walks of life. It's also a must-read for leaders—of both genders—who want to be authentic, love life, and find a way to their true passion and purpose. I believe Maya's story will help and guide so many people on their journey on this earth."

—**Elham Binai**, VP People & Culture, The Adecco Group

"A magical and immersive experience into a journey of transformation, self-awareness, and alignment to living a life of meaning and connection. The heartfelt story of one woman's path and those that she touches as it unfolds is filled with unexpected shifts and turns, just like the flight of the butterfly and just as beautiful and mesmeric to follow."

—**Dawn Brown**, Business Development Director and Coach

Fly, Butterfly

Annicken R. Day

RIVER GROVE
BOOKS

This book is a work of fiction. Names, characters, businesses, organizations, places, events, and incidents are either a product of the author's imagination or are used fictitiously. Any resemblance to actual persons, living or dead, events, or locales is entirely coincidental.

Published by River Grove Books
Austin, TX
www.rivergrovebooks.com

Copyright ©2019 Annicken Roed

All rights reserved.

Thank you for purchasing an authorized edition of this book and for complying with copyright law. No part of this book may be reproduced, stored in a retrieval system, or transmitted by any means, electronic, mechanical, photocopying, recording, or otherwise, without written permission from the copyright holder.

Distributed by River Grove Books

Design and composition by Greenleaf Book Group
Cover design by Greenleaf Book Group
Cover and interior images used under license from
©Shutterstock.com/Lightspring; ©Shutterstock.com/littlenySTOCK;
©Shutterstock.com/Oliver Klimek

Grateful acknowledgment is made for copyright permission to reproduce lyrics from "Bali H'ai."

"Bali Ha'i" by Richard Rodgers & Oscar Hammerstein II. Copyright © 1949 by Richard Rodgers and Oscar Hammerstein. Copyright © Renewed. Williamson Music Owner of Publication and Allied Rights Throughout the World. International Copyright Secured. All Rights Reserved.

Publisher's Cataloging-in-Publication data is available.

Print ISBN: 978-1-63299-212-3

eBook ISBN: 978-1-63299-213-0

First Edition

To my Butterfly Girl

There is freedom waiting for you,
On the breezes of the sky,
And you ask, "What if I fall?"
Oh but my darling,
What if you fly?

—ERIN HANSON

We delight in the beauty of the butterfly,
but rarely admit the changes it has gone
through to achieve that beauty.

—MAYA ANGELOU

THE
BEGINNING

There is nothing in a caterpillar
that tells you that it is going to
be a butterfly.

R. BUCKMINSTER FULLER

LAST CALL

"Last call for Hawaiian Airlines flight 51 to Honolulu! Can passenger Maya Williams please contact gate forty-nine? The gate is about to close."

Shoot! Would I ever learn to not wear high heels in airports? Already late to begin with, I had been detained for an extra security check because of that stupid water bottle in my carry-on. Typical.

"Please, please, please wait for me!" I shouted silently as I ran toward the gate. I had forgotten how big JFK was, especially when in a hurry.

"Twenty more seconds, and we would not have let you on board," the strict-looking woman at the gate said. I was too short of breath to even speak, so I just smiled thankfully, scanned my ticket, and entered the plane.

As I walked through the business class section where passengers were already sipping expensive champagne, I silently cursed TechnoGuard Inc.'s travel policy. Only executives were allowed to fly business class. Since I was just a simple vice president overseeing five hundred salespeople—selling cybersecurity for a billion dollars a year—I was only permitted to fly coach. Or cattle class, as I secretly called it.

I left the calm and luxurious business class section and stepped into a world of crammed seats crowded with families dressed in matching tracksuits, elderly couples in Hawaiian shirts, and shouting children with chocolate-covered faces jumping up and down in their seats.

Eleven hours of this. Sigh.

In my charcoal-colored suit, high heels, and black leather briefcase, I definitely did not fit in. I guessed by the way the other passengers looked at me that they agreed.

A large man, who seemed as though he was about to burst out of his trousers, struggled with getting his oversized bag into the overhead compartment. I tried to be patient and not make a face, but on the inside, I was rolling my eyes. The things I had to endure . . . I only hoped it would all be worth it in the end.

And as if all of it wasn't enough already, when I finally arrived at my seat on the thirty-fourth row, I realized I would be sandwiched between one of those elderly couples in matching Hawaiian shirts. They both had raised eyebrows, as if they were constantly surprised. I nodded toward the seat between them, indicating it was mine.

"Hello, doll. Give me a moment so you can get to your seat," the funny-looking woman said with a heavy Southern accent and smiled cheerfully. I struggled to match her level of enthusiasm.

Just getting up from her seat seemed to require all her strength, and I was near panic, just thinking about sitting between the two of them for the next eleven hours.

"Is there any chance I could have the aisle seat?" I asked carefully. Maybe they would have mercy on me.

The woman looked at her husband, or was he her twin? "Engelbert, hon, let's give this little creature some space," she said and moved into the middle seat, which could hardly contain her large body.

"Thank you," I said and sat down in my seat with a silent sigh.

Maybe there was a God after all.

When the cabin attendant announced that boarding was complete and the plane started taxiing out to the runway, I leaned back in my seat and closed my eyes. I thought about the past day and what must qualify as some of the strangest thirty-six hours of my forty-three years. Little had I known when I woke up yesterday that today I would be on my way to Hawaii, of all places . . .

TECHNOGUARD INC.

I had been even more stressed than normal for the first Monday of the month. It was an important day. My monthly thirty-minute presentation to the executive team was my moment to shine, impress my boss, and demonstrate my accomplishments as a VP of sales.

I had worked all weekend and stayed up until 3:00 a.m. the night before, leaving nothing to chance.

"Fail to prepare, prepare to fail" was my mantra. I had been promoted to vice president of sales only one year earlier. This was no small feat in itself, as I was the *first* female VP in TechnoGuard's twenty-year history.

My ultimate goal, however, was to be promoted to *executive* VP of sales, with a corner office (and business class tickets!) to go with it. But to get there, I knew I would constantly have to prove myself to my boss and the other men on the executive team.

At times, it both frustrated and exhausted me, but I knew that if I wanted to continue my way up the corporate ladder, I didn't have any other choice than to continue playing the game. A game I, by the way, had become so good at that I sometimes forgot I was playing it.

Before I left my apartment on the Upper West Side of Manhattan, I checked my look in the mirror. I had decided to go with a black skirt and white, low-cut blouse.

I was pleased with the way I had learned to master the art of classic corporate with just a dash of sexy. It was an important part of the game. The effect high heels, red lips, and a little bit of skin had on a man's concentration and his willingness to negotiate never ceased to surprise—and amuse—me.

In fact, often my clients, mostly male, didn't realize what had happened until the deal was done and I had their signature on a piece of paper. It felt like a little victory every time. Payback for all the looks, comments, and condescending attitudes I'd had to endure as a woman in business.

Today, however, it wasn't a client but the executive team I needed to dazzle. I had an important message to convey; I didn't particularly look forward to delivering it, but I knew I didn't have a choice.

After I passed my own final inspection, I took the elevator down to the ground floor, said hello to Fred, the doorman, and stepped out on the pavement. It was 6:15 a.m., and the streets of New York were bustling with cars and people. Everyone was in a hurry, and most people seemed to be even more stressed than I was, which said a lot.

It was still dark outside when I got into the back seat of the yellow cab Fred had waved in for me. "Have a beautiful day, Ms. Williams," he said with a bright smile and opened the car door for me. I had no idea how he did it. Rain or shine, he always had a friendly smile and remark for everyone.

"Thanks, you too, Fred," I said and smiled back as I sat down in the back seat of the car. It took me less than five seconds to discover that the cab driver didn't have Fred's good mood. I watched from the back as he honked and screamed at the other drivers, and when there was no one else to swear at, the man swore at himself.

It was just a regular morning in New York City.

I put on my headphones to drown out the cabbie and listened to the morning news while browsing through the emails on my phone. I had one hundred new emails since I had checked earlier that morning.

As I quickly browsed through my inbox to see if any needed an immediate response, one email in particular caught my attention. The subject line read, "Invitation to speak at a Young Professional Women's Network (YPWN) event."

The network's chairwoman, Cynthia Jones, wanted me to come and speak to their members about how to become a successful business-woman in the male-dominated corporate world.

I looked out the window of the cab for a moment. Men and women in similar attire were rushing up and down the streets, their blank faces revealed by the lights of hundreds of cars aggressively making their way through the heavy southbound traffic.

I sighed. What could I possibly tell these young professional women that would help them become successful in today's corporate world?

"Work hard, much harder than the men."

"Learn to adapt—to be treated as less worthy."

"Be smart, but not so smart that you intimidate your male colleagues."

"Look good, but not so good that you attract your male boss."

I felt a bit nauseous. No, I couldn't say that. Someone might get curious and start asking questions. And that was the last thing I wanted and needed right now. I decided to decline.

As soon as the cab arrived at the office building on 57th Street, I hurried in and took the elevator up to the thirty-sixth floor. I always arrived in the office before seven and expected my team to do the same. Never mind that we usually stayed until eight or nine in the evening. If you wanted to get ahead, you needed to put in the hours. The competition was fierce. "Eat or be eaten," that's what my dad had always told me. He had forty years of experience; I only had fifteen, but I knew he was right.

Many members of my team were in the crowded elevator. I nodded to a few of them before I stared down at my phone, making sure no one felt invited to start a conversation. I neither had time nor interest to engage in meaningless chitchat.

Once on the thirty-sixth floor, I noticed that most of my sales staff were already inside their cubicles staring at their screens with their headsets on.

The few people who stood by the coffee machine hurried toward their cubicles when they saw me. I pretended not to notice.

RUTH

Right outside my office, Ruth was already at her desk. She looked like a picture cut out of a glossy magazine that featured smart, professional women in their mid-fifties. With an extraordinarily organized mind to go with her professional look, Ruth was a dream of a personal assistant.

As soon as she saw me, she stood up, followed me into my office, locked the door behind us, and handed me a cup of freshly brewed coffee, like she did every morning.

"Ready to kick some ass?" She smiled.

"Always," I said.

Ruth sat down opposite me, legs folded, with her iPad in her lap, and looked at me over her 1950s-style, black-framed glasses.

"OK, boss. This is what your week will look like."

Little did we know that it wouldn't end up looking anything like that.

I first met Ruth five years ago. It was the day I had been promoted to senior sales manager. She had knocked on my door, introduced herself, and said that she wanted to work for me.

"If you are serious about getting somewhere in this company," she said, "you need someone who knows people, who can give you the

information you need, including the kind you're not supposed to have."
She winked.

I admired her gumption.

Two weeks later, her boss, the director of marketing, was fired. That
is when I realized how well informed Ruth was. She'd known about his
firing long before her boss did.

The day after he left, she started working for me.

I know it's unusual that a personal assistant chooses her boss and
not the other way around, but there was nothing ordinary about Ruth.

"We women need to stick together," she said. I knew the kind of
women she meant: ambitious, determined, and perhaps a bit more
ruthless than most.

. . .

From that day on, my journey up the corporate ladder accelerated.
Skillfully guided and advised by Ruth, I learned where to be, what to
do, and what to say to whom at what time.

Soon I was promoted to sales director, and then senior sales director, and then to my current position as VP of sales.

I wondered how much longer it would be until I could call myself
Executive VP and move into my own corner office on the thirty-seventh floor.

The alarm on my phone beeped. It was 8:45 a.m. and my presentation to the executive team was scheduled for nine.

On my way up to the executive suite, I thought about some of
the nicknames the execs apparently had given me: "Hot Lips," "Ice
Queen," and "Little Miss Lonely Pants."

I knew it was their hurt male egos talking. The majority of them
had once, in one way or another, tried to pick me up or insinuated
that they wouldn't mind getting into those "lonely pants" after a few

too many drinks at one of the dreadful social gatherings I had forced myself to attend.

They had all, of course, been rejected. Not as mercilessly as I would have liked, but considering no one had tried to pick me up twice, I must have made myself pretty clear.

THE
THIRTY-SEVENTH FLOOR

T he thirty-seventh floor was like a different world—with big empty spaces, heavy brown furniture, wooden floors, and two massive brown leather sofas in the middle of the room.

Every office was the size of ten of the cubicles on the thirty-sixth floor, the corner offices even bigger. The doors were always locked, and a red or green light outside signaled whether it was OK to knock or not.

I took a seat in the waiting area that looked like a set from the TV show *Mad Men.* The décor was old-fashioned, heavy and dense, with an air of power, testosterone, entitlement, and greed.

The receptionist, Agnes, fit perfectly into the picture. Dressed in a tight blouse that left little to the imagination, the size of her cleavage could easily hold ten pencils upright at any time. I was amazed that the chief financial officer, who apparently had a thing for big-breasted women, didn't screw up the numbers more than he already did.

Thanks to Ruth, I knew most of the things that happened on the executive floor.

It fascinated me that the executives, who I am sure considered themselves of above-average intelligence, were stupid enough to think that their assistants kept their bosses' shady affairs and dirty little secrets to themselves. The executive assistants were treated like dirt and expected to be dumb and loyal, but I knew that these women were neither.

Every last Friday of the month the executive assistants met for "therapy night" at a local bar. Over pitchers of margaritas they complained about their horrible bosses and swapped stories, each more outrageous than the last. On the following Mondays, Ruth was always eager to share with me what she had learned about the politics, dysfunctions, power struggles, and secret lives of the executives.

It was the highlight of the month.

I knew about Agnes and the CFO, who apparently worked "overtime" quite a bit. One time, during a late-night teleconference call, someone had heard the CFO groan "Ohhhh yeeeessss!" in the middle of a discussion they were having about new accounting practices. "Our CFO sure loves his numbers," one of his colleagues had commented dryly.

Another story was about the chief marketing officer, who usually welcomed his new team members with a wrapped package of marketing books that he wanted them to read, all written in the early 1980s.

One time, however, he gave a new team member the wrong package. He realized his mistake when the call girl he was seeing had phoned him and asked what he wanted her to do with all those books.

As soon as he realized what happened, he rushed his assistant down to the marketing office to retrieve the package for the newly hired marketing assistant, but it was too late. She was already sitting at her desk, staring down in shock at a giant pink dildo.

The mother of all stories, however, was the one about the executive VP of products known for his macho leadership style and sexist behavior. When he didn't show up at work one day or answer any calls or text messages, his assistant Sasha became worried and called his wife, who was out of town. The wife got worried too and asked her to go check on her husband, saying that the doorman would give her the keys to their apartment.

Inside their Park Avenue penthouse, Sasha found her boss on the floor—shouting and growling, feet and hands tied behind his back, wearing only a diaper and a pink tutu.

"I was drugged! I've been robbed! It's not what it looks like!" he screamed when he saw her.

"Right," Sasha thought to herself and hurried to the kitchen to look for a knife. As she loosened the tight rope around her boss's ankles and wrists, her eyes fell on a note on the table.

"This is what happens to cheap, lying sons of bitches. Get yourself another babysitter," it said. Beside the note was his open wallet. Except for a few credit cards, it looked empty.

As her boss quickly wrapped a blanket around his body, the tutu below giving him a funny shape, he simultaneously threatened and begged her to never tell anyone. She would be richly compensated with "shitloads of TechnoGuard shares," he said.

Sasha had managed to keep a serious face and told him that his secret was safe with her, then left the apartment for her boss to get dressed.

Her silence didn't last for long, though.

On the next "therapy night" she completely spilled her guts by the time she had finished her second margarita. Fueled by the effects of the alcohol and the camaraderie with the other executive assistants, Sasha simply couldn't contain herself anymore. Laughing so hard that she was barely able to speak, she gave a detailed description of what had happened, which ended with two of the other girls lying on the floor laughing hysterically and one of them peeing her pants.

Ruth didn't particularly enjoy the assistants' get-togethers, but she still attended them, knowing the information shared one day might come in handy.

For both of us.

THE PRESENTATION

At 9:10 a.m., Agnes told me that the executives were ready for me.

The executive meeting room had floor-to-ceiling windows overlooking Central Park and a sizable wooden table that made the men around it look a lot smaller than they really were. I doubted they were aware of how ridiculous they looked, like little boys pretending to be men.

As I entered the room, they were in deep conversation about some delayed product release and hardly noticed me.

Sometimes I'd been tempted to imply what I knew about them, especially when they displayed their oversized egos, smug grins, and condescending attitudes while I was talking. But knowledge is power, whether it's used or not. Knowing what I did about them gave me a psychological advantage the executives didn't even know I had.

After all, it's very difficult to be intimidated by a man's power plays when you know that the origin of his enormous ego is that he has small-penis issues or is compensating for a lack of motherly love.

There were other stories I'd heard from Ruth that actually troubled me much more than their ridiculous sexual escapades—things like unethical business deals, filthy power plays, and illegal business practices. I often wondered whether my boss, Alistair Parker, knew about these stories too, or if he even was involved in them.

A couple of times I had thought about telling him what I'd heard. If even half of it was true, it could seriously hurt the business. But I also knew that whistle-blowing rarely was a good career choice. To keep quiet and just do my job was probably a better strategy than trying to be the Mother Teresa of the company.

Besides, this was business, a world full of gray zones, where the lines between right and wrong were often blurred, where truthfulness and honesty were hardly considered an advantage, and where the ones in power called the shots.

Even if they got caught wearing pink tutus and diapers on occasion.

. . .

I plugged my laptop into the projector and looked around the table, waiting for the men to quiet down. On the opposite side of the conference table was Mike Harrow, the chief technology officer. He was the joke of the engineering team, as he strolled around, wearing his ill-fitted suits and colorful ties among the T-shirt and sandal-wearing engineers.

He had no idea what his team was doing and didn't seem interested in finding out either. He was more than ready to take credit for their hard work, though. His lack of knowledge and huge ego were a dangerous combination. Some of the engineers had expressed concern that he would rather see the whole team fail than admit any of his own shortcomings—a fear that was proven right when he fired some of the most brilliant engineers because they had questioned his judgment.

To my right, the chief financial officer, Harry Johnson, was studying some papers in front of him. He was a dry-looking accountant type, whose mantra was "If it's not in a spreadsheet, it doesn't exist." I couldn't help thinking about those late-night conference calls that

sounded anything but dry. No wonder he opposed the idea of install-
ing videoconferencing in his office. For a moment I had to concentrate
on my laptop to keep myself from laughing.

Next to Harry was Brad Miller, the chief marketing officer—a bald,
overweight sixty-something who defined marketing as putting an ad
in the newspaper. He looked like a grandfather, but that hadn't stopped
him from suggesting that he and I should get away on a business trip
together one day, wink-wink. He's lucky I treated the executives with
way more respect than they deserved.

On my left was the chief executive officer, Alistair Parker. My
boss was an intelligent and skillful corporate politician. He had
slowly and carefully climbed the ranks at TechnoGuard until he'd
become the CEO seven years ago, a few months before I'd joined
the company. Always well dressed, well groomed, and handsome in
a subdued, modest way, Alistair was one of the few men in the company who didn't seem intimidated by me. He'd never flirted with me
or thrown any sexist comments my way. He was also the one who
ultimately would determine whether I would get a seat at the executive table one day.

"Let's get started," Alistair said, and the men around the
table quieted.

My PowerPoint presentation showed last month's sales numbers
and explained how they had flattened out a bit, but that we still were
reaching our targets. Corporations around the world were waking up
to the fact that everything could be hacked, and with our well-estab-
lished cybersecurity solutions, their fear was our gain.

Most of the executives paid attention as I shared our prospects and
new customer deals. Only Mike Harrow seemed to have better things
to do—he constantly looked down at his phone.

I spoke up a bit more. I wanted him to listen to what I was
about to say.

"After months of negotiations, we seem to be close to signing deals with a number of highly prestigious federal clients," I said, then paused and leaned forward with my hands firmly on the table. This is what I had stayed up all night practicing for.

"However, something has come to my attention that may jeopardize contracts somewhere in the neighborhood of $50 million next month."

I studied the men. The tension in the air was palpable.

"I've been told by several people in R&D that there is a bug in the cybersecurity system we have installed with a number of our federal clients."

I looked around the room to be sure everyone had heard my message.

"As you all know, this is an extremely serious matter. And needless to say, there is no way we can sign any new contracts until this has been resolved." I paused briefly before I continued, "I know I don't need to tell you the consequences this could have on our reputation, our sales numbers, and ultimately, our share price."

The last bit hit closest to home. All the executives around the table had indecently generous stock-option plans, so they would feel any change in share price directly in their wallet, which, I had come to realize, was the only thing they really cared about.

Of course, Ruth had been the one to tell me first. A quick visit to the engineering team had confirmed the story. There was a bug in the system that no one knew how to fix. Apparently, Mike Harrow had fired the person who first addressed it, and who also—as it later turned out—was the only person who knew how to fix it.

When I prepared for my presentation to the executive team, I had suspected I might be throwing a truth-bomb into the room. But it wasn't until it detonated that I realized the size of it.

Alistair narrowed his eyes as he turned his head and looked at Mike, who in a matter of seconds had started sweating intensely. By the streams of sweat running down his forehead, I gathered he had known, and that he had hidden the information from his boss.

Mike desperately tried to avoid Alistair's eyes.

"Is this true, Mike?" Alistair asked.

"I was going to . . . to . . . mention it," Mike said, his eyes looking anywhere but at Alistair. He looked terrified, like a naughty boy caught with his pants down. It was almost painful to watch.

"You *were* going to mention it?" Alistair sneered through clenched teeth. I had never seen Alistair Parker like that. He was fuming with anger. Everyone around the table looked terrified.

Alistair turned toward me, his eyes cold.

"That's quite enough, Maya. You can leave now. You and I will talk later."

I swallowed hard and nodded, closing my laptop. As I left the meeting room, I threw a glance at the men around the table. How did you all get here? I wondered, and then closed the door behind me.

On my way back to my office, I thought about the saying in the company—that TechnoGuard's achievements were *in spite of* the executive team, not *because of* them. And the more I was exposed to these men, the more I had to agree.

In a way I was glad to not be part of that group of arrogant, self-absorbed, executive fools. On the other hand, I couldn't help thinking that if I'd been there, things might have turned out a bit differently.

LISA

My work life was pretty intense, but my social life was not much to write home about. Many friends had given up on me a long time ago. I guess there is an upper limit to how many times you can say no to invitations and not return someone's calls or texts before you never hear from them again.

It was different with Lisa, though. She and I had been friends since kindergarten. She was the sister I never had. Whenever I needed to escape corporate insanity for a few hours, Lisa was my go-to person.

Lisa used to work in the corporate world herself, before she decided it was "soul-sucking and meaningless" and quit her job as VP of marketing for a big PR firm and went to India to train to become a yoga teacher instead. Even though we had chosen different paths, and would sometimes go without seeing each other for months, every time we met it was like no time had passed.

Lisa now dedicated her life to helping stressed-out corporate executives and their victims by offering yoga and meditation classes along with nutritional advice. She loved telling people that I was her most hopeless case so far. She had not been able to get me into a yoga studio, do a single meditation class, or stop me from eating whatever I came across in my hectic life.

For the past year, ever since I got the role of VP of sales, Lisa and I had a standing appointment the first Monday of the month. It was the evening of the executive meeting, and I needed the distraction—and the alcohol—to get whatever had happened out of my system.

This Monday was no exception.

For once, I arrived at Tony's before her. Tony's is an Italian joint with the best pizza in the neighborhood and the most generous glasses of wine. It was also only two blocks from my apartment, which was a big plus, considering how I always ended up having a bit too much to drink on those Mondays.

"You're like a one-day-a-month-alcoholic," Lisa told me, seeing how I transformed into a calmer and more balanced person as soon as the alcohol took effect.

"You could try yoga instead, you know," she once tried, but the look on my face stopped her from ever suggesting that again. Besides, we agreed that it was really nice to have these monthly get-togethers. They were usually our only chance to meet. The rest of the month I worked my butt off, and Lisa was busy trying to get people like me to relax and embrace a healthier lifestyle.

I had eaten a handful of black olives and was already half through my first glass of house red, a nice Valpolicella, when Lisa arrived. She stopped by the bar and said hello to Antonio, the owner, and ordered a glass for herself. I was relieved every time I saw Lisa drinking alcohol. I had nightmares about her insisting we should start having our monthly meetings at the local juice bar instead.

As Lisa walked toward me, I could see how Antonio followed her with his eyes. It was not hard to see that he had a total crush on her, but then again, who didn't? Whenever she flashed her white smile or showed off some of her ridiculously fit yoga body, men started drooling.

Lisa was not one for small talk. As soon as she gave me a hug and sat down, she put an olive into her mouth and asked, "How was the treatment?"

She was referring to my appointment with her Swedish friend Gustav, who apparently was the best holistic body therapist in New York City.

I had no idea what that even meant, but I agreed to see him, as Lisa said he would be able to help me with the neck and back pain I had been struggling with for the past seven years.

"A total disaster, thank you very much," I said, rolling my eyes.

Lisa looked at me, surprised.

"Why?"

"Well, to begin with, he hardly examined me at all. He just asked me to lie down on a bench and breathe. I did what he said, but he kept on telling me to pull the air deeper into my stomach."

Lisa looked like she was hanging on to every word I said, so I continued.

"He ended up diagnosing me with something he called 'shallow breathing syndrome' and told me that my back and neck pain probably comes from not getting enough oxygen into my blood cells and muscles."

Lisa nodded eagerly. "How interesting!" she exclaimed. "So, what did he suggest?"

She seemed to be taking the whole thing a lot more seriously than I did.

"Well, that's the disaster," I told her.

Lisa looked puzzled. "What do you mean?"

"When I asked if he perhaps could prescribe me some oxygen pills, he just laughed. Apparently, he thought I was joking."

Lisa laughed out loud. "You are unbelievable, Maya Williams."

I shook my head and continued. "And then he scribbled something down on a paper and gave it to me."

I opened my wallet and showed Lisa the note:

"*Do NOTHING for fifteen minutes every day. Take five deep breaths three times a day. Go for a walk. Have some fun. Chill.*"

Lisa smiled as she read the note. I didn't understand why she didn't laugh.

"Honestly, Maya. This is the best prescription you could possibly get. In fact, this is exactly what you need!"

She leaned forward and took my hand, as she often did when she wanted to make a point.

"Look at you; always busy, always working, always doing something, checking your emails, being on the phone, never resting, hardly sleeping. You need a break, to relax a bit, have some real chill-time. Maybe even get laid."

Getting laid was Lisa's go-to solution for most problems in life.

"I don't have time to do nothing," I said. "And honestly, Lisa, getting laid is about the last thing on my mind right now."

I moved toward the bar for another glass of wine, but Lisa took my hand and gently held me back, so I had to sit down on my chair again.

"I know, but it's been the last thing on your mind for seven years," she said, leaning over the table and reaching for my other hand. She was clearly not letting me escape this time.

"He was a jerk, Maya. He took advantage of you. And he almost raped you. But most men are not like him. And you have to stop thinking that they are." Lisa teared up. I could see her jaw clenching. I knew I was scarred by the incident, even though I'd done my best not to dwell on it. Still, it always took me by surprise, being reminded of how sad and angry Lisa was about what had happened to me, even after all this time.

"I still can't believe you let that bastard get away with it. He was your goddamn boss! *He* should have been punished. And instead, *you* were the one who lost your job."

I carefully patted her hand. "It's OK, Lisa. I've moved on. You should, too."

"But that's the thing," Lisa said, and looked at me with teary eyes. "You haven't."

An alert on my phone saved me.

"Just a moment," I said, ignoring Lisa's rolling eyes.

It was a text message from my boss.

"Be in my office tomorrow, 7 am. Alistair."

I felt like I'd just been kicked in the stomach.

"What's wrong, Maya?" Lisa asked, concerned. "You look pale."

I swallowed hard and heard my own voice as if it came from far away.

"Sorry, but I have to go. I think I might get fired tomorrow."

ALISTAIR PARKER

The next day, at 6:50 a.m., I walked into the office building and took the elevator straight to the thirty-seventh floor. Agnes was already there, milling around her desk with some of the other executive assistants. She looked surprised to see me.

"I'm meeting with Alistair at seven," I said, looking over at Alistair's closed office door. The indicator lamp was glowing red.

Agnes looked down at her iPad, then looked up at me and shook her head with a slightly condescending smile.

"Sorry, you're not on Alistair's agenda today. Do you want me to schedule a meeting for you another day?" Her smile was as cold as ice.

I don't know quite what got into me, but I lashed out: "I don't care whether I'm on your stupid agenda or not. Alistair sent me a text last night. We're meeting at seven, so can you please drop the attitude and let him know I'm here?"

I was as surprised as Agnes by my outburst.

I was wondering whether to apologize when Alistair opened his door and waved me in. Agnes didn't look up when I passed her desk.

I walked into Alistair's office and stood in front of his desk, waiting for my sentence, like a convict in front of the judge.

Alistair sat down in his brown leather chair behind his large mahogany desk and waved his hand toward the smaller leather chair on the opposite side.

"Have a seat, Maya," he said, and I sat down carefully on the edge of the chair. I looked directly at him and was surprised by what I saw.

The always groomed, well-dressed Alistair Parker looked terrible, as if he hadn't showered or slept for days.

"You opened up quite a can of worms yesterday, Maya," he said, removing his glasses and rubbing his eyes. "That unresolved bug cannot become public knowledge," he continued after a brief pause. "Any doubt whatsoever about the safety of our products could destroy everything we have built over the last twenty years."

I wondered if this was his warm-up to firing me.

After another moment of silence, he continued. "Tomorrow afternoon there is an important investors' conference where I am scheduled to speak. We show up every year, together with ten other tech companies, fighting for investors' money, impressing the hell out of the financial analysts, and making sure that faith in our company continues to grow."

I remained quiet, waiting for him to explain why he was telling me this.

"I can't leave the office until the issue has been resolved. But if we don't show up at the conference, rumors may start."

For the first time that morning, Alistair looked directly at me.

"I've seen you with customers, and I've seen you onstage, Maya. You are knowledgeable, trustworthy, and ruthless. I need you to represent me at the investors' conference tomorrow."

I just stared at him. I guess I should have been relieved—at least I wasn't getting fired. But this? Representing TechnoGuard's CEO at an investors' conference?

"I want you to go on that stage and tell the analysts and investors that all is well, that our cybersecurity solutions are 100 percent reliable, and that their money is entirely safe with us."

"So, you want me to lie?" The words jumped out of my mouth and sounded way more critical than I had intended. Alistair's eyes turned to ice.

"I want you to do your job, to do what is best for the company. If that means to lie, then, yes, you will do that. And in case you thought this was a question, it wasn't. It's an order."

Those three words rubbed me the wrong way, but I was smart enough not to let it show.

"By the way," he continued, "the conference is on the island Kaua'i in Hawaii, so I suggest you go home and pack. I'll tell Agnes to book you on a flight that leaves this afternoon. I'll send you the PowerPoint presentation with my speaker notes. You'll have plenty of time on the plane to memorize it all."

When he finished, Alistair looked back at his computer screen, gesturing with his hand that I was dismissed.

As I was about to leave his office, he called out: "And by the way, Maya. If you can pull this off, the Executive VP title and the corner office will be yours when you return. Mike won't be needing it any longer."

OK, I might not like being given orders, but I did like the reward for following them. I decided to push away the uncomfortable feeling in my gut and tell myself that it would be worth it in the end.

I would finally achieve my career goal, get the corner office, be in power, and become everything I'd ever dreamed of.

But I wasn't naïve. Fifteen years in the corporate world had taught me this: nothing comes for free.

There is always a price to pay to get what you want.

A WALK
DOWN MEMORY LANE

As I leaned back in my seat, exhausted after the mad dash through the airport, I thought about the long flight ahead of me: first to Honolulu, then another forty-minute flight to Kaua'i.

I had never been to Hawaii before and never had any desire to go there, either. I dreaded the idea of Hawaiian shirts, leis, mai tais, and mass tourism, and decided to do my best to stay away from it all.

I would do my job and then get my butt back to New York as fast as I could.

In less than four days it would all be over, and I'd be back in the city, busy moving into my new office on the thirty-seventh floor. Maya Williams, executive vice president of sales. I certainly liked the sound of that.

As soon as the plane was up in the air and the captain had turned off the fasten-seatbelt sign, I opened my computer to have a look at the PowerPoint presentation Alistair had sent me a few hours earlier.

The first slides were about customer testimonials and case studies, market share, and some new technology releases. It looked fine. I continued clicking through the slides, feeling better about the whole

thing, when suddenly a slide I recognized showed up. It was a slide
from the presentation I had shared with the executive team the day
before, but something was different. The numbers had been changed.
Sales were increased by 20 percent, next quarter's prospect had been
increased by 25 percent, and it said we had closed some deals that I
knew we were still working on and probably would not get.

My heart started racing. This was not good.

When I clicked to the last slide of the presentation, it stated that
TechnoGuard's cybersecurity products were 100 percent reliable and
safe and had never experienced any security issues. I closed my laptop quickly.

It was one thing knowing that other people lied and acted unethi-
cally, but it was something entirely different to be told to do the same.
I didn't know how to think or feel. I needed a drink.

The cabin attendant approached with the beverage cart, and I asked
for two glasses of white wine. I downed one of them even before she
had finished serving me the other.

"A bit nervous about flying, are we?" She looked sympathetically at me.

"Yes." I nodded and took a sip of the second glass, happy to have
an excuse.

A chubby hand patted my knee. "No worries, we'll be looking
after her." Mrs. Hawaiian-shirt, on my right side, winked at the cabin
attendant.

Oh, Lord. If I survived this, I would deserve way more than a new
title and a corner office.

"I'm Betsy, by the way," Mrs. Hawaiian-shirt said to me.

I nodded and attempted to smile.

She pointed over to her sleeping husband. "And that's Engelbert,
my husband. He always sleeps," she giggled. "He's kind of cute, isn't
he?" She gave me a friendly bump with her shoulder.

"Peaceful as a child," I said, thankful for the calming effect the wine
was already having on me.

I leaned back in my chair and closed my eyes. My mind went back to the presentation on my laptop. Damn it. This was not OK. This was borderline fraud. Still, what choice did I have? Alistair had made himself very clear. This was an order.

I took a deep breath. You can do this, Maya. You're just doing your job. It's only business. And sometimes the goal justifies the means. Every successful businessperson knows that.

The self-talk and second glass of wine calmed me down.

I decided I needed some distraction and started browsing through the in-flight movies. The first one that popped up was *King of Lies*, about Bernie Madoff. Nope. Then there was *The Wolf of Wall Street* with Leonardo DiCaprio. Double nope. Then *The Devil Wears Prada* with Meryl Streep . . . Geez, was someone trying to tell me something, or what?

I went to the Classic Movie selection instead, and the picture of the musical *South Pacific* from 1958 showed up on my screen. Suddenly, I was overwhelmed by memories. I leaned back in the chair and closed my eyes.

It was the early 1980s and I was back at the old movie theater in Brooklyn, where my mom and I used to go and watch classic Hollywood movies a few times a month. I was about six years old when we first started and ten and a half when we stopped. We never told my dad about our trips to the cinema. Mom used to say that it was our little secret. Nor did we tell him about Giorgio, the old Italian cinematographer who opened up his little cinema for us on any afternoon we wanted to come by and watch a movie.

The movie theater didn't look like much on the outside. It was a small house squeezed in between two taller buildings, with a worn-out "Cinema" sign and a few movie posters on the wall that looked like they had been there since the house was built.

But on the inside, it was like stepping into a magical world—with rows of big, comfortable red velvet chairs, and in between them small tables with tiny, old-fashioned lamps, and in the corner of the lobby, a big popcorn machine. I was allowed to eat as much popcorn as I wanted on those visits, and I never let the opportunity pass me by.

Giorgio was a tall man with gray hair and sad brown eyes that always lit up every time he looked at Mom.

My mom was beautiful. Old Hollywood beautiful. While most women embraced shoulder pads and neon-colored tights in the 1980s, my mom wore dresses from the 1950s, red lipstick, and sometimes even a scarf over her hair, just like Audrey Hepburn. Giorgio said she looked like a mix between Doris Day and what he thought Pocahontas might look like, with her blonde curls and almond-shaped brown eyes. She had laughed out loud and thanked him for the compliment.

"And what do my two favorite movie stars want to see today?" Giorgio always asked with his strong Italian accent as soon as we stepped through the doors of his cinema.

"*South Pacific!*" we usually shouted and laughed. It was our absolute favorite movie. We knew all the songs by heart and sang along during the movie, and when it ended, we always agreed that it was "the most wonderful movie ever made."

With music and lyrics from the composers Rodgers and Hammerstein, it is a light-hearted, fun musical that addresses serious themes such as racism and prejudice alongside the telling of two love stories.

What I remembered the most from the movie was the song about Bali Ha'i. Every time I watched the movie and heard the song, my heart yearned for this mysterious place.

Bali Ha'i will whisper
Any night, any day
In your heart, you'll hear it call you
"Come away, come away."

Hand in hand, on our way home from Giorgio's cinema, Mom and I often talked about how we wanted to visit Bali Ha'i one day. I loved those afternoons, and I loved our dreams.

Mom and I were best friends. My dad was working all the time and usually ate his dinners in the city, so most of the time it was just her and me. And since she couldn't stand cooking, we just ate whatever we felt like, whenever we felt like it.

Our house was a happy mess, which often annoyed my dad; but Mom would just laugh and say she had more important things to do than to cook and clean, which I knew was true.

Mom was a very talented artist, known for her happy and colorful paintings that sold for a lot of money at a gallery in Lower Manhattan.

"Always make sure to earn your own money, Maya," she used to tell me.

I knew when she was telling me something important, because she had a certain look in her eyes, and a determined sound to her voice.

"Only be with a man—or a woman, should you prefer that— because you want to, not because you have to."

I would nod in serious agreement when she spoke like that, trying to memorize every word she said.

Most of the mothers of the children in my class were stay-at-home moms. I often saw them together, sitting in the park drinking coffee or standing outside the school chatting. I never saw any of them speak to my mom.

"Your mom is weird!" one of the boys in my class shouted to me one day, when I wouldn't let him have the swing.

"She looks funny and acts weird. No one likes her and no one likes you," he shouted before one of the teachers came running and hushed him.

After that I stopped bringing classmates home. Not because I was embarrassed, but because I didn't think they deserved to spend time with my wonderful mom. I knew she was different from the other moms. And I wouldn't have had it any other way.

One of my favorite things to do was to watch her turn blank canvases into explosions of color. Whenever she painted, her eyes sparkled, and it was like she disappeared into something or somewhere only she could go. She could paint for hours, and when she did, it was only she and her painting that existed.

I would often sit on the floor of her studio and do my homework. Sometimes, I would even make my own drawings, but I quickly found out that I didn't have my mother's artistic talent. One time she joked and said maybe I had inherited my dad's talents instead and would be an amazing lawyer one day.

I remember being scared by that thought. I didn't want to be like my dad. I wanted to be like her: artistic, happy, and free. My dad was always so serious. He worked all the time and didn't seem to know what it was like to have fun.

Every night before I went to sleep, Mom would make up bedtime stories to tell me. She spoke of kings and queens, dragons and fairies, heroes and heroines, world travelers and time travelers, life under the ocean and life among the stars. Her imagination was as vast and vivid as her paintings, and I looked forward to those stories each night.

My favorite story, however, was one from real life. It was the story about a young, handsome, fair-haired sailor from a land far, far away who fell in love with a beautiful Native American woman on a stop-over in New York and proposed to her after only two days. The woman, known for her ability to navigate ships by looking at the stars, had been waiting for her blond prince.

"Our story is written in the stars," she had told him. They had gotten married, and two years later, Stella, their little baby girl, was born.

Stella grew up at sea, on boats and ships, and traveled to every corner of the world together with her adventurous parents. When the day came for her to start on her own journey, as a student at the San Francisco Art Institute, the eighteen-year-old girl was left by the harbor in San Francisco.

"The stars will be watching over you," was the last thing her mother had said before she and her blond prince sailed away, hand in hand, into the sunset.

That was the last time my mom saw her parents. Two months later their boat disappeared somewhere in the middle of the South Pacific Ocean.

"And now they live among the stars," Mom told me.

Every night we went out in the garden and waved Grandma and Grandpa goodnight. Sometimes, I thought I could see a star blinking, and Mom told me it was them, waving back at us.

My own parents had met at an art exhibition when Mom was twenty-two and Dad was thirty. Serious, quiet, and modest, my dad couldn't have been more different from my mom. I think they really loved each other, but they disagreed on many things. One of them was about my upbringing.

One day I heard them argue.

"You have to stop making her believe in fairy tales!" I heard my dad say. He didn't like her magical stories or that every night we waved goodnight to the stars.

"Just because you don't believe in it, doesn't mean it doesn't exist," she replied. I remember the frustration in her voice.

"I only believe what I see," my dad responded.

"And some things you have to believe to see," my mother replied.

Sometimes, I could see a sadness in her eyes. I never knew where the sadness came from, and I never dared to ask.

The happiest days of my childhood were the days when Mom and I had picnics with sandwiches and lemonade in our garden.

Afterward, we'd lie on our backs, my head resting in the softness between her breast and her shoulder. Looking up at the sky, we talked about everything between heaven and earth, discussing the funny shapes of the clouds in the daytime and gazing at the stars at night.

Whenever we saw a shooting star, Mom would whisper, "Make a wish, make a wish." I always made the same one: that Mom and I would be happy and together forever.

One day when I was playing alone in the garden, I saw a beautiful butterfly sitting on the grass. I managed to capture it in a small glass jar and ran proudly into the house to show it to Mom.

I remember being startled by her reaction.

"Poor little thing!" she exclaimed. She quickly took the glass jar from me, ran out in the garden, and opened the lid. Her movements were tense and hurried, as if every second mattered.

"Butterflies need to be free to fly, Maya," she said, as we watched the butterfly fly back to its freedom. Then she took both my hands in hers and looked me in the eyes. She was smiling, but her voice was serious.

"All life is precious, my dear. But a butterfly's life is not only precious; it is also very short. Only a few days ago, maybe a week, that beautiful butterfly was just a caterpillar. And, in a few weeks, her life may already be over. Between now and then, all she wants is to be happy and free, to dance and to enjoy every moment she has. We don't want to take that away from her, do we?"

I shook my head and looked sadly into my mom's eyes. I knew I would never capture a butterfly again.

To lighten the mood, Mom started tickling me.

"Let's pretend we are happy butterflies, too," she laughed, then started running around in the garden with her arms out, pretending she had wings.

Soon I was doing the same.

"We are butterflies! We are butterflies!" We laughed and danced around the garden. And then she lifted me high up in the air, so I could feel what it was like, to be free to fly.

· · ·

I don't know when I first started noticing that something was wrong with Mom. Maybe it was when she canceled our visits to the cinema because she needed to sleep. Or when I saw more of the sadness in her eyes, even when she was painting.

Maybe it was when I started noticing that her clothes were too big for her. Or the whispered conversations between her and my dad and the looks they gave each other when they thought I didn't notice. Never had I seen their eyes so sad.

A few months before my eleventh birthday, my parents told me that Mom was very sick. I don't remember much from the time that followed. Mom got smaller and weaker by the day, and one day I overheard the doctor telling my dad that it had spread much faster than they'd expected.

One night when I was lying beside her in bed, almost afraid to touch her because she was so small and fragile, Mom stroked my hair and whispered: "Don't be afraid, my darling Maya. I will never leave your side. I will live inside your heart. I will wave to you from the stars, and dance around you like a butterfly. Remember that even though you won't see me, I will still be there."

She was exhausted after speaking, and I thought she had fallen asleep, when she opened her eyes again. Her eyes were shining and sparkling, like the stars in the sky, when she looked me in the eyes and whispered: "My only wish is that you live a happy life and enjoy your time on earth, until we meet again among the stars. I love you so much, Maya. Go fly, my little butterfly girl."

One week after my eleventh birthday, Mom took her last breath. And life as I knew it ended.

I don't remember much about the time that followed, except my dad's stone face on the day Mom was buried, and the sound of my cries as her coffin hit the ground.

The only thing that prevented me from jumping into the grave with her was Lisa's firm little hand holding mine tightly, and the words she whispered in my ear. "Your mom's not there, Maya. Remember, she is among the stars."

That night, alone in the garden, I looked up and for the briefest of moments, I saw a star expand into a giant light, only to disappear and leave no trace on the deep, blue sky.

· · ·

I had fallen asleep in my seat and woke up confused. My throat had dried out, and for a moment I panicked and gasped for air.

"It's OK, doll. Just take some deep breaths. Everything will be just fine. You are safe."

Betsy spoke to me with a soft and calm voice. I took some deep breaths and a sip of water and felt the panic slowly fade away. I gave her an embarrassed smile and leaned back into my seat.

I glanced at my watch. Eight more hours to go.

The picture of *South Pacific* was still on my screen. I reached over and put on my headphones. Why not? It wasn't like I had anything better to do.

Watching *South Pacific* was like being pulled back in time again, back into the cinema, with my little hand in Mom's. And when the Bali Ha'i song started playing, I could feel the same longing in my heart as I remembered feeling all those years ago.

Bali Ha'i will whisper
On the wind of the sea
"Here am I, your special island!
Come to me, come to me."

Tears were running down my cheeks and a paper towel was handed to me from my right side.

"Bali Ha'i always makes me cry too," Betsy said and smiled warmly.

I paused the movie and thanked her as I dried my eyes and blew my nose.

For someone like me, who was neither used to, nor comfortable with, public display of emotions, this had turned out to be a highly disturbing flight.

I didn't understand what was happening to me.

"Isn't *South Pacific* just the most wonderful movie ever made?" she said with a dreamy voice. I stared at her, but she didn't seem to notice. "Are you going there?" she asked.

"Going where?" I asked, confused.

"To Bali Ha'i!" she said.

I still didn't understand what she was talking about and suddenly she burst out laughing, started clapping her hands, and jumped up and down in her seat, causing the entire row to shake.

"Oh, my goodness, you don't know, do you? *South Pacific* was filmed on Kaua'i! Up on the North Shore of the island. And Bali Ha'i exists. It's called Mount Makana. I've seen it myself!"

She was unstoppable now. And I was too shocked to speak.

"Years ago, Engelbert and I went to Kaua'i and attended a *South Pacific* tour that took us to all the beautiful sites where the movie had been filmed. That was something, I'll tell you!"

Betsy was nearly jumping out of her seat from the excitement.

"I sang and danced for one week straight. Even Engelbert was tired of me after a while," she giggled.

I had to smile.

"You only live once, right?" She laughed. "It was one of the best experiences of my life."

Betsy told me that she and Engelbert couldn't afford to go back to Kaua'i for all these years, and how they couldn't believe their luck when a company invited them and offered to pay for their plane tickets and hotel.

She talked and talked, but I only half-listened to what she said. My head was still spinning as I processed the information.

South Pacific was filmed on Kaua'i? Bali Ha'i was a place I could go? What a strange and funny coincidence! Maybe I should go there and take a look. Just for the fun of it.

Then, I realized the ridiculousness of it all. I was there to do a job, not to relive some silly childhood fantasy.

I gratefully accepted the coffee the cabin attendant handed me and hoped it would help clear my head. As I sipped my coffee, I opened my laptop and reviewed the speaker notes from Alistair's presentation. In forty-eight hours, I would be finished, and on my way back to New York and my new executive life.

I couldn't wait.

THE CONFERENCE

I had dressed to impress and felt good in my tailored Armani jacket and pencil skirt, wearing my highest heels, which made me about six feet tall.

I was prepared.

I'd spent half the night and most of the morning practicing my speech. As always, I was leaving nothing to chance.

As I left the hotel room, I decided to leave my cell phone behind. I needed my mind to stay laser-sharp and focused. Besides, I would be back in the room in less than an hour—with mission accomplished. I couldn't wait.

When I entered the large conference hall, located on the ground floor of the hotel, I noticed that the room was packed with people.

I walked over to the technician's table and got mic'd up, and ten minutes later the voice on the loudspeaker called out my name.

"You can do this, Maya," I told myself. Of course I could! After all, I was a pro.

I calmly and confidently stepped up onstage.

The room was dark and the spotlight strong. I could only see the people in the first few rows. They were mostly men, and they all looked like they'd come directly from Wall Street.

In their dark suits and white shirts, they stood in stark contrast to the colorfully dressed tourists I had met on my way from my hotel room.

The room was quiet, and I started to speak.

It started out well. I knew all the slides by heart and had practiced exactly what to say and how to say it. I'd already detached myself from the actual content. I was like an actor onstage, playing the part I'd been told to play.

I was pleased with my ability to elegantly serve one lie after the other without even blinking.

I realized I didn't mind it as much as I thought I would. After all, the women and men in the room were all financial analysts and professional investors, dealing with other people's money. They knew what they were doing and had enough experience and critical judgment to make whatever investment decision they believed in. If they were unlucky with one investment, they would have another good investment to even it out. It was all a big money game, and I was just playing my part in it.

Halfway through the presentation, my mouth started to dry out, so I went to the left side of the stage to drink some water from the glass I had left on a table. My eyes had finally adjusted to the spotlight, and I could see the people farther back in the room now.

Suddenly, something surprising caught my eye. In the middle of all the black suits, there was an island of color. When I looked closer, I noticed that most of these people had gray hair. Some were even wearing hats.

A hand went up, and somebody in the middle of the colorful crowd was eagerly waving to me. What? Was that Betsy from the flight? With her sleeping husband, Engelbert, beside her? I was confused. What the hell were they doing here? And who were all their friends?

Then, as if hit by lightning from above, I suddenly understood. It was something Betsy had said on the plane, about being invited by some company. While I had only partially listened to her, I now understood what kind of company had invited them.

A number of financial investment companies specialized in bringing elderly people to holiday retreats, pampering them, and making them feel special. In return, the seniors had to show up at these kinds of meetings, where the goal was to trick them into investing their hard-earned savings in company shares, with no other guarantee than the indecently high commissions the so-called financial advisors would walk away with.

The dark-suited financial people suddenly all looked like sharks to me. Greedy, mean sharks, fooling senior citizens, with no concern as to whether their investments would be good or not, as long as the commissions paid for their own high-flying lifestyles.

How could they do this to these old, innocent people?

And how could I?

I realized, as I was standing up there, that I was no better than they were. I was telling lies to these elderly people, giving them false information to get them to invest in our company, even though I knew that their money could be gone within seconds, should the truth about TechnoGuard come out.

My mind was racing.

What should I do?

I started speaking again, surprised to hear myself continue. It felt like I had been standing there, silent, for several minutes, but it had probably been just a few seconds.

No one seemed to have noticed.

"As I said, the company has never been in better shape," I said, even though I saw images inside my mind of TechnoGuard going bankrupt, and all these old people losing their savings, living the rest of their lives in poverty. And me, living with the knowledge that I could have prevented it.

How could I do that to Betsy and Engelbert and all those other people who had no idea that they were being tricked into something they might regret for the rest of their lives?

While all these thoughts spun around in my mind, an angry, agitated voice began shouting inside my head:

"Stop this nonsense, Maya! You're just doing your job. Finish the job you came here to do. It's not personal. It's only business."

The voice in my head grew louder and tried to squelch my doubt and hesitation.

"Remember what's at stake here. Everything you have ever wanted and dreamed of. Who cares about some old people? An executive vice president title and a corner office. *That* is what you care about. Look after yourself. That is all that counts. Eat or be eaten, remember?"

All of a sudden, I felt ashamed. I had been taught and trained to become a shark. But was I really like them? I looked at the people in suits and then back at the colorful island of gray-haired people.

Then, as the yelling voice inside my head took a break to draw its breath, I heard another voice softly whisper: "Who do you want to be, Maya? Who do you want to be?"

And suddenly, I just knew.

I turned off the presentation and cleared my throat.

"The business world is a tricky place," I said and looked out over the crowd.

I let my eyes rest on Betsy and the group surrounding her.

"PowerPoint presentations aren't always consistent with reality. And reality is an ever-changing thing. The presentation I just shared with you is based on the way we would like things to be, and how they might have been, if it hadn't been for a number of unfortunate events as of late. Now, I could just stand here and pretend that those things never happened, and that everything is as great as this presentation is trying to tell you. I could do that, but I won't. Because I simply wouldn't be telling the truth."

The room went dead quiet. It felt as if everyone was holding their breath.

"But this is the truth." I took a deep breath.

"Every morning at TechnoGuard, we go to work, driven by our mission to keep our customers' data safe. We have been providing cybersecurity solutions to millions of users over the last twenty years, and we intend to continue doing so. But if you choose to trust us with your money, I think you should know what you are investing in. You should expect honesty, transparency, and trustworthiness in all your interactions and transactions with us. And that is what I intend to give you."

I walked over to the side of the stage, picked up the glass of water, and took a few more sips. I studied the audience as I walked back to the podium. All eyes were on me. My voice was surprisingly calm, and so was I.

"I want to inform you that TechnoGuard has detected a bug in one of our cybersecurity systems that we have not been able to resolve yet. Our brilliant engineers are working around the clock to fix it, but until they do, we simply cannot guarantee 100 percent security for our clients." I could see people were sitting on the edges of their seats now, and some of the people in suits were picking up their phones.

"I am sharing this with you so you can make an informed decision. I assure you we are doing everything we can to remedy this matter as quickly as possible. However, until this is resolved, you might want to wait on investing your hard-earned money in TechnoGuard."

I looked directly at Betsy when I said this. Her eyes were shining stronger than the spotlights.

I took another deep breath and looked over at the crowd again. I decided to leave things there.

"Good luck with your investments, everyone! Thank you."

The room was quiet for a few seconds before it exploded with analysts shouting into their phones, "Sell! Sell! Sell!"

I slowly removed the microphone, walked off the stage and down the aisle, toward the big doors at the back of the room.

"Keep on walking, keep on walking," the soft voice whispered.

I could feel my legs turning into jelly. My heart pounded so hard that I was afraid it would jump right out of my chest. As I opened the doors leading to a big green lawn, the shock of the sunlight nearly knocked me to the ground.

All I could think was, "What have I done? What have I done?"

And then I just kept on walking.

THE BEACH

I walked across the lawn, passing a large swimming pool surrounded by palm trees, sunbeds, parasols, sunbathers, and children playing in the water with their inflatable toys.

I felt dizzy and strange but kept walking until I found myself on a beach. The sunlight hurt my eyes, so I covered them with my hands, kicked off my shoes, and continued all the way down to the water.

The sand was intensely white and the ocean crystal blue. Everything looked and felt as unreal as the whole situation I was in.

I took off my jacket, rolled it up as a makeshift pillow, and lay down in the sand. My mind was empty, my body was heavy, and I didn't know what to think or feel. I just lay there, listening to the sound of waves and thinking how I probably had just screwed up my entire career and everything I had ever worked for. A lifetime of hard work, and I had managed to destroy it all within a matter of minutes.

The sand warmed and comforted my skin, and the sound of the waves hypnotized me into a dreamlike state. I allowed myself to drift away. Away from reality. Away from what I had just done.

Suddenly, I was back onstage, telling lies and doing high-fives with the sharks. Betsy was sitting in a chair, all alone in the dark conference room. She was crying. Then Alistair Parker's face showed up. First, he was laughing, then he was screaming. There was no sound, only froth coming out of his mouth. My dad was there, too, looking judgmental and disappointed. And in the background my mom was dancing, wearing her 1950s dress and humming a song from *South Pacific*.

Dad spoke: "You better watch out, so the tide doesn't carry you out and feed you to the sharks."

His voice was different. In fact, it didn't sound like him at all. Whose voice was this?

"Aloha, lady. Are you alive?" It was as if someone touched my shoulder, and I gave a little scream and quickly sat up in the sand. I had water up to my thighs and pulled myself farther back on the sand, dizzy and confused. Where was I?

A warm and friendly laugh came from above.

"Sorry, I didn't mean to scare you. I just didn't want to see you ending up as shark food on this beautiful day."

A young man with shoulder-length blond hair was staring down at me with a big smile on his face.

Suddenly it all came rushing back to me.

"Oh, nooooo," I said out loud and covered my face in my hands.

"Nice to meet you, too!" the man laughed.

I slowly removed my hands from my face and looked at him. Tanned and fit with sun-bleached hair and dressed in a white T-shirt and long, colorful shorts, he was the poster child of a surfer dude. He carefully sat down on the sand beside me.

"I don't mean to intrude or anything. I just want to make sure you're alright."

He had a very friendly and open face, and his eyes were the bluest I had ever seen. It was almost difficult to look into them.

I suddenly felt a bit self-conscious, realizing I must look like a crazy woman in my corporate outfit covered with sand. The surfer dude seemed to enjoy the situation.

"Now, this is what I call beaching in style," he teased.

Realizing the absurdity of the situation, I couldn't help but laugh.

"Thank you. I figured bathing suits were so last year."

"Beach fashionista with a sense of humor. I like it!" He grinned. "I'm Josh, by the way."

"Maya," I nodded, smiling at him.

He seemed charming and friendly, in a non-intrusive way.

We sat in silence for a little while and just looked out over the ocean. I was still mortified over how my presentation at the conference had turned out.

I glanced over at Josh. I couldn't help thinking that he was one of the most beautiful men I had ever seen, like a blond Greek god. He looked very young, maybe twenty-five. Yet something about him felt very old.

He looked back at me and smiled. "So, what have you been up to today, Maya?"

I shook my head. "Oh, you don't want to know."

"Try me!"

I looked at him; his eager face and kind smile were hard to resist.

"OK. Well, I just blew up my entire career and everything I have been working toward for the last fifteen years because I wasn't able to lie to a group of seniors and tell them to invest in something they shouldn't."

Josh grinned. "Cool," he said and continued looking out over the ocean.

I started laughing. I guess I shouldn't have expected any other remark from a surfer dude.

"So, do you regret telling the truth?" he asked.

I was silent for a while. Did I regret it?

"No," I finally said. "I honestly don't think I would have been able to live with myself had I deliberately lied to those people." I let out a sigh. "But even though I think I did the right thing, it still feels like shit right now."

Josh looked at me. It felt as if his crystal blue eyes could see right through me. He smiled. "Do you want some words of wisdom?"

"Yes, please!" I figured I could use all the wisdom I could get.

"Shit happens! But life goes on." Josh grinned.

I laughed out loud. Was this guy for real?

"I guess it does. But right now, I have absolutely no idea what's next."

"You'll figure it out," Josh said.

Then we sat quietly again, overlooking the ocean, listening to the calming sound of the waves.

"So, how are you liking the island so far?" Josh asked and leaned back on his elbows in the sand.

I was still trying to find a comfortable way to sit, feeling a bit awkward about the way my pencil skirt curled up toward the top of my thighs.

"I honestly have no idea. This is the first I'm seeing of it." I looked around. "But from what I can see, it looks pretty good."

"Well, if this is all you've seen, you're in for a treat."

"I don't think so." I shook my head. "I'm actually leaving tomorrow."

Josh just smiled and sat quietly and looked out over the ocean. I had the feeling he would rather be in water than on land.

"So, do you surf?" I asked, feeling a bit stupid, asking such an obvious question.

Josh slowly shook his head and sighed.

"I used to, but not anymore." He fell quiet again. I sensed he didn't want to talk about it.

"So, what's it like? To surf, I mean." It felt like a safe enough question.

He smiled widely and let out a happy sigh. "It feels like heaven."

I was mesmerized by the sparkle in his eyes.

"Surfing was my life. I used to jump out of bed every morning and I'd be out in the water at sunrise, eager to hit the waves." He took a deep breath and looked out over the ocean. "It was like having a love affair with the ocean—a loving, passionate, but unreliable lover. Some days, she made my life feel like heaven. Other days, it felt like hell."

Josh fell silent, his eyes resting on somewhere far away.

"If I didn't listen or acknowledge her, she would punish me, but when I communicated softly with her, and showed her that I loved and respected her, she would send me one perfect wave after the other. She gave me experiences of pure bliss, like nothing I've ever experienced before. Whenever I wasn't with her, I longed for and dreamed about her."

I smiled. It really *did* sound like he had a love affair with the ocean.

He went silent again, and when he continued, sadness came into his voice. "One day she was in a really bad mood. I should have read the signs, listened to her warnings, and not gone out that morning. But I was stubborn. I wanted the bliss. I was selfish, and I just went for it."

He stopped speaking, and again his eyes looked at something far away. Beyond the horizon.

"So, what happened?" I asked.

"I had an accident and that was the end of it."

I didn't ask anymore. I could tell how painful the memories were. It must have been a pretty bad accident.

We sat quietly for a while and looked at the ocean. It sparkled, as if it was covered with diamonds.

It was strange to sit and do nothing with a stranger, yet it felt surprisingly comfortable at the same time.

"You know, there is a saying that no one leaves Kaua'i the same as when they arrived," Josh suddenly said and looked at me.

"Ha, well that sounds about right. I came here with a job and will most likely leave without one," I said dryly.

He smiled gently. "You shouldn't be so hard on yourself, Maya."

I guessed my face gave me away.

Josh added, "It might feel like crap right now, but this could be the best thing that has ever happened to you."

"And why would you think that?"

"It's just a feeling I have," he said.

I looked at him, waiting for him to continue.

"It takes a lot of courage to do the right thing," he said. "It might be a hard choice to make, but in the long run, I don't think anyone regrets listening to their heart."

I thought about what he just said. I couldn't say "listening to my heart" had been a great priority in my life. Yet, somehow, I knew Josh was right.

"And life is pretty amazing, you know," he continued. "When one door closes, another one opens."

"Oh really?" I said and pretended to look surprised. "Where I come from, we say that when one door closes, you're screwed."

Josh laughed.

He had the nicest laugh. It was deep and warm. I loved how we could joke and be serious together, at the same time.

"Well, if you hang around on the island and chill for a while, you may start seeing things differently."

"Funny how I keep getting that advice." I shrugged. "To chill, I mean." I looked over at Josh. "But to be quite honest, I don't even know how to do that."

"Oh, that's really easy," he smiled, "just do like this." He leaned all the way back into the sand, arms spread out, and gave a happy sigh.

"OK, I think I can do that," I said and followed his example. It felt nice to let myself rest in the warm, soft sand. I even made my own happy sigh.

"Good girl. You're getting the hang of it."

We just lay silently in the sand for a while, looking up at the bright blue sky. A bird was gliding through the sky, its wings spread out, doing nothing but floating through the air. Imagine being that free.

The tide was getting closer, and suddenly a wave came all the way up to where we were lying. We both jumped to our feet with a laugh and relocated a bit farther up the beach. I brought my curled-up

Armani jacket with me. It was soaking wet and filled with sand. I was pretty sure this was not part of the designer's vision for it.

We just sat and listened to the waves for a while. The sun was slowly making its way toward the horizon, and the ocean was transforming into a blanket of silver.

"Wow," I sighed. "I must say, I really do like this whole chilling thing."

"Yeah, me too," Josh said, and then we were silent again.

A young couple strolled by, arms intertwined, gazing toward the horizon. A little girl was building a sand castle, while her mother relaxed in a beach chair next to her.

After a while, Josh spoke again. "Chilling is not only about relaxing, you know," he said. "Chilling is just as much a way of thinking and approaching life."

"Like having a very relaxed lifestyle?" I grinned and looked over at him. He sure seemed to have figured that one out.

He smiled back at me. "Yeah, but it's more than that too. It's about living in the moment. Enjoying what is, instead of overthinking the past or worrying about the future."

I had to admit that sounded a bit difficult. I always analyzed what had been and anticipated what would come. Even now, my head was drifting back to what had happened on that stage and worrying about what messages I would find on my cell phone when I got back to my room.

"This moment is all there is." Josh spread his arms. "Everything else is irrelevant. The past has already happened, and the future is yet to come. The only thing within your power is *this* moment, this exact second. And what you choose to do with it determines what comes next."

I nodded. What he said made sense. Yet, it was far from how I used to think.

Josh took a deep breath, and I instinctively followed his example, taking another deep breath and then another one. My lungs filled with clean, salty ocean air. It felt as if it was washing me clean from the inside. Even my mind felt clearer.

Josh was right. I couldn't change what had happened at the conference earlier or control those missed calls and messages waiting for me. But I could decide what I wanted to focus on right now.

I felt the sand below my feet and the ocean breeze on my face. It was as if my heart slowed down a bit and a new sense of calm came over me.

I turned my head and smiled at Josh. He smiled back at me. No words were needed.

The sun was starting to set. It looked like a giant fireball going down into the ocean. I hadn't watched a sunset for as long as I could remember.

"It's breathtaking," I said, feeling as if I had just witnessed a miracle.

Josh nodded. "It sure is."

And then we were silent again.

After the sun had set, a chilly breeze came in from the ocean. I was still wet and was starting to get cold. It felt like reality was sneaking its way back into my life.

I stood up and tried dusting the sand off of my skirt but quickly realized it was a lost cause.

"I'd better go back to my hotel room now, before I catch a cold," I said. "Besides, I have a feeling there will be a few missed calls waiting for me."

I told Josh I hadn't been away from my phone for this long since the invention of the smartphone. "It feels weird. Like a body part has gone missing," I said.

Josh laughed, and then we slowly walked side by side toward the hotel.

Neither of us said anything, but now and then we looked at each other and smiled. It was nice to not have to fill the space with words. I don't think I had ever felt this relaxed around a man before. There was nothing threatening about Josh. It was just comfortable. And really, really nice.

When we arrived at the hotel, he turned to me and said, "Should you change your mind and decide to hang around the island for a few days, I'll be up at Kealia Beach tomorrow, just chilling. You're more than welcome to come and join me."

I had to admit it sounded really tempting, but not like something that was likely to happen.

"I would love to, Josh, but I honestly have no idea what the next few days will look like."

"Good," he said. "When nothing is certain, everything is possible."

I smiled as I watched him disappear into the night.

THE DREAM

I was flying, dancing, and gliding through the air. I was having fun, high up in the sky, above the clouds, bathing in the sunshine, and enjoying the wind in my hair. My big wings carried me wherever I wanted to go, without a care in the world. There were no expectations, plans, or places to be. I could do and be anything I wanted. I could go anywhere I pleased.

Why hadn't I spread my wings earlier? Why hadn't I known I could fly? Had I forgotten how? I had never felt so free, so lighthearted, so happy. I was laughing until my belly hurt. I knew I was just where I was supposed to be, and I wanted to stay up there forever. What else in the world could I possibly want but this?

I was aware of the ground below me, but I didn't look. A soft voice whispered, "Look forward," but another voice shouted, "Look down!"

I knew I shouldn't. But the shouting voice was very persistent. As I decided to take a quick look, just to see what all the fuss was about, I felt the ground beneath me start pulling me down. I desperately fought against it, but it was too late. Gravity was stronger than I was.

My body was being pulled toward the ground, faster and faster. Suddenly my wings were gone. Below me everything looked gray and dark. Little creatures were scurrying up and down on narrow streets, in and out of big black buildings. First, I thought it was people. Then, I realized they were ants. Giant black working ants. With no will of their own. No souls. No life.

Suddenly, I was on the ground. Trapped inside a big black, ice-cold body. I was shivering and screaming with fear, but no one could hear me. Then I realized why. Ants don't have a voice.

I screamed and gasped for air. I had fallen asleep in the bathtub. The water was ice cold, which caused me to shiver. I quickly got out of the bathtub and wrapped the bathrobe around me, stepped over my wet and sandy clothes that were still lying on the floor, and went onto the balcony. I was shaken to the core by the vivid dream. The feeling of being trapped had been so real. But so had the feeling of being happy and free, without a worry in the world.

The air outside was warmer than the air in the room. I sat down on the balcony chair and looked out over the silvery ocean, illuminated by the star-covered sky. I tilted my head back and looked up. I hadn't seen this many stars since the nights when Mom and I waved Grandma and Grandpa goodnight from our garden.

Suddenly, a shooting star zoomed by and lit up the sky.

"Make a wish, make a wish," I heard Mom whisper. I could almost feel my little hand in hers.

"Please show me the way," I whispered into the air.

Then I went back inside, crawled into the big, comfy bed, and fell into a deep sleep.

THE DAY AFTER

The phone in my hotel room woke me up. I quickly put a pillow over my head, desperately wanting the ringing to stop. I wasn't ready to face reality yet. And why would anyone call this early anyway?

A glance at the alarm clock told me it was 11:00 a.m. What? How was that even possible? Last time I looked it was 10:00 p.m., which meant I had slept for thirteen hours!

The phone rang a few more times before it stopped. I sighed and threw my head back on the pillow. Finally, some peace and quiet.

Then there was a knock at the door.

"Miss Williams, Miss Williams, are you in there?" The person on the other side of my door tried to come in. Thankfully, I had the security chain on, so it only opened a bit.

"Miss Williams, this is Jorge from the front desk. Are you alright? We are receiving calls from people who are worried about you. No one seems to be able to get a hold of you. Do you need any help?"

I felt embarrassed and was glad Jorge couldn't see me.

"I'm fine, thank you. Tell anyone who calls that everything is fine and that I will call them back. Thank you, Jorge."

"Thank you, Miss Williams," Jorge said politely and closed the door.

I sat up in bed. I still hadn't checked my cell phone. When I got back to the room last night, I was starving, so I ordered a pizza, but fell asleep in the tub before I ate it. Thank goodness I'd stayed away from the wine. Normally, after a day like yesterday, I would have drowned my frustration in alcohol. But after spending time with Josh on the beach, I had actually felt calmer and more balanced than I had felt in a long time.

It was time to get up. The bathrobe from last night was still wet, but there was a spare one in the bathroom. I wrapped it around me and walked over to the table and took a quick bite of the cold pizza. Yuck. It tasted like paper. There was an electric kettle and some instant coffee on the desk in the corner, so I prepared myself a cup of coffee, still moving slowly.

I was procrastinating, trying to postpone the inevitable, but I finally had to admit to myself that the grim circumstances waiting for me weren't going anywhere.

"Get a grip, Maya," I said out loud and walked decisively across the room, rummaged through my leather briefcase, and retrieved my cell phone from the bottom of it.

I took a deep breath and quickly scanned my call history. Seventy-seven missed calls and thirty new text messages. I quickly browsed through the texts. Three of them were from Alistair Parker.

"OK, here we go," I said with a sigh, then walked over to the bed and sat down.

I opened the first message: "What the hell were you thinking????"

The second one read: "The deal is off!!!"

And the third: "YOU ARE FIRED!!!"

I read the last text over and over. I wasn't surprised about the message. I was more surprised at my reaction to it.

I felt nothing. No anger, no disappointment, no sadness, no remorse, no regret, nothing. It was as if I couldn't care less, as if that message had nothing to do with me at all.

I had worried about being fired since the day I joined TechnoGuard, and now that I had been, I didn't even care. I shook my head. Something weird was going on with me.

I looked back at my phone. Some of the other missed calls and messages were from Lisa and Ruth, in addition to a lot of unknown numbers.

Ruth had texted, "I'm with you, boss. Always!" Lisa had sent about ten texts, all of them saying the same thing: "CALL ME!"

I dialed Lisa's number and even before I got to say hello, Lisa shouted, "You crazy, crazy, wonderful woman!" I had to hold the phone far away from my ear. Lisa has a very loud, high-pitched voice when she gets excited.

"I can't believe what you did! I am so goddamn proud of you! You did the right thing, Maya. Screw anyone who doesn't get that!"

I smiled, bringing the phone a little closer to my ear and thought how lucky I was to have a friend who loved me no matter what.

"How are you?" Lisa asked.

"I'm surprisingly well," I replied. "Alistair just fired me, and I don't even seem to care. I'm probably going insane or something!"

Lisa laughed. She sounded relieved. "Have you seen the papers?"

"Nope!" I said as I took a sip of the weak coffee. "And I'm not planning to either," I went on, walking into the bathroom to pour the rest of the coffee down the sink.

"Oh my God!" Lisa shouted, her voice bursting with excitement.

I moved the phone away from my ear again. "Maya, you *have* to check it out! You're famous! You're on the front page of *The Wall Street Journal* and *The New York Times*!"

"I'm what?" Now I was the one shouting.

"Listen to this! *The Wall Street Journal:* 'IT Executive Maya Williams Tells It As It Is.' And there's a big picture of you from the conference yesterday, looking smashing hot in that pencil skirt, and a facial expression that clearly says, 'Don't you dare mess with me.'"

I quickly grabbed my laptop and Googled myself. I read along as Lisa shared articles with me over the phone.

"Has a new wave of transparency finally arrived in Corporate America? In an unprecedented, candid, and brutally honest presentation for analysts and the investor community, TechnoGuard's VP of sales, Maya Williams, confirmed the rumor that there is an unresolved bug in the company's cybersecurity system. Now the big question is: Will Maya Williams be celebrated or punished for speaking the truth?"

"Well, we know the answer to that one, don't we?" I said dryly before I continued to read along with Lisa:

"The TechnoGuard stock (TECGD) dropped 10 percent when Nasdaq opened this morning, then took a surprising turn, rising 20 percent since the market opened. Senior analyst at Goldman Sachs Bernie Walters says he believes the market's reaction to Williams' presentation yesterday comes from 'Wall Street's hunger for authenticity and trustworthiness in an age of alternative facts, lies, and greed.'"

"Maya, you're making history!" Lisa shouted.

I continued reading as Lisa shared the next article from *The New York Times,* which had a similar spin.

"Maya Williams, VP of TechnoGuard Inc., has demonstrated what the corporate world lacks and investors desperately seek: radical openness, real integrity, and the courage to stand up for the truth, however inconvenient it may be."

"Wow, Maya. Just wow!" Lisa read on, citing a third article, in *The Washington Post,* written by one of their most prominent columnists.

"Enough is enough. TechnoGuard's VP of sales, Maya Williams, took the stage and showed us how it's done. With yesterday's speech,

she demonstrated that business and integrity are not mutually exclusive. Let's hope this ends one era and begins a new one."

I was shocked. Not in my wildest dreams had I seen this coming. I suspected that Alistair Parker hadn't either.

While Lisa read more of the articles to me, I went back to the text messages Alistair had sent. They were all from last night, before the papers had come out. I didn't think it would change anything. I had still done the unspeakable and would never be forgiven for that, but the news reports felt like a small victory, regardless.

"So, what are you going to do now?" Lisa asked when she had finished reading the highlights to me.

I rifled through my unpacked carry-on and found my plane ticket. My flight was leaving in four hours.

"I have absolutely no idea," I said as I sat back down on the bed. It felt weird to say those words out loud. I always knew what to do. I always had a plan. And now I didn't. What was wrong with me?

"Hey, why don't you hang around on the Garden Island for a while?" Lisa asked.

"Garden Island?" I asked, confused.

"Kaua'i, silly. It's called the Garden Island. It's supposed to be one of the most beautiful places on earth. You should totally check it out. Get some sun, sleep, eat some pineapples, and just chill for a while. Get out of your head and have some fun."

And then it hit me. Yes, of course.

"You know what, Lisa? I think I'll follow your advice."

"You will?" She sounded surprised.

"Yes. Sorry, I have to run. I have somewhere I need to be! I'll call you later and explain! OK?"

"You go, girl!"

I smiled as I hung up the phone.

It was time for some major chilling.

CHILL

Relax. Nothing is under control.

ZEN PROVERB

THE KEY TO PARADISE

"And now, ladies and gentlemen, I'll be playing the good old classic 'Knee Deep,' by Zac Brown Band and Jimmy Buffett, for you all," the radio host said in a laid-back voice. "Whether you live here or are just visiting, make sure to get your feet wet and sandy, and immerse yourself fully into the aloha spirit and endless days of chilling. And know that you have just found yourself the key to paradise."

I turned up the volume. It felt as if the radio host were speaking directly to me.

"I am Casey Kamaka, your favorite host on Island Radio, 98.5 FM. And this, my friends, is music that will make your feet stomp and hearts sing!"

As "Knee Deep" streamed out of the loudspeakers of my rental car, I stepped on the gas pedal and watched the hotel disappear in the rearview mirror. I could hardly believe I was doing this. I was going to live in the kind of world Zac Brown Band and Jimmy Buffett sang about for a whole week!

A strange, unfamiliar feeling bubbled up inside of me and came out as a loud "woooohoooo" as I waved my left hand up in the air.

A passing car honked and waved back at me and I laughed. Never had I felt so crazy, bubbly, and free. I had absolutely no idea what was happening to me. But I loved it!

After a quick search online, I had found a beach house on the North Shore of the island, only a two-hour drive from where I was.

When I'd phoned the airline to cancel my flight, the airline agent asked, "And when will you be returning, Ms. Williams?"

"You know what?" I replied. "I'm actually not sure."

The agent was quiet for a moment, and then she sighed, "You lucky thing."

"I sure am." I laughed before hanging up.

The car made a funny sound, like it had an engine too big for its size. I had never driven a Jeep before and realized it would take some getting used to. I chuckled as I realized I'd probably get used to the car long before I got used to my new outfit.

The lady in the hotel souvenir shop had been thrilled and clapped her hands with excitement when I, still dressed in high heels and my charcoal suit, my only clean clothes, had asked for an entire wardrobe for a week's stay on the island. She came running with dresses, swimwear, shorts, T-shirts, and lots of sarongs. That is when I learned that Hawaii doesn't do clothes without rainbow colors, flowers, palm trees, or "aloha" written all over them, at least not according to the lady in the souvenir shop.

"Happy colors, happy people," she exclaimed eagerly when I tried on all the different items she brought me.

Not in the mood for going shopping anywhere else, and eager to explore the island as quickly as possible, I bought most of the things the sweet lady suggested. I figured I could give it all away when I left the island in a week.

As I was about to leave the souvenir shop, carrying a big shopping bag with "Live with Aloha" written all over it, the sales woman came running after me. She had a pink flower in her hand and wanted to put it in my hair.

"The crown jewel," she said.

I tilted my head, a bit confused.

"You single lady, right?" Her English was decent, but she spoke in fragments.

"Is it that obvious?" I grimaced.

"Very easy. You pay for your own things. Don't ask man for advice. You self-sufficient woman. I like," she said and signaled that I should lower my head so she could put the flower in my hair.

"Flower on right side means you are single, flower on left side says you are taken. Very important you wear flower on right side. If not, no hanky-panky while in Hawaii."

I couldn't help but laugh. "No hanky-panky wherever I am or however I wear the flower," I said.

The old lady looked at me, worried. "Why no hanky-panky?" she asked. "Everyone do hanky-panky."

I laughed and shook my head. Her face suddenly lit up.

"You wear this flower, and I promise you hanky-panky very soon. You come thank me after. After hanky-panky."

I didn't want to hurt her feelings, so I lowered my head so she could put the pink flower over my right ear.

As I left the shop, I knew I probably looked ridiculous, but I smiled politely and waved the sweet old lady goodbye.

I was a bit nervous about bumping into someone from the conference, but when I threw a glance at myself in the large mirror in the lobby, I realized it wouldn't really matter. I doubted anyone would recognize me in this get-up. Hell, I couldn't even recognize me.

I smiled and stepped harder on the gas pedal.

Soon the road turned right and not long after, the ocean appeared directly in front of me, crystal blue and covered with sparkling diamonds. I took a deep breath and let out a happy sigh.

Being here was like being in a dream.

I turned left and followed the road alongside the ocean. Apparently, it was the only road heading north, so I didn't need to worry about getting lost.

Keeping my eyes on the road, however, was more of a challenge.

With the ocean on my right and green lush mountains covered with waterfalls to my left, it was like driving through a painting, with colors almost too intense to be real.

After a while, I passed a cute little town called Kapa'a, with low pastel-colored buildings, food trucks, and surf shops on every corner.

I was hungry so I stopped at a rainbow-painted food truck by the main road. The tiny courtyard in front of it was packed with young people, all looking like ridiculously happy and healthy surfer types. Some were waiting in line, others were hanging out on the grass, eating sandwiches out of small paper bags.

While waiting for my turn, I asked a girl dressed in shorts and a bikini top where Kealia Beach was. "Three minutes north, right by the cemetary," she smiled. Then she added, "The waves are awesome today. You'll have yourself some serious fun!"

I thanked her and laughed silently to myself. Now, wouldn't that be a sight for sore eyes.

After finishing my sandwich and kombucha, a cold fermented tea the girl behind the counter insisted I should try, I got back in my car and continued further north.

A few minutes later I saw the cemetary on the left side and pulled into the beach parking lot on the right. The large white beach was almost empty. It was easy to spot Josh. He was sitting peacefully on the sand, watching some surfers playing in the waves.

JOSH

"Aloha, Maya!" Josh's voice was warm and welcoming, as if he'd been expecting me. "Well, well, what do you know," he said with a big grin, checking out the "new" Maya.

I lowered my head, feeling a little self-conscious.

"From corporate fashionista to chill Hawaiian babe in less than twenty-four hours. Not bad at all." With sunglasses on I was able to see him more clearly. I realized he was a bit older than I first thought, maybe thirty. And just as beautiful. I don't think I'd ever met a man more fitting to that word.

"I decided to follow your advice to stay and chill for a while," I said.

Josh patted the sand beside him, inviting me to sit down.

"I'm very glad you did," he said, and I could feel that he meant it.

As I sat down, I noticed something I hadn't seen the day before. On his right arm he had a tattoo of an orange butterfly. It looked so real, as if it had just landed there and was having a little rest before it would continue to fly on to new adventures.

Josh must have noticed my stare.

"Once upon a time, I dreamt I was a butterfly," he said, "fluttering hither and thither. I was conscious only of my happiness as a butterfly, unaware that I was myself. Soon I awaked, and there I was, veritably myself again. Now I do not know whether I was then a man dreaming I was a butterfly, or whether I am now a butterfly, dreaming I am a man."

"Wow," I said and shook my head in awe. "Did you write that?"

Josh chuckled warmly.

"I wish," he said. "But no. I borrowed it from the great Chinese philosopher Zhuang Zhou, who—almost 2,500 years ago—was able to put words to something that resonates so deeply with me today."

I nodded and smiled at him. Then I looked back at the butterfly on his arm.

"It looks so real," I said, wanting to trace it with my finger but stopping myself, realizing that might come across as a bit strange.

I was quiet for a moment, then said, "My mom used to call me her little butterfly girl." I'd known Josh for less than twenty-four hours, but still it felt like the most natural thing in the world to share that memory with him.

He studied me silently with his warm and friendly eyes, waiting for me to continue.

"Right before she died, she told me to look out for butterflies, because they would be there to tell me that she was fine and that she was watching over me."

"And did you?"

I shook my head slowly at the memory.

"I think I tried, but then Dad told me I had to stop believing in all that sort of nonsense. To him, things that cannot be rationalized or scientifically explained don't exist."

Josh smiled and nodded knowingly. Something told me he'd been told the same once.

"And what do you think now?" he asked.

"Well, my dad trained me well, so I guess I have become more like him than my mom, who looked at everything in life as if it were a miracle. I used to believe in the things she believed in, but I think all of that died with her."

Josh nodded and was quiet for a while.

Then he took a deep breath and mused, "I guess it's all about how we choose to see it. Life can be serious and rationalized, or it can be playful and full of miracles. And whatever we choose to believe ends up becoming our reality."

At that moment, an orange butterfly flew by. I couldn't remember the last time I'd seen one.

"Look," I said. "It looks so happy. And so free."

"Yes, doesn't she?" Josh said. "She lives in the moment and enjoys every second of her short life. I think humans have a lot to learn from butterflies."

I smiled and looked from the real butterfly to the one on his arm. They were hard to tell apart.

"Is that why you got your butterfly tattoo?" I asked, even though Josh didn't seem to need that reminder.

"Yes," Josh nodded. "Nobody is born a butterfly, you know. We all start out as caterpillars and have to go through the journey to become a butterfly."

His words struck at something deep inside of me. Was that what we all were? Caterpillars? Without even being aware of it?

Pictures flashed through my mind: the blank faces rushing through the streets of New York, the dead eyes in front of the computer screens in the office, my own tired face sometimes reflected in the car window on my way to work. I shook it off—I didn't want my mind to go there.

I looked over at Josh again. A light wind blew his blond hair away from his face. He lifted his face toward it and gave a contented sigh.

"Did you grow up on the island?" I asked, realizing how little I knew about him.

"Nope. I am not from here," he replied. "I was born and raised in Detroit."

I didn't even try to hide my surprise. "Detroit? Really? So how did you end up here?" I scooped my arms around my knees, curious and eager to hear his story.

A modest smile flashed across his face. He seemed more comfortable talking about me than about himself. It was endearing and very different from most men I had met.

"It's kind of a long story," Josh warned.

I smiled. "I have all the time in the world."

He nodded and laughed softly.

"My dad was an accountant, working for one of the car companies," he began. His eyes were distant, as if he were searching for the memories.

"Every morning he got up at 5:30 a.m. and left for work at 6:30 a.m. He came home at 6:30 p.m. Then he ate his dinner, watched TV, complained about everything that was on it, went to bed, got up, and the next day looked exactly the same. What I remember about him was his miserable face, morning and night, and his mantra, the lone sentence that he repeated constantly: 'I can't wait till I retire.'" Josh had a painful expression on his face, as if he could feel his father's despair.

"First time I remember hearing him say that he longed for retirement, he was in his mid-forties and I had just turned twelve. That was when I started thinking that if this was what life was about, I couldn't see much point in it. My mom worked as a cashier in the local supermarket four days a week. She didn't hate her job as much as my dad did, or at least she didn't complain as much about it, but she didn't like it, either."

I shook my head slowly. "So many people feel like that," I said as an afterthought, maybe more to myself than to him.

Josh said, "'We work to pay the bills. Period,' was what Mom told me when I asked her why she and dad were so unhappy about their jobs."

After a brief pause to gather his thoughts, he continued. "Pretty soon I started noticing that it wasn't only my parents; most grown-ups had the same dull expression on their faces, as if all life had been sucked out of them."

I recognized what he was talking about. "Is that why you chose to leave?" I asked.

Josh nodded. "I knew I didn't want to live my life like them, but I had no idea what the alternative could look like."

He paused again for a moment. I could almost feel his frustration as he spoke. It was strange to think about Josh as a young, frustrated boy in Detroit.

"Then one day, when I was fifteen, I was on my way back from school, and I passed the local movie theater."

I smiled. I wondered whether his cinema was anything like the one Mom and I used to go to.

"I saw they were showing a movie called *In God's Hands*. The movie was about three surfers who traveled the world looking for the perfect wave. They discovered some of the most amazing places on earth, and Hawaii was one of them."

Josh was quiet for a little while, resting his eyes on the young men and a dark-haired woman who just had joined her friends in the waves. They looked like they were having so much fun, howling and laughing every time one of them caught a big wave.

I waited patiently for Josh to continue. I was eager to hear more.

"I saved my lunch money for a week to afford a ticket to a matinee," he continued. "The movie transported me to a world as different from mine as you could possibly get. I had never seen the ocean, much less surfed on it, but ten minutes into the movie, I knew that I had found my calling and that there was nothing else in the world I wanted to do."

"Wow," I said. "I love that the movie was just right there waiting for you."

Josh nodded. "It was pretty incredible. It gave me something to work toward, something to dream about and hope for."

"What did your folks say about your career plans?"

"I didn't tell my parents. I knew they wouldn't approve. Instead, during my remaining high school years, I took every job I could get and saved all the money I earned, with only one goal in mind: to get myself a one-way ticket to Hawaii and become a professional surfer."

Josh fell quiet and looked out over the ocean again.

"That's amazing, Josh. And you did it!"

How I admired that young, determined boy who wouldn't let anything, or anyone, stop him from pursuing his dream.

"So, how did you parents react when you left?" I asked.

Josh shook his head and laughed dryly.

"My parents took my choice as a personal insult to their way of life. They called me an ungrateful son and said I was bringing shame on the family. They were worried about what the neighbors would think."

I could hear in his voice that the memories stirred a lot of emotions.

"But regardless of their resistance, I knew I had to leave. I would have suffocated and died a slow death had I stayed. The life they had chosen for themselves was not for me, and I refused to let them or anyone else define what kind of life I should live."

"Did you ever return home?"

Josh shook his head. "On my way out, they told me I needn't come back. So, I never did. I tried calling and sent them postcards and invited them to come stay with me over Christmas every year, but they never responded."

"Family. It's a tricky thing," I said. I thought about my own dad, with whom I didn't exactly have the warmest relationship. Ever since my mom died, I felt I had done everything I could to please and impress him, but he never seemed to approve of anything I did. I felt ridiculous for still trying, for still caring.

"It's not an easy thing to stand up to your own parents," I said, as much to myself as to Josh.

"Standing up for ourselves, in whatever situation we find ourselves, is not an easy feat," Josh replied.

"When I was about sixteen years old, I came across an article by e. e. cummings called 'A Poet's Advice to Students,'" Josh continued. "The article stressed the importance of being true to yourself and resisting becoming the person everyone else wanted you to be. Reading those words gave me the strength and courage to follow my own dream and not the path of my parents, which I knew would never make me happy. So that is what I did. And that is why I am here."

I had noticed the strained expression on his face when he talked about his old life, but as he leaned back in the sand and turned his face toward the sun, I had no doubt that he was a happy man now.

"That's an amazing story, Josh," I said. "I'm really glad you chose to follow your dream, but I understand it couldn't have been easy."

Josh nodded. "The best things in life usually aren't," he said and smiled warmly to me, then looked back out over the ocean.

We watched one of the surfers catch a huge wave and heard the others howl and cheer her on. We laughed and clapped our hands as she made a pirouette inside the wave, then elegantly continued surfing it.

"Incredible!" I laughed and shook my head.

Josh nodded and grinned. "That girl will go far."

Then we were quiet again.

I took a deep breath and let the ocean air fill my lungs. Suddenly I was overcome by an emotion that only could be described as . . . happiness! What a funny feeling.

Josh smiled and studied me.

I sighed. "It's just so wonderful to be here."

Josh was still smiling, but the seriousness in his eyes reminded me of Mom's, whenever she wanted me to understand something important.

"You deserve to be happy, Maya," he said, holding my gaze.

I nodded. Something hurt deep in my chest.

I looked out at the water. A father was playing with his little daughter in the waves. Their happy, cheering voices filled the air.

Farther out, I could see a boat in the horizon, slowly making its way to its destination.

After a while I looked back at Josh.

"How did you do it, Josh? How did you break free from your old life? All the patterns, expectations, judgment, self-doubt?"

Josh smiled. "I just decided to ignore the boxes."

He noticed the puzzled expression on my face and continued.

"Most people live their entire lives inside a box, without even realizing it. They don't understand that they could be so much more and live a much richer life, had they only dared to step outside of their boxes. People think the boxes they live in are made of brick or stone, but, in fact, they are only made up of air. They think all the limitations surrounding them are real, while in truth they are only illusions."

I was silent for a while, trying to understand what he had just said.

"So, if limitations are illusions, they actually don't exist. Which means we can just go ahead and do whatever we want to, because what we think stops us isn't really there?" I asked.

I meant to challenge his thinking, but Josh only smiled and nodded.

"Yes, that's exactly it. But very few get this," he said eagerly.

I had to admit, I struggled a bit with following him.

"You see Maya, most people don't understand their full potential. Just like the caterpillar doesn't understand it can become a butterfly."

I reflected on what he was saying. In some strange way it actually made sense.

"So, what's stopping us?" I asked after a while.

"Fear is," Josh replied. "Fear of failure, fear of uncertainty. Fear of being ridiculed, fear of not belonging, of not being good enough. Fear of being too good. You name it."

I nodded. I was very familiar with all of these fears.

"You see, fear is the opposite of love and joy," Josh explained. "Fear is what keeps us in those boxes and makes us live our lives as caterpillars. When we let fear be our master, we cannot be free and happy as the butterfly. But when we choose to trust the journey and embrace love and joy, we are free to fly."

A gentle breeze came and took the pink flower the shopkeeper had placed behind my ear. We both watched as it blew along and landed softly on the waves.

"So, you leaving Detroit for a surfer life in Hawaii, that must have been a really scary thing," I said after a while. "And you did it anyway."

"Yes, it was scary. But for me, staying in the box, living the life of my parents, that was just as scary as diving into the unknown. So, since I was scared anyway, I decided to go for the one that most likely would lead to the kind of life I wanted for myself."

"You were such a brave kid," I said. I realized I had a lot to learn from young Josh.

"Maybe I sound braver than I was," Josh replied. "I wanted to escape the life laid before me as much as I wanted to pursue the dream ahead of me."

I nodded. "In a way you were lucky, because you actually had a dream. You knew what you wanted to do. What about those of us who haven't found our dream yet?"

Josh leaned forward and looked me in the eyes. If I hadn't had sunglasses on, I might have drowned in his crystal blue eyes.

"Don't worry, Maya, you'll find your dream too. Just give it some time. Don't overthink it. Finding your dream is a bit like chasing butterflies. If you run after it, it will fly away. But if you sit still, it just might land on you."

And as if on cue, the orange butterfly came fluttering back. It gently circled around us and landed softly in my lap.

"Now, if that isn't a sign, I don't know what is," Josh laughed.

In the water, a child laughed. The butterfly lifted, danced around our heads, and then continued to new adventures. The little girl out in the water screamed joyfully when the big waves came, and her dad lifted her high up in the air.

"How wonderful to be a happy, innocent child," I said.

Josh nodded.

"If I had children, I would do everything I could to keep them that way," he said. "And when they grew up, I'd encourage them to go out in the world and do whatever makes them happy. To live their lives to the fullest."

"Wow, those would be some lucky kids," I said. "But wouldn't you also want to prepare them for the brutal realities of life?"

Josh shook his head.

"I believe what you send out is what you attract. If you believe that the world is a mean and unfriendly place, that is probably what you will experience. If you choose to believe the world is a good and friendly place, that is what you will find. I would teach my children to always look for the good in others."

"Do you always look for the good in others?"

"Yes. And that is why I always find it."

I shook my head and laughed. "You are a remarkable man, Josh."

"There, look. You did it, too! You just found the good in me! Wow, you are such a fast learner, Maya!"

We both laughed.

I could have stayed on that beach with Josh forever, but I realized it was getting late. I had an appointment with the landlady of the house I was renting.

"The woman who is renting me a beach house told me to meet her around sunset. I don't even know when that is."

Josh laughed. "That's the island style. We orient ourselves after the sun instead of the actual time. I haven't owned a watch in years."

"What about a cell phone?"

"Don't need one," he said.

We stood up, and Josh walked me back to the car.

"So how can I get in touch with you? For some more life wisdom, I mean." I didn't want to come on too strong or insinuate anything.

"When you want to find me, you will," he winked.

"OK," I laughed. This whole island style would take some getting used to.

"Hey, can I give you a ride somewhere?" I asked when we got to the parking lot. I noticed there were no other cars but mine there.

"Thanks for asking, but that's not necessary. I live just across the street."

"Ah, lucky you," I smiled as I looked over at the other side of the road. There were a number of small pastel-colored houses to the left of the cemetary. "Great view."

"You bet!"

A soft breeze came and blew my hair away from my face. I looked over at Josh. He had closed his eyes and lifted his face to the wind.

"Do you feel it, Maya?" he asked. "The winds of change?" He opened his eyes and smiled at me. "I think great things are about to happen."

I smiled back at him. "I think they have already started."

I climbed into the Jeep and started the engine.

"Thank you so much, Josh. For everything."

"Thank you, Maya," he said, and smiled warmly. "Go fly, butterfly girl."

I smiled, waved him goodbye, and pulled out of the lot. Back on the highway, I waved a last goodbye, but Josh was already gone.

I turned on the radio and stepped on the gas. And would you believe it? "Knee Deep" was playing again. I turned up the radio and cheerfully sang along.

Knee deep, indeed!

THE BEACH HOUSE

The house I had rented was an elevated plantation-style beach house with a big lawn, surrounded by lush and colorful bushes and two tall palm trees with a hammock hanging between them.

Inside, it had two bedrooms, a big kitchen, and a cute living room with flowery curtains, beachy furniture, lamps shaped like pineapples, and paintings of hula dancers, surfboards, and palm trees on the walls.

Big windows and a small door led out to the large wraparound veranda, or "lanai," as the landlady called it, with an unobstructed ocean view on one side, and a view of the green mountains on the other.

The place was as different from my minimalistic Manhattan apartment as it possibly could get, and I loved it!

I couldn't believe how lucky I had been to get this house on such short notice. While the landlady showed me around, she told me that the house was usually rented out six months in advance, but they had received a last-minute cancellation just a few hours before I booked it.

"Looks like you were meant to have it," she said. "It's also available for the next three weeks, if you decide to stay longer."

"I'm planning to go back to New York next week," I explained, "but thank you anyway."

As wonderful as it all seemed, I couldn't see myself staying any longer than a week. It was already way more time off than I'd had in years. For all I knew, I might be bored after a few days, but then I could just go home.

After the landlady had left, I unpacked the "Live with Aloha" bag with all my new clothes as well as the groceries I picked up in Hanalei, the little town I had passed on my way here.

I realized I was getting hungry. The giant pineapple I had selected with some skillful help from the man in the store looked very tempting.

"This one is as ripe and juicy as it gets," the man had said proudly, as if he had picked it from the tree himself. Come to think of it, maybe he had.

I found a knife in one of the drawers and cut some slices. As I did, dark yellow juice seeped out onto the counter. I tried a slice. Oh my. The man hadn't exaggerated. It was by far the sweetest and juiciest pineapple I had eaten in my entire life.

I sliced a few more pieces of pineapple and some bread and cheese, poured myself a glass of Chardonnay, and went barefoot out on the veranda. A big couch with thick, flowery cushions faced the ocean. I set down my plate and glass on the wooden table and sank down in the soft cushions with a happy sigh.

As I sat there, looking at the ocean, listening to the sound of the waves, eating the juicy pineapple, and sipping my wine, it felt as if all my senses were vibrating. Like an instant injection of oxygen into every cell of my body. I had to admit that Gustav and Lisa had been right all along: this was by far the best medicine I could get. No need for those oxygen pills anymore, I smiled to myself.

On my first day in the house, I slept until noon. I was a bit confused and disoriented when I opened my eyes, but when I saw the pineapple-shaped fan over the bed and heard the enthusiastic bird choir and the loud sound of waves, I remembered where I was.

I wrapped a sheet from my bed around me and walked into the

kitchen to make myself some coffee. Outside the sky was blue and the sun was shining. Lucky me.

There was a classic Bialetti espresso maker on the stove. I filled it with water and the freshly roasted coffee I had bought the day before, and then just stood and watched it slowly percolate.

A memory came back to me of my mom standing beside the stove, quietly relishing the scent of coffee slowly filling the room. I used to stand there silently with her, feeling I was part of an important ritual. The ritual of welcoming a new day.

I leaned over the coffeepot and took in the aroma. It smelled heavenly.

When it was ready, I poured the coffee into a mug with rainbows on it and walked barefoot onto the veranda. Still wrapped in the thin white sheet from my bed, I sat down on the top of the stairs that led down to the lawn and looked around.

Large, colorful bushes separated the intensely green lawn from the sand, and behind it was the crystal blue ocean for as far as I could see. It looked like diamonds were dancing in its waves.

I didn't know that colors like these actually existed in real life. The only time I had seen colors this intense had been in Mom's paintings. "These are the colors of paradise," she had told me. And I realized that was where I was. In paradise.

As I sipped my coffee, a little bird with a red Mohawk landed on the stairs just below me. It tilted its head as if to say, "And who are you?" Three hens and a rooster walked right in front of me and carried on as if I weren't even there. I was surrounded by life. And no people. This was paradise, alright.

A bit later, as I walked back into the kitchen to refill my cup of coffee, a familiar voice jumped back into my head. "Fine, Maya, here we are. Now what? What's the plan? How are you going to spend the next week? And more importantly, what do you intend to do when you get back to *real* life?"

I shook my head. No way. I just got here. I am not going to listen to that voice today. "Shut up and give me a break," I growled.

And with that, the voice disappeared just as quickly as it had arrived. Thank goodness. Not only did I not want to listen to it judging me for not having a plan, I *definitely* didn't want it around when I put on my new bathing suit.

In my defense, the suit was the only one they had in my size in the souvenir shop. Pink, with a white sash across it that read "Aloha Baby," I wish I could say it was fun, ironic, or that I at least wore it well. Regretfully, all I could say about it was that it was better than being naked. But who cares? It wasn't like I needed to look good for anyone on the beach anyway.

I tied a sarong around my hips and walked barefoot across the lawn toward the beach. The grass was thick and coarse; it felt like getting a foot massage on the short trip over the lawn. As I stepped onto the soft sand, I took a deep breath and let out a deep, happy sigh. It was like the warm sand hugged my feet and sent happy chills through my entire body. I was surprised to see many people on the beach: sunbathers, children playing in the sand, people in the water, and couples walking hand in hand along the shore. I realized the sounds of chirping birds and waves hitting the shore must have drowned out all the other sounds.

An old man who looked a bit like a sailor with his navy blue-and-white-striped T-shirt and white hat was sitting in a chair on the beach right outside the house next door. He gave me a smile when I looked over at him.

"Hello," I said, smiling back.

"Hello. Welcome to paradise."

"Thank you, it certainly feels like it," I replied and was about to walk toward the water when something caught my eye.

I turned my head to the left of the beach. In the distance was a sight I never could have prepared myself for.

Bali Ha'i! Large, green, majestic, it looked like it was floating on a sea of liquid gold. The mountain seemed to be vibrating from inside, its peaks stretching up toward the sky, like fingers pointing upwards toward the heavens. Overwhelmed by emotions and memories, I just sat down in the sand and took it all in.

Suddenly I felt something tickle my arm. I looked down. An orange butterfly was dancing around me. It flew so close that its wings brushed my arm.

I followed the butterfly with my eyes as she flew toward the neighbor's house and landed quietly on a rose bush right behind the old man's chair.

GEORGE

"She's quite a beauty, isn't she?" the old man said. At first I thought he was talking about the butterfly, but then I noticed he was nodding toward Bali Ha'i.

His voice was deep and strong and sounded much younger than he looked.

"It's out-of-this-world beautiful," I said.

"Have you seen the movie *South Pacific*?" the old man asked.

I smiled and nodded eagerly. "At least thirty times. It was my mom's and my favorite movie of all time."

The old man smiled. Then, with a deep baritone voice, he started singing a familiar tune.

Most people live on a lonely island
Lost in the middle of a foggy sea
Most people long for another island
One where they know they will like to be
Bali Ha'i may call you
Any night, any day
In your heart, you'll hear it call you
"Come away, come away"

Bali Ha'i will whisper
On the wind of the sea
"Here am I, your special island!
Come to me, come to me."

The whole situation was so unreal; for a while, I thought I was dreaming. I just sat there, in the sand, listening to the old stranger with the stunning voice, singing the song that had meant so much for Mom and me, at this place that we had dreamt about visiting, without even knowing it existed for real.

When I realized I wasn't dreaming, that I was actually here and this was really happening, it was almost more than I could handle. Tears were streaming down my face.

How I wished Mom had been here to experience this with me. Then I had to smile. It was like I could see her here, dancing barefoot in the sand, dressed in a beautiful dress and with the happiest of smiles on her face.

As the old man finished the song, the orange butterfly lifted from the rosebush behind him, circled around his head, and softly landed on another flower, closer to my house.

I dried my tears and walked over to him.

"Wow. Just wow. I am speechless. Thank you so much!" I extended my hand. "I'm Maya. I'm renting the house next door."

His handshake was strong and firm. "Delighted. I'm George." His face wrinkled up in a friendly smile.

"Are you a professional singer or something?" I asked.

The old man seemed pleased.

"I used to be. Many, many years ago." He was beaming. "I was actually one of the singers in the movie."

I could feel my jaw drop. "In the movie? You mean *South Pacific*?"

He laughed and nodded. "I was young. It was only a tiny part, and if you blink you will have missed me, but I was there, alright."

When he smiled, I could see how handsome he once must have been. And charming, too. I bet all the ladies on set had swooned over him.

"You know, Maya. You're standing on the beach where many of the scenes in *South Pacific* were filmed."

He pointed to his left.

"Just over there is where Lieutenant Cable and the marines came the first time they visited the island of Bali Ha'i—which of course, as you can see, isn't a real island. You know, what is Bali Ha'i in the movie is actually the mountain of Mount Makana. But many of us still, affectionately, like to call her Bali Ha'i."

I recognized the spot and started to replay that scene in my mind. I still couldn't believe this was happening for real.

"What was it like here back then, when you were filming? Did it look the same?"

"Yes, pretty much," George said. "You should have seen it—the cameras, the crew, actors running around preparing for their scenes."

He pointed toward my beach house.

"In your backyard, there used to be a food truck where they fed the entire crew. The food was dreadful. But it was the only food around, so we ate it anyway."

I laughed. This was all too much.

"So, how did you land a role in *South Pacific* and get to experience all that?" I was curious to hear George's story. I had a feeling he was only happy to share.

"Please, have a seat," he said and opened the folded beach chair that was resting in the sand beside him.

I sat down next to him. He seemed to be just as eager to tell as I was to listen.

"It was 1956. I had just arrived in Los Angeles from Chicago. I was one of the many hopefuls that wanted to make it in the city of lights."

I could easily envision a young George stepping off a Greyhound bus, wearing his best suit and carrying a small, worn-out suitcase in his hand.

"Hollywood was at its most glamorous. You could bump into Marilyn Monroe or Cary Grant in one of the fancier lunch places in town, and whether you were cleaning floors or standing in front of the camera, you were part of that big adventure called Hollywood."

"Amazing! I can't believe you were actually there." I shook my head in awe. Listening to him speak was like being transported to a different place and time.

"I was working as a driver for one of the movie studios. Mostly I drove crew here and there, but sometimes I was lucky enough to drive a movie star or one of the big powerful film moguls. One day I was driving Joshua Logan, the famous film director, to the airport. He was complaining to his secretary that two of the actors in his upcoming film had been in a fight over some girl in a bar and were facing prosecution, so they would not be allowed to leave the city for the next couple of months."

My eyes widened. He knew *the* Joshua Logan?

George didn't seem to notice my awe. Instead, he continued, as if what he was talking about was the most ordinary thing in the world.

"With filming starting in less than a week they wouldn't have time for new auditions, and Mr. Logan told his secretary that he didn't have any hopes of being able to find anyone on the remote island where they were going to shoot the movie."

As I listened to George, the bird with the red Mohawk flew over and landed next to me in the sand. I watched as it tilted its head and looked back at me, then at George, who continued with his story.

"Sometimes we are given unique opportunities in life, and it's up to us whether we act on them or not. That day I had my big chance, and there was no way I wouldn't take it."

The red-headed bird inched closer to George's chair.

"'Sorry for eavesdropping, sir,' I told the famous film director. 'But if you need an actor that can sing, he just might be right in front of you.'"

George and I chuckled. I couldn't wait to hear what came next.

"Mr. Logan just stared at me, then continued talking to his secretary as if he hadn't even heard what I had said. With nothing to lose, I started to sing that song from *Oklahoma*, 'Oh What a Beautiful Morning,' and boy, did I give it my all."

I laughed. This was unbelievable!

"When I finished, he was quiet for a while. Then Mr. Logan said, 'Go home and pack your bag, son. You're coming with us to Hawaii.'" George grinned. "And that was the end of my life as I knew it—and the beginning of an entirely new life."

I was enthralled by his story.

"Life is a funny thing," George continued, "the way one choice, one chance, one opportunity, can entirely change the course of a life. That is, if we let it. I thought being rich and famous and living in Hollywood was my calling, but then I came to Kaua'i in 1957 and found what I really wanted. Something way better than being rich and famous."

"And what was that?" I asked.

George smiled. "I found love. I found happiness. I found paradise."

He took a deep sigh and looked over the ocean. I could see he was overwhelmed by all the memories.

When he looked at me again, he had tears in his eyes.

"Her name was Aimee. She was one of the actresses in the movie. First time I saw her was on set. She came walking toward me, wearing a white dress, looking directly at me, and I had this strange feeling that I had seen her before. When I looked into her eyes, it felt like coming home, and I just knew she was the woman I would spend the rest of my life with."

My hand went to my heart. I had always been a sucker for romantic stories, even though I was rarely part of them myself.

"It took some convincing, but on the last day of filming, right here on this beach, I asked her to be my wife in front of the entire crew. Two months later we were married. We spent the next fifty years together, on this beach, where we first met."

Tears continued to well up in his eyes, and he dried them off with the back of his hand.

"This always happens when I remember her," he said.

I was starting to tear up, too, but had to smile when our little bird friend circled above our heads and landed on a small log in the sand right in front of us. It seemed to be a sucker for romantic stories too.

"We had a wonderful life together. So many happy memories. I only wished it had been longer. Ten years ago, she passed away. I know she is waiting for me on the other side, but I am apparently not allowed to join her just yet. It seems like my life still has some kind of purpose, that there is something else I should do before I leave. I just don't know what it is. At least not yet."

His eyes were sad now. I wondered what it would be like to love someone that much. My heart was aching for him and his lost love. And it was aching a little bit for myself too. I'd never felt that kind of love and probably never would.

"Did you ever consider living anywhere else than here?" I asked.

"No, never. We knew that life would be much tougher for us on the mainland, because she was Tahitian. Interracial marriages were still taboo back then. Even today some people seem to have a problem accepting that people are people, regardless of the color of their skin or the shape of their eyes."

George's story stirred something deep inside me. I thought about Mom again.

The orange butterfly that had been sitting silently on a purple flower lifted softly and circled above our heads. George followed my gaze and smiled, then looked back out over the ocean.

"Aimee and I just wanted a happy life for ourselves and our son, William. We couldn't have asked for a better or happier life than the one we had right here. After all, how many people can say they have spent their lives in paradise on earth?"

For a moment, he seemed lost in the memories.

Then, as if just waking up, he shook his head and shifted in his chair. He leaned forward and looked directly at me with the warmest of smiles.

"But enough about me. What is your story? What is a beautiful woman like you doing all by herself in one of the most remote places on Earth?"

The little red-headed bird was still there and cocked its head, as if it wanted to hear my story too. What a funny little creature.

I told George about my mom, about our trips to the cinema, and about losing her when I was eleven. How I always tried to make my dad proud and had studied and worked hard my entire life.

I told him about how I had made a career in the corporate world and what I had come here to do—and then couldn't do it. How I had gotten to know Betsy and found out that Bali Ha'i existed for real and suddenly had just known that I needed to come here.

"Of course. Bali Ha'i was calling for you. I saw that the moment that you stepped on the beach."

I nodded. "I think you may be right. This feels weird to say, but I have this strange feeling that I belong here."

"I think so too, Maya. Believe it or not, I normally don't sing for strangers. But for some reason, for you, it just felt like the right thing to do. I thought you deserved a proper welcome." He smiled, his whole face wrinkling up again.

"Well, I certainly appreciated it." I smiled warmly back at him.

George reached over to the side of his chair. "Please excuse my bad manners. I haven't offered you anything to drink."

He reached his hand into a beach bag resting in the sand beside his chair and pulled out a thermos and two coffee mugs, one orange and one blue, both with "Aloha" painted across them in a child's handwriting.

"Care for some coffee?"

"Yes, please. Nice cups," I said.

He looked proud. "Yes, aren't they? My son William made these for Aimee and me when he was ten years old. We have been drinking from them ever since. I still bring Aimee's cup with me down to the beach. Somehow, I feel she is a bit closer to me when I do. Sometimes, in the wind, I can still hear her voice."

He filled the orange cup up and handed it to me.

"No one else has ever drunk from this before, but I know Aimee would be honored to have you drink from it."

My throat tightened. I thought it was one of the most beautiful gestures anyone had ever made to me.

We drank our coffees in silence and looked out at the ocean. I was fascinated by George and his story. Imagine living your entire life on one of the most remote islands in the world and being so happy. I assumed it would have its challenges, too, as with most things in life.

"Do you have any regrets?" I asked, realizing it was a very personal question, but still feeling it was OK to ask.

"No," he said and shook his head slowly. "I don't regret a single thing. I wake up every morning and go to bed every night with gratitude in my heart for my life, for the people in it, for what I've experienced and what I have learned."

He leaned forward in his chair. There was so much warmth in his eyes.

"I always told Aimee and William how much I loved them. Every day. I tried to be and do good, and if I didn't, I apologized afterward. I don't have any enemies, and there are no people in my life that I don't truly care about. I've laughed a lot and I've had a lot of fun. All of that makes up a good life in my book."

I nodded. It did sound like a very good life.

George paused, and then continued, "But that doesn't mean life has always been easy. There have been ups and downs, as in everyone's life. But even in the toughest and saddest days, I've always found something to be grateful for. I think life is a gift and whatever circumstances and challenges we meet, it is up to us whether we let them break us or make us a better version of ourselves." He smiled. "And now I am doing my best to enjoy the time I have left on this earth, knowing that when I have fulfilled my purpose, I will join Aimee on the other side."

I was moved by his firm belief that there was another side.

"So, what do you think the other side looks like, George?"

He spread out his arms.

"Like this! Times ten. And with Aimee in it."

"That certainly does sound like a perfect place," I said and smiled. George nodded, and I could see how his mind drifted away again. I followed his gaze and for a while we sat there in comfortable silence. Looking at the horizon and listening to the waves filled me with so much calm. A kind of calm I could not remember ever having felt before.

After a while the little bird flew back to its perch on the steps of my beach house. I took it as a sign that I should head back, too. I stood up and thanked George for the coffee.

"Any time. May I ask how long you are planning to stay on the beautiful isle of Kaua'i?" He pronounced Kaua'i differently from what I had heard before, with an accent on the "i" at the end.

"I don't know yet," I replied. "Yesterday I was thinking that a week would be more than long enough, but today I'm already feeling that it will be too short. I may stay for another week or two. It's not like there is any rush for me to go back to New York or anything."

"I hope you will stay," George said. "Next week we have a ceremony on the beach. It is the tenth anniversary of Aimee's passing. All our friends will be there, and my son William will fly over from San Francisco to be with us. I would love for you to come."

"Thank you so much," I said. "If I'm still here then, I would be honored to. Thank you again for the coffee, and the song and the stories. It's been magical."

I didn't use those words lightly.

"I'll see you again very soon, George."

I smiled as I walked back to the house. Within thirty-six hours I had made two new friends, one young and one old, both by far the sweetest men I'd ever met. It gave me hope for the future.

· · ·

I was in a haze the next few days. I slept and relaxed and then slept and relaxed some more. I practically lived in the hammock between the two palm trees in the garden, listening to the ocean sounds and the songs from my little friend the red-headed bird. It was the perfect backdrop to process everything I had experienced and learned over the last few days.

The nagging voice that wanted me to start planning my future jumped into my head now and then, and one day it almost convinced me to call the headhunters that had been chasing me with different job offers during the past year.

But just the thought of talking about work, or having to go back to New York for meetings and interviews, filled me with dread. I knew I would have to at some point, but I decided to postpone the inevitable for another couple of weeks. It wouldn't make much of a difference anyway. I could always find a job. But how often would I have the chance to totally chill?

Three weeks in paradise. I decided I deserved that, after everything I had been through. Reality could wait.

My landlady happily extended my stay, and once everything was settled, I messaged Ruth, Lisa, and my dad to let them know everything was OK and that I would head home by the end of the month.

"I'm happy & proud of you," Lisa texted.

"Let me know if there's anything I can do," Ruth wrote.

"Have you gone out of your mind?" Dad replied.

Apparently, back in New York, everything was the same.

As the days passed by, I gradually adjusted to island life. I had hardly looked at my cell phone or laptop since I'd arrived at the beach house. It was liberating, not thinking, caring, or worrying about the external world. To just relax, chill, and enjoy the moment I was in, for once.

I'd never felt better.

George and I chatted for a bit every day after my morning swim. He served me coffee and talked about life on the island. He also shared funny stories from the set of *South Pacific* and sometimes he talked about his son, William, who apparently was some Silicon Valley hot shot.

When I asked him if he had any grandchildren, he just laughed, explaining that William was way too busy for that. He mentioned that William had dated a sweet woman for a long time, but they were taking a break, so he'd pretty much given up his hopes for grandchildren for the time being.

I enjoyed my chats with George. In addition to our morning coffees and my daily swims, I continued spending a fair amount of time in the hammock. I had started picking up some of the books that the previous tenants had left behind and I devoured novels, biographies, and even some business books. It had been ages since I'd carved out the time to just sit and read a book. I'd forgotten how much I actually enjoyed it.

One day, a week after I first had arrived, I was resting and reading in the hammock, when that familiar voice snuck back into my head. "OK, you needed the rest. That's fine. Been there, done that. Now, you need to get on with your life. You're not planning to wander around like some barefoot goddess in funny-looking clothes your entire life, are you? You're being ridiculous. Imagine if people back in New York saw you. They'd think you'd gone insane. And what about your poor dad? His only daughter, once a promising businesswoman, now nothing but a lazy beach bum. Maya Williams, it's time to get real!"

I sat up in the hammock. For a moment I wondered whether I should open my laptop and check on what was going on in the world. Maybe I should contact those headhunters after all. But just the thought of doing that made me queasy. I wasn't ready yet.

Instead, I put on some clothes and took the Jeep into Hanalei. Maybe a change of scenery would be good for my mind and keep that nagging voice at bay.

When I got there, I found a farmers market on the lawn next to the little green church right outside Hanalei. The market was crowded with locals and tourists. The stands were stacked with avocados, mangos, coconuts, and pineapples. Two young men were playing their ukuleles and singing traditional Hawaiian songs. In Kaua'i, even grocery shopping was chill.

After filling my bag with fruit and vegetables and chatting with the local farmers about the perfect ripeness of a mango, I walked over to a nearby café. I had never been a great cook, and not even the magic of the island could change that. Without my daily fast-food habits from New York, the shorts I had bought a week earlier were starting to get loose around my waist. I didn't mind that at all. Being more curvy than skinny, I could stand to lose a few pounds.

"It's stress fat," Lisa had explained to me, showing me scientific research that stress was the worst threat to the waistline. Another good reason to hang around on the island and chill some more.

LANI & LIAT

The café was crowded, so the waitress asked a mother and a daughter who were seated at a four-person table if I could join them.

"Absolutely, Jesse," the woman at the table said. "We'd love some company."

Normally I would have hesitated to join some strangers, but this was Kaua'i, and I was the new, improved, and chill Maya. Besides, the mother-daughter duo looked very sweet.

"Hi, I'm Maya. Thanks for letting me crash your party," I said as I sat down. The mom looked like she was in her mid-thirties, with shoulder-length brown hair, big almond-shaped eyes, and a small emerald-stone nose piercing. She laughed and reached out her hand to welcome me.

"Hi, I'm Lani. And this is my daughter, Liat."

"Hi, Lani—and hi, Liat," I said and shook the little girl's hand. "What a pretty name you have."

Liat looked pleased. She had the cutest little dimples when she smiled.

I looked around the room. The café was crowded with small wooden tables and had a large bar in the corner. The two young men behind the counter were laughing and throwing glasses in the air, clearly trying to impress two young women sitting by the bar. Soft island music was playing in the background.

"Nice place," I said.

"The fish tacos are delicious," Lani said and nodded toward the menu in front of me.

"I'll follow her advice then," I said and smiled at Jesse who was waiting to take my order. "Fish tacos and a kombucha, please."

I turned around and looked at Lani and Liat. "So, do you two live here, on the island?"

Liat nodded eagerly and picked up one of the crayons in a small glass jar on the table.

"Yes, we're both born and raised on the island," Lani said. She nodded toward my shopping bag. "My parents are local farmers, and I used to help out at the farmers markets from when I was a little girl." Liat looked admiringly up at her mom. "And then you left," she said before she looked down again and started drawing on the white tablecloth.

"Yes, that's right, doll face," Lani smiled and tenderly stroked her daughter's hair.

"When I was nineteen I went to Honolulu to study to become a teacher, and when I finished, I decided I needed to widen my horizons, so I moved to New York," she explained.

"Nice, I'm from New York," I said.

Lani nodded and smiled. I had a feeling she had already picked up on that.

"I loved New York—and my work there," she continued. "I worked at an elementary school in Harlem. God how I loved those kids." Her eyes crinkled up in an affectionate smile. "But when I got pregnant with Liat, I decided to move back to Kaua'i. I can't imagine a better place to grow up. Now I teach at the local school here in Hanalei, and I love that too."

Lani exuded life, strength, and positivity. I imagined she would love whatever she did.

"And I'm in first grade!" Liat exclaimed proudly. She had lost both of her front teeth, and the way she pronounced "first" was unbelievably cute.

I didn't ask about Liat's father. I had a feeling he was no longer in the picture.

"What about you?" Lani asked. "What brought you to the island?"

I meant to give her the short version of my story but ended up telling her about everything that had happened in the last weeks, including my performance at the conference and my meetings with Josh and George on the beach.

"Way to go, sister," she said. "Sounds like you're on quite a journey. I'm really excited for you."

I felt that she really meant it.

"And you've definitely picked the right place to come to figure things out. This island can do wonders for people who are open to it."

I nodded. I was starting to realize that Kaua'i was a special place.

I turned towards Liat, who was deeply focused on transforming the white paper tablecloth into a big colorful rainbow.

"What a beautiful drawing!" I told her.

"Yes, isn't it?" Her dimples were truly adorable.

"I love drawing rainbows," she continued. "Mom says it's because I am a Rainbow Child."

She didn't look up, but I could hear the pride in her voice.

"What is a Rainbow Child?" I asked.

Liat looked up at me and then at her mom and they both started to giggle.

"Shall we tell her?" Liat asked and looked eagerly over at her mom. Lani smiled at me.

"Why don't you come and check it out for yourself?" she said a bit cryptically as her daughter nodded eagerly.

"Once a month the Rainbow Children meet up for a fireside chat on Ke'e Beach, overlooking Mount Makana. We usually don't invite grown-ups, but something tells me that you would really enjoy it, and the children will love having you there."

"I would love to!" I said.

"Phones are not allowed at the fireside chat," Liat added and pointed to my cell phone, which was lying beside me on the table.

"I promise I won't bring it," I said earnestly and put it into one of my grocery bags. I had brought it with me to take pictures and soon realized how hard it was to not look at all those emails, missed calls, and ignored text messages just waiting for me. I felt a tightness in my neck and stress in my body when I had the phone around. I had already decided I would put it back in my suitcase as soon as I got back to the house.

Lani turned toward me.

"Even here in Kaua'i, kids just five or six years old are getting addicted to their devices. I want to bring children together, device-free, so they can learn to really connect with each other and have real in-person conversations."

"Mom always says that if you can't say something to someone's face, don't say it at all."

"Yes, I do," Lani smiled. "And what else do I say?"

"That you should only say things that come from a kind place, because you mean the other person well. And if you don't mean well, don't say it."

"That's right, my sweet little angel."

Liat responded to her nicknames as if it was the most natural thing in the world. It was really adorable to watch. Lani and Liat reminded me a lot of my mom and me. In spite of the age difference, they seemed to be best friends.

"You know, Maya, the world you and I grew up in, the world before the internet, smartphones, and computer games, was so much simpler than the world children grow up in today."

I nodded.

"Kids today need help to sort out all that information, to make sense of things in a different way, and to learn how to be humans in a world where the difference between the virtual and the real is increasingly difficult to separate."

I nodded. "Yes, times definitely have changed, haven't they?"

Lani smiled as she looked down on the table that now was covered with every color of the rainbow.

"Nice work, princess." She gave her daughter a kiss on the cheek. Then she looked back at me and continued, "Today, many kids don't get to use their imagination. They are receivers, not creators, playing on their phones and computers all day. And while they are becoming increasingly good at playing violent video games, they are getting worse at empathy, communication, and normal human interactions."

Not having kids myself, I hadn't given this much thought, but I had to admit that it sounded like a scary scenario for young children.

"I want to help children make sense of this world, to grow up to be kind and sensible but also dreamy and courageous human beings. And most of all I want them to be happy, and to learn that true happiness comes from within."

Her words moved me.

"So, what made you decide to do what you do?" I asked.

"When I grew up, my parents always told me that if I didn't like something, I should try to change it," Lani explained. "And that is what I am doing. Trying to change things for the better. For one child at a time."

Listening to Lani speak, I couldn't help thinking how meaningful and personally rewarding her work with children must be.

I was almost embarrassed about how important I always had thought my work had been.

When my food arrived, I was left to my thoughts while Lani chatted with her friend Jesse, and Liat continued her drawing in deep concentration.

I thought about the boxes Josh had talked about, the ones with the imaginary walls. I realized I had spent most of my life inside one, thinking it was solid and that there was no other way to live my life.

Meeting Josh, George, and now Lani made me realize that life could be so different and much more exciting than I had ever been able to imagine.

Now I also understood what Josh meant when he said, "When nothing is certain, everything is possible." I felt excited to realize I had no idea what to do next or what was waiting around the corner. Thoughts like these usually would cause me to go into a tailspin, because I always wanted to have everything carefully planned and thought out. I hardly recognized myself now, and somehow, that was a big part of the thrill.

When it was time to pay the check, Lani insisted on buying me lunch.

"I get the friends and family rate." She winked.

I smiled. "Only if next time it's on me, at a place where you don't get that."

"Deal," Lani said and gave me a fist bump. I made a mental note to practice my fist bump technique.

Before we said our goodbyes, Lani asked if I wanted to join her for sunset yoga on the beach that evening. I hesitated for a moment. I might be the new and chill Maya, but I wasn't sure if I was *that* chill yet.

"I've never done yoga, and I don't have any yoga clothes," I explained, hoping that would qualify as a no.

Lani just laughed. "Don't worry about that, girl. This is island beach yoga. People show up as they are, in T-shirts and shorts, swimsuits, or whatever they feel like. It's easy and fun. Just bring a towel, and you'll be good to go."

ISLAND BEACH YOGA

"Inhale. Exhale. Breathe in. And breathe out."

We were sitting on the soft sand, just breathing. There were about twenty of us, women and men of all ages and sizes, and not a fancy pair of yoga pants to be seen.

In front of the group, with her back to the ocean, was our instructor, Ava. Long gray hair, mid-sixties, with the body of a thirty-five-year-old, she was dressed in a blue bathing suit and white shorts. She looked like a goddess who'd just stepped up from the sea.

Her voice was deep and soothing: "Feel the humidity of the ocean cleansing you with every breath you take. Breathe in the beauty, the purity, the happiness, the love. Breathe out any feelings that don't make you happy. Breathe out any thoughts that don't make you feel great."

I could have sat there for hours, listening to her and just breathing. Who knew that just sitting and breathing could feel this great?

After a while, Ava told us to start moving, and I followed her lead. Every movement was done in a very soft and calming way. We did downward dog, sun salutations, peaceful warrior, tree pose, and child's pose. I had seen it all demonstrated by Lisa before, but I'd never tried any of it myself.

It was nothing like I'd expected. While I'd always thought yoga was a bit pretentious, something you already had to be super fit and smashing hot to do, no one in the class seemed to fit that description. Except Lani, but she used to be a yoga teacher back in her New York days, so she didn't count.

In between guiding us through the different poses, Ava spoke softly about life philosophy and how important it was to speak to ourselves like we would speak to someone we loved. She said our bodies were listening and that every thought we had, every word we said, counted. When she started talking about the two conflicting voices in everyone's heads, I paid close attention.

Ava called the two voices the voice of the ego and the voice of the soul.

"Most people go through life thinking that the voice of the ego is the real voice, so every day they listen to that angry, critical voice that tells them they are not good enough, not clever enough, not good looking or successful enough, that they're not worthy of love. The voice of the ego judges, criticizes, and shouts. But that voice is not the real you. It's just a part that pretends to be you. You are not your ego. You are your soul, the voice that whispers and has nothing but love, compassion, and understanding for you, who only wants the best for you and who thinks you are perfect just the way you are."

She paused for a moment. "How many of you have, within the last thirty minutes, been thinking that you aren't good enough at this yoga thing, worried that you look ridiculous, or maybe even been telling yourself you have more important things to do than sitting on a beach and breathing?"

We all started laughing and almost everyone's hands went up.

"That's your ego talking, my friends. You can recognize it by how it does everything it can to take the joy out of the moment you're in."

I was glad to know I was not the only one struggling with the judgmental voice.

"So, when you are standing barefoot in the sand in paradise and have every reason to be blissfully happy and enjoy the moment, the ego hurries in with all the reasons why you shouldn't enjoy it."

The voice had jumped into my head a few minutes earlier, but I had firmly shut it down. I realized I was starting to get the hang of it and felt secretly proud.

Ava continued, "The ego will never stop trying to bring you down. It will keep coming back with all the reasons you should not be happy, but every time you quiet it down by ignoring it, it will get weaker and weaker."

I closed my eyes and took a deep breath.

"It takes a lot of practice, but in time you will be able to control it, to turn down that angry voice that lives in your mind and turn up that loving voice that lives inside your heart. Listen to your heart. It always knows best."

Listen to my heart. Yes, I could do that. At least I wanted to try.

I watched as Ava started to lean backward.

"Back-bending is a great way to open your heart. Just lean back into the sand and open your heart to all the love and goodness the universe has in store for you."

Standing on my knees toward the ocean, I leaned back so my hands touched my heels and tilted my head backward. It wasn't as difficult as it looked.

I could see everything upside down, and I heard Ava's voice from afar, "Now stretch and open those beautiful hearts of yours. Don't hold back. Whatever comes up, just let it out. Let it pour down into the sand."

For a moment all sound disappeared, and I felt a tingling, itching sensation around my heart. Then it spread throughout my entire body, like soft electricity pulsating through my veins. I sat back up, feeling my throat tightening, and suddenly I started to cry.

No one seemed to notice or mind, and Ava continued teaching while she slowly walked toward me. She put her hand on my shoulder and looked at me with warm eyes. "This is good, you are opening up, just let it all run down into the sand," she said, and then she moved on. The urge to cry disappeared as quickly as it came, and when she invited the whole class to walk with her down to the water, I followed.

In downward dog, with our backs toward the beach and our heads between our arms, we watched the ocean and the sky upside down.

"Who decides what is up and what is down?" Ava asked.

How interesting. I'd never thought about it that way before.

"Who decides what is right and what is wrong? It is all about perspective and what kind of lenses you choose to see the world through." She walked between us, speaking with a gentle voice. "Dr. Wayne Dyer used to say that when you change the way you look at things, the things you look at change. Keep that in mind, my friends. Things aren't always the way they seem."

Toward the end of the class we were just lying in the sand, breathing, and listening to the waves. It was perfect. And when we all sat up again with our hands in prayer, agreeing to live from our hearts, bowing with a heartfelt namaste, I started crying again. What was happening to me?

After class, Lani walked me to my car.

"You did really well," she said with a big smile.

She was wearing a T-shirt that read "Hanalei Queen." She caught me staring at it and laughed, pulling it down to straighten out the lettering.

"Liat gave me this shirt. She gets so happy every time I wear it."

I had to agree with Liat. Hanalei Queen was a very fitting name for Lani.

"I can't believe I started crying in class," I said when we got closer to our cars, feeling a bit embarrassed about it.

"Many people cry the first time they do yoga," Lani explained. "It's a good thing. It means you're doing it right. It's a happiness cry, really. Your body is thanking you for stretching and freeing up all those old, stuck emotions. Don't be surprised if you cry more later. Or get really hungry for sex. As you stretch and open up, the blood starts running through your veins, and maybe into places it hasn't been for a while."

She winked at me. "First time I did yoga I was so horny afterward that I almost picked up the first man I met on the street." She laughed.

I laughed with her. She reminded me of Lisa.

"OK, thanks for the warning, Lani. I'll make sure to lock myself in the house tonight."

She gave me a hug before she climbed into her pickup truck.

"See you at the fireside chat on Thursday?" she asked out her window.

"Definitely!"

"Great! We start at sunset. See you then!"

On the rear bumper of her truck there was a big sticker that read, "Life's a beach."

It sure is, I thought.

ANOTHER KIND OF DREAM

That night I had a sex dream, which was something I hadn't had in a very long time. In fact, I had started wondering whether I even had it in me anymore, if maybe I was done with sex forever.

Once upon a time I thought that not wanting to have sex must be really sad. But that was before I was nearly raped by my previous boss. Since then, I had been so shut off that neither my body nor my mind seemed to remember what was so great about it.

In the dream I was lying on the beach right after sunset. The sky was pink and orange, the ocean silvery blue. I was all alone. The sand felt like velvet. The water was soft and warm. I was lying on my back in the sand with my eyes closed and my legs in the water.

The soft waves were touching my toes and feet and the lower parts of my legs. The way the water softly caressed my skin felt soft, loving, and sensual, like it was kissing and carefully licking my legs. The water moved a little bit farther up with every wave.

Every time the waves receded, they returned a little bit firmer and went farther up my legs. I was starting to shiver, feeling how I wanted the waves to go even higher up. Breathing a little bit faster, I felt a tingling in my body, in my breasts, and between my legs.

I was starting to feel impatient, so I slid my body down, closer to the water, and opened my legs a little bit more for every wave that came, feeling more and more aroused.

Then I heard it: the ocean collecting all its power. As I opened my legs wide open, a big wave hit right between my legs, and riding on a giant wave of ecstasy, seeing the stars and universe exploding, I screamed out loud.

My own scream woke me up. Shocked by the vivid dream and the emotions it unleashed, I just lay there for a while, staring at the pineapple-shaped fan in the ceiling, going round and round.

I could feel something building up inside, big waves of emotions surging through me. I didn't know where they came from or what they were, I just knew they needed to get out.

And for the first time, for as long as I could remember, I decided to let them.

It started as a careful sob that quickly grew into a cry. And before I knew it, I was roaring with fury, bawling with hurt, and weeping like a child—sad, frightened, and lost.

I continued crying until there was no more crying left in me. And when I was empty, I crawled back under the sheets and fell into a dreamless sleep.

I woke up hours later, bathing in sweat. I slid out of the bed, walked into the bathroom, and turned on the shower. As I was waiting for the water to warm up, I turned around and studied my naked body in the mirror. I realized I hadn't looked at myself in a long time.

I touched my hips softly with my hands, then moved them over my stomach and my breasts. It felt strange touching myself, like I was touching someone else's body. But the more I touched it, the more I recognized it. My breasts were fuller than they used to be. And my hips and belly were rounder than when I was in my twenties and thirties. But the more I looked at myself, the more beauty I recognized. I was a woman. I looked like a woman. But for a long time, I hadn't felt like one.

As the bathroom filled with the warm humidity from the running water, I stepped into the shower and let the water caress my body while I continued to run my hands over it. I knew I had ignored my body for such a long time, but as I stood there, naked and wet, soft and warm, it felt like it was coming back to me. But then I realized: it wasn't my body coming back to me; it was me coming back to my body.

After my shower, I put on my swimsuit and walked barefoot over the lawn. The grass was covered with morning dew. I couldn't wait to just sit on the beach and breathe, like Ava had taught me in yoga class yesterday. Fresh oxygen, ocean air, peace and quiet was exactly what my mind and body wanted and needed this morning.

And I intended to oblige . . .

CHILL BEACH BABE

The sand was cool, almost wet. The ocean was still.

I sat down in lotus position, closed my eyes, and did what I had learned: Breathe in. Breathe out. Breathe in loving thoughts. Breathe out judgment and criticism. It felt good. I felt a wave of calmness spread through my body and a little tingle at my crown. It must be all that oxygen pouring into my body.

Hello breathing, hello yoga. Where have you been my entire life? I couldn't believe how well I was doing with this whole chilling thing. Lisa wouldn't have believed her eyes, and I think even Josh would have been proud of me.

I ignored the familiar, critical voice that told me I probably looked more like a pink walrus than a yogi. "I'm not listening to you," I said and continued breathing—and lo and behold, the voice disappeared.

The sound of the waves and the sight of the ocean washed away all unwanted thoughts, made me feel like I was one with the elements and that nothing in the world could disturb my peace of mind.

I closed my eyes for a new, deep, peaceful breath in, when I suddenly heard someone shouting. The next thing I knew I was attacked by a large, furry beast from behind!

I screamed and instantly jumped to my feet. A big white hairy dog was jumping eagerly around me with an enormous tongue hanging out of his drooling mouth. I noticed a dark-haired man walking toward us.

"Doggy, doggy, come to Papa. Leave the little meditation lady alone."

I couldn't believe my ears. Little meditation lady?

First, this man sent his beast to attack me and then he has the nerve to make fun of me.

And in an instant, the calm, chill Maya was gone.

"How dare you?" I shouted and tried to push away the dog that still was jumping on me. "Get that ugly thing off me!"

The dark-haired man laughed out loud.

"Yes, really funny, isn't it," I sneered. "Why don't you go screw yourself. Both of you." I stomped furiously through the sand, ignoring both the man and his dog, and rushed back to the house.

I could still hear the dog-owner's laughter as I angrily climbed the stairs to the house. What a jerk!

Back at the house I slammed the door behind me, still fuming. But as soon as I was inside, I sank down to the floor with my face in my hands.

Oh nooooo. No no no no. What had happened out there? What happened to the cool, chill island Maya?

I had freaked out when I got attacked. And the man was clearly an idiot. But still.

I stood up. OK. Deep breaths. No harm done. I'll probably never see him again. I'll just stay away from the beach today. It'll be fine.

I carefully peeked from behind the flowery curtain to see if the man and his ugly dog were still on the beach. They weren't. Instead, the man was walking across my lawn, heading toward my house, looking awfully relaxed, confident, and smiling.

And then it hit me. It was something in his posture, the way he held his head, the laughing eyes. He reminded me of someone I knew. And suddenly I realized who he was.

I wanted to sink into the ground, hide under the table, or pretend I wasn't home, but it was too late. He'd seen me peek at him from behind the curtain.

Red-faced, I opened the veranda door and reluctantly walked out to meet him.

"Hi, Maya. I'm William, George's son," he said and shook my hand. He was taller than his dad and had brown messy hair and brown eyes. But the smile and the firmness of his handshake were the same.

"Hello, William," I said, wishing I had a magic wand that could make me evaporate into thin air.

"I'm really sorry about what happened down there," William said and nodded toward the beach.

Even his voice reminded me of George's.

He had stopped laughing, but there was still a lot of laughter in his eyes.

"I tried to stop the dog, but it all happened so fast, and you got so angry. It all looked so funny, and I just couldn't help myself from laughing. It wasn't very nice of me, though. I'm really sorry!"

My face got even redder.

"So that dog—it wasn't yours?" I asked, mortified.

"Nope. Never seen him before," he said.

I hid my face in my hands. I didn't know what else to do.

When I looked up again, he was still there.

"This is very embarrassing," I said, my voice sounding weaker than normal.

"Don't worry about it, Maya." He grinned. "Dad pointed you out to me. I was just on my way over to introduce myself and remind you about the ceremony tonight."

I nodded.

"Yes, of course, thank you. Please tell George I will be there."

"Great. See you right before sunset, then," William said as he waved goodbye.

I followed him with my eyes as he walked back to George's house.

I hadn't expected William to be like that.

And I hadn't expected me to still be like this.

One week with a chill attitude apparently doesn't erase all those years without it. You can take the girl out of New York, but you can't take New York out of the girl, I suppose.

I was deeply embarrassed but tried to remind myself of Josh's advice of not being so hard on myself. I would make sure to pass that advice on to the judgmental voice that just noticed that I had been wearing the pink Aloha Baby bathing suit the entire time.

"Relax. Nothing is under control," the soft voice whispered.

That much I was beginning to understand.

CONNECT

Somewhere, something incredible is
waiting to be known.

CARL SAGAN

AIMEE

It was close to sunset when I left the house. I was wearing the only pretty dress I had in my Kaua'i wardrobe. It was long and low-cut in different blue tones, and made me feel like a mermaid. With a slight tan and a little bit of makeup, I looked better and healthier than I had in a long time. I felt a lot healthier, too. I hadn't eaten any junk or drunk much alcohol since I arrived on the island. I hadn't really felt like having it. It was almost like I wanted my insides to reflect my surroundings: clean, fresh, and pure. I think it would have put Lisa in a state of shock if she'd seen me.

As I walked down to the beach, I saw the big bonfire right below where George sat every day. It was the spot where he had proposed to Aimee and where they had exchanged their wedding vows sixty years ago. It was also where they had gathered to spread Aimee's ashes over the Pacific Ocean ten years ago, just as she had wanted.

"We both decided early on that neither of us wanted a gravestone. This island that brought us together and the memories held in our hearts were all we needed," George had told me one day as we drank our morning coffee.

To me, that made perfect sense. I had only visited Mom's grave a few times since she died. I never felt she was there.

A group of about thirty people were standing around the fire, with drinks in their hands, chatting. Everyone seemed to know each other well. A man was playing the ukulele and singing Hawaiian songs.

George was sitting in a chair a bit outside the group, looking out at the ocean, while William welcomed the newcomers. William looked over at me and gave me a little wave when I arrived, but he didn't come over. I couldn't blame him after our encounter earlier.

I walked over to greet George, who stood up and introduced me to a large dark-haired man with a ponytail. The man offered me a drink, which I received thankfully. It felt good to have something to hold on to. The drink tasted of coconut and rum, and it was pretty strong. Already after two sips, I could feel the warming sensation of alcohol in my blood.

After William had chatted his way around the group, he finally came over to me. "Thank you for coming. It means a lot to us," he said, nodding to his father, who was chatting with some of the other guests.

"Of course. I was looking forward to it," I said. I felt I should clear the air but didn't quite know how to begin.

William eyed my glass. "Can I get you another drink?"

He was polite, a gentleman, just like his father.

"Thanks, I'm good," I said. "My body needs to adjust slowly to the rum."

The warmth of his smile helped me summon enough courage to say what I needed to say.

"William, I need to apologize for earlier. I don't know what came over me, and I'm really embarrassed about it. It's really no excuse, but the dog kind of freaked me out."

At the mention of the dog, we both started laughing. And I realized that the whole situation was pretty funny. The tension was gone, and it suddenly felt friendlier and more relaxed between us.

"Frankly, Maya, I have to say that I found your temper quite refreshing," William said.

"Oh really?" I said. "What makes you say that?"

"When Dad pointed you out to me, sitting in your meditation pose on the beach, I thought you would be another one of those soft-spoken, tree-hugging, new-agey types that this island attracts in hordes. Not that there is anything wrong with that. It was just refreshing that you weren't one of them." He smiled and walked away to attend to some other guests, leaving me there, wondering whether I had just received a compliment or not.

The group suddenly became quiet when the large dark-haired man with the ponytail stood up and announced, "Aloha, friends."

I realized he was some sort of minister.

"We have gathered today to remember a beautiful soul, known to you as Aimee, who ten years ago crossed over to the other side."

He got quiet. A few seconds later, a strong, warm voice filled the air.

Facing the ocean, George began singing "Some Enchanted Evening," the song from *South Pacific* that he had sung to Aimee on the day they got married.

Everyone stood still and watched George as he walked down to the water, carrying a big lei, made up of flowers of every color. He finished the song at the exact moment that the sun set in the ocean, then he threw the lei out on the water.

We watched the flowers dance on the soft waves, while the man with the ponytail said a prayer in Hawaiian. When he finished, William walked down to meet his father at the shore and put his arm around him. Together they walked back up to the group still standing quietly around the bonfire.

William nodded to the ukulele player, who started playing again. People resumed talking and laughing, and the ceremony became a cheerful party again.

Suddenly, William was right in front of me again.

"Enjoying yourself?" he asked, flashing his boyish smile.

"Yes, I am. I've never attended a ceremony like this before, where sadness and happiness go hand in hand."

"Mom always liked a good party," William said with a smile. "She would have hated it if we just sat around with sad faces and mourned her on a day like this."

We watched an elderly couple dancing to the music from the ukulele. The old man was leading, and the woman was in his arms, smiling up at him like a schoolgirl. It was endearing to watch.

"Can I get you another drink now?" William asked. "That is, if your body has adjusted to the rum yet?"

I laughed and nodded. "I'd love one."

I had never been a fan of hard liquor, but coconut and rum was surprisingly enjoyable, especially in these surroundings.

A few minutes later William was back with a new drink. I realized I had been following him with my eyes the entire time, noticing how he walked, how he talked, how he poured the drink, the way he held his head, how he smiled, how he laughed, and how warm and friendly he was with everyone.

"Careful, Maya," a voice inside of me said, but I wasn't sure which one it was.

When William came back and handed me my drink, our hands touched for a moment and a shiver ran through my body.

He gave me a concerned look. "Are you cold? Can I get you a blanket?"

"Thank you, that would be nice," I said, even though I wasn't cold at all.

As he carefully put a blanket over my shoulders, his hand touched my back, and I shivered again. What was happening to me? This was very unlike me. I decided it must be the rum going to my head. I made a mental note to be careful with the alcohol. I didn't want to embarrass myself in front of William—again.

It was a nice party. Everyone seemed to be enjoying themselves, and when it got dark, one person after the other started to leave, hugging George and William goodbye as they left. Pretty soon, it was just the three of us left around the bonfire.

William was sitting with one arm around his father, the other holding George's hand. The love expressed between them was moving. I felt I was intruding on something deeply personal, so I stood up, signaling that I would leave as well.

"Can't you stay for a little while longer?" George asked.

William smiled and patted the pillow beside them.

"Yes, please, Maya, do join us. We still have plenty of rum to finish," he said and poured me another drink.

I smiled and sat down on the pillow beside William. I had a warm sensation in my body, and it wasn't only because of the rum.

For a while we all looked silently into the bonfire, sipping our drinks, listening to the sound of burning fire mixed with the ocean waves.

"What a beautiful ceremony it was," I said after another moment of silence. The two men nodded and smiled back at me, their faces lit by the warm light from the flames.

"Cheers to Mom," William said and lifted his glass.

"Cheers to my love," George chimed in.

"Cheers to Aimee, whom I wish I had met," I said as I raised my glass.

A big wave hit the shore and I took a deep breath. The sand was starting to get cooler under my feet. I moved closer to the fire and wrapped the blanket tighter around my shoulders. Thousands of stars were lighting up the sky, one of them shining brighter than the others.

While William put another piece of wood on the fire, I thought about how little I knew about the woman these two men had loved so much.

"What was Aimee really like?" I asked, when William sat down again.

George and William exchanged glances, and then they both burst out laughing.

"You go first," George said.

"No, you go, Dad. After all, you're the one who chose to marry her."

"OK," George said and took a deep breath. "To describe Aimee is like describing the island of Kaua'i, I guess: magical, beautiful, powerful, emotional, and strong."

I smiled. There was so much love in George's eyes.

"She was someone you definitely didn't want to mess with! Aimee fascinated me from the moment I met her. She was not like any of the other women on the set."

William smiled at his father. He had clearly heard this story many times before.

"While the other actresses seemed to accept and do what they were told, Aimee was opinionated and passionate and quickly became a headache for the film director. She didn't believe in following orders. She always had her own ideas for things, including the scenes she was in."

George was looking into the flames, smiling.

"In the scene when the marines were visiting Bali Ha'i for the first time, they were welcomed by the local girls. Aimee was supposed to wear a white dress and put a lei over the head of one of them when they stepped on land. But when she showed up for her scene, her white dress was torn and muddy and full of sand, and her hair was a mess. She was smiling from ear to ear, and her eyes were shining like two happy stars. I had never seen anything so beautiful in my entire life."

I looked over at William. He was chuckling, as he anticipated the next part of George's story. I couldn't help but smile. It was nice to be included in the telling of these stories.

"When Joshua Logan saw her, he shouted, 'What the hell, Aimee?' He scowled at Aimee as she lifted her stubborn little chin and looked the famous film director right in the eyes. She said, 'Don't you find it strange that on a desert island, far out in the South Pacific, hundreds of local girls are wearing clean white, starched dresses and have perfectly coiffed hair? I'm just helping you make the scene a bit more believable.'"

Now I was chuckling. Aimee sounded amazing—strong willed and fearless.

William leaned over and put another piece of wood on the bonfire while George continued his story.

"Needless to say, she was taken out of the scene, and the role was given to someone else. She was such a rebel, so full of laughter and heart. And even though there are hardly any traces of either of us in the final version of the film, I know the whole purpose of us being in it was so we could meet."

George smiled and gave William a little shove. "Which you should be really happy about, by the way."

William laughed and teasingly nudged his father back.

"Now it's your turn," George said, turning toward his son. "Tell us what it was like having Aimee as a mother."

William laughed. "What can I say? It was like being on a never-ending adventure. Mom didn't believe in strict rules or punishment like many other parents do."

George smiled, proud and happy to hear his son share his story.

"'You'll end up doing whatever you want to do anyway,' she used to tell me. And, of course, she was right."

I put my drink down in the sand. There was something about Aimee that reminded me of Mom.

"This is perhaps common knowledge now, but in the seventies this was pretty radical parenting. I remember learning right from wrong by observing my parents and by making my own mistakes and learning from them.

"If I wanted something, I needed to make good arguments for it and build my case. If I disagreed or didn't want to do something, and I had good enough reasons for it, she gladly let me convince her or change her mind. And I never needed to keep any secrets from her, because I always felt that she supported me and respected my decisions, even when they were really stupid."

George was still smiling. William stood up to refresh his drink. He gestured to me, to see if I wanted more, and I shook my head. I'd lost count of the number of drinks I'd had, and even though it was just a short walk back to the beach house, I wanted to be able to make it on my own.

William took a sip of his drink and continued, "One time my friends and I decided to hike down the Nā Pali Coast, also known as the Kalalau Trail, which is strictly forbidden if you don't have a guide or a permit, or—in our case—adult supervision.

"We were fifteen, cocky, and way too sure of ourselves, and decided to go it alone. Mom knew of our plans and asked if we had thought it through, if we realized the risk, and if we were willing to take the consequences should we get caught or should something happen to us. I said yes to it all, and she didn't say anything else except, 'Bring enough water and food and wear something warm.'"

George nodded at the memories. The reflection of the flames danced in William's eyes as he continued telling his story.

"Two hours into the hike, we were surprised by the weather. We had checked the forecast, and it looked good, but the weather can be very unpredictable around here, and if there is somewhere you don't want to be in a rainstorm, it's on the Kalalau Trail. The rain soon turned the trail into a mudslide that could have pulled us right down the rocky side of the mountain."

I held my breath, waiting for him to continue his story.

"There were five of us. We were all used to nature and climbing, but we were terrified. We simply couldn't move. There was nowhere to hide from the rain, and we all knew the dangers of mudslides."

My eyes widened as I looked over at George, who nodded to punctuate the gravity of the situation. I think the two of them enjoyed keeping me on edge with the vivid story.

"No one knew where we were except my parents. All the other boys had told their parents they would be sleeping at each other's places. They knew they would never be allowed to hike the Kalalau Trail by themselves."

The tide was getting closer and almost reached our chairs and pillows. We all stood up and moved to the other side of the bonfire.

"Then what?" I asked. I could almost see the terrified boys in front of me.

"I'll never forget when I heard the voices of Mom, Dad, and the park ranger," William said, with relief in his voice.

"They showed up with ropes and blankets and helped us back to safety. When we got back, Mom made sure we all had warm showers, dry clothes, sandwiches, and hot cocoa in front of the fireplace. There was no judgment or criticism. She just washed everyone's clothes to get rid of the mud, made up beds on mattresses on the living room floor, and woke everyone up for breakfast the next morning."

"That's incredible," I said.

William nodded. "Over breakfast she asked us to share what we'd learned over the past twenty-four hours. After everyone had shared their lessons, she nodded and smiled. 'As long as you all learn,' she said. Then she told us we all had to work for half a day each to pay the park ranger back as a thank you for helping with the rescue."

George smiled and nodded knowingly. He clearly liked this part of the story.

"Some had to cut the lawn. Others had to pick up trash on the beach. She gave all of us different chores that she paid for, and then asked us to personally go and pay the ranger and thank him for what he did."

My admiration for Aimee grew. I couldn't let go of the feeling that my mom probably would have done something similar.

William continued, "She never told any of the boys' families and said it was up to them if they wanted to share what had happened. In fact, we never spoke of the incident again until many years later. I asked Mom how come she hadn't tried to stop me from going on the trip when it was clearly a bad idea."

I looked over at George who beamed with pride as his son spoke of Aimee.

"She just looked at me and asked whether it would have made any difference, and I told her that I probably would have found a way to do it anyway."

Aimee clearly knew her son very well.

"So, what did she say then?" I asked.

William laughed. "Mom just looked at me and said, 'Well, there you go. Life is full of choices and risks, and we all have to learn from our own mistakes. And you clearly needed to learn a lesson to not make the kind of mistakes that could kill you.'"

William smiled and shook his head. "I definitely learned from that one, and so did my friends."

George chuckled. "What your mom never told you was that we notified the park ranger before you left, and we were just twenty minutes behind you. We let you stand in the rain for a while, to make sure you learned your lesson."

A smile broke across William's face. He grabbed some sand in his hands and threw it playfully toward his dad.

"You bastards! You never told me that!" He laughed and then turned to me.

"See what I was up against?"

George and I both laughed.

"Aimee sounds like such an amazing woman," I said.

"She certainly was," George said and smiled warmly into the fire. "And not only as a wife or mother. She was also one of the most accomplished businesswomen on the island."

"Really?"

George chuckled at my reaction and continued, "When William was just two years old, she started her own business. She'd been out shopping for children's clothes one day and thought the clothes in the stores were too expensive and of poor quality, so she started making her own clothes out of good material, with fun, playful designs.

"When the other parents saw William dressed in the clothes that

Aimee had made for him, they asked her if she could make clothes for their children, too. Pretty soon, more parents started contacting her, and the demand for her clothes exploded among all the parents on the island."

William smiled. Now he was the one who looked proud.

"She quickly outgrew our living room and rented a house to use as a makeshift factory. She hired some local people, trained them, and pretty soon, she had her own clothing brand and a chain of stores that became hugely popular on Kaua'i and quickly expanded to the other islands as well.

"And the funny part is that she ended up employing Dad," William added, laughing.

I laughed, too. This was all too much.

"She needed someone loyal and handy to help her build and open new stores, so Dad got the job, and she bossed him around and made him travel around to the different islands while she was here on Kaua'i, running the company and raising me."

"Which by the way was a much tougher job than managing the company," George teased.

William laughed and gave his dad a playful noogie.

"Aimee was a super woman in every sense of the word," George said, "but also the warmest, sweetest, and most fun-loving person you'd ever met."

William said, "Remember how Mom and I used to go body surfing, Dad? We were out in the waves for hours, and then we ate grilled fish and played cards afterward. Of all my childhood memories, those are some of my favorites."

"And my best memories are from after you went to bed," George teased as his son rolled his eyes and pretended to put his fingers in his ears.

"I'm too young to hear about this," William said, and they both laughed.

I don't know if it was the stories, the rum, the magical night, or the feeling of Aimee's spirit embracing us all, but there and then I thought to myself that I could not remember the last time I had felt so much happiness, joy, and love.

It was getting late and even though I felt I could have sat with those two men the entire night, I didn't want to keep them up too late.

"Gentlemen, this has been the nicest evening I've had in a very long time. Thank you for the drinks and the stories. I adore Aimee even more after this evening." I wanted to add, "and the two of you," but I didn't.

I felt warmly toward George—I had become really fond of the old man.

But watching William also made me feel warm, though in a very different way.

In a way I wasn't used to feeling.

WILLIAM

The next morning, George was not in his chair when I went down for my morning swim.

After my swim, I brought a sandwich and a book with me to the hammock, but I had trouble concentrating. I kept thinking of William: the way he embraced his dad, the love in his eyes for his mother, and the way he had smiled at me.

I'd finally managed to focus on my book when I heard a familiar voice.

"Hey, Maya."

It was William. I quickly sat up, trying to do it elegantly, which of course is an impossible feat in a hammock. Instead, I rolled over and fell right to the ground.

William laughed and helped me back up.

"You are quickly becoming one of the cutest girls I have ever come across," he said.

My heart leapt until I realized that "cute" probably meant "weird and clumsy."

I smiled as I dusted myself off with my book.

"Gabriel García Márquez, huh?" William said. He clearly knew his books better than I did, but I was pleased to impress him. No need to mention I had only read three pages.

"So, Dad and I were wondering whether you had any plans for tonight."

I smiled, thinking I could get used to all this attention.

"Since we only served you booze yesterday, we'd like to make it up to you with a proper meal tonight. That is, if you are free."

I nodded, maybe a bit too eagerly. "No plans. And yes, I'd love to."

"Great, see you at sunset then," he smiled.

I watched him walk back to his father's house and sighed.

Back in the hammock, I tried to concentrate on my book again, but the butterflies that had been dancing above my head earlier seemed to have found their way into my belly. And they gave me no rest.

. . .

Dinner was lovely. William grilled fish, and George made a rice dish that apparently had been Aimee's specialty. They served chilled white wine, and we talked and laughed like old friends all evening. I already adored George. And my fascination with William continued to grow, the more I got to know him.

William was a rare breed, a combination of playful and funny, intelligent and kind. He was confident in his own skin and not afraid to show his vulnerabilities. His love for his father was obvious, and when Aimee's name came up, he often had tears in his eyes. It was heartwarming to see.

William asked a lot of questions. He was curious about my life and what I thought about things and wanted to learn my likes and dislikes. He shook his head in disbelief when I told him some of my corporate stories and high-fived me when I told him what had happened at the investor conference.

When he asked the "what now?" question, he must have noticed my hesitation, so he quickly added, "I guess that's what you're here to figure out."

I nodded and was thankful that we left it at that. I asked William about his company and was amazed by his story.

Five years ago, he and his friend, Ray, a former Silicon Valley engineering star, had decided to start a company that developed software that could make robots mimic human emotions, like joy, sadness, and compassion. They got the idea from a conference they both attended, about how artificial intelligence and robotics would transform the human experience in the next ten years and how people will need to get used to the idea that robots, instead of humans, may be the ones that take care of them when they age.

William and Ray had gone from friends to business partners within a week. They were still best friends, after building a company that now employed two hundred people and was still growing. They had already installed their software in a number of existing robots, including one that was on trial in a retirement home.

William explained how the robot, Agatha, was dressed up as an old-fashioned maid with a white apron and hat. He said it was programmed to serve the elderly coffee and tea in the afternoon, while asking them questions about their days and showing appropriate human emotions, depending on what the elderly people said. When a man told Agatha about his hip pain, the robot appeared compassionate and caring and said she hoped he would feel better soon.

And when an old lady told Agatha that her grandchildren would come to visit, Agatha clapped her hands and smiled and said, "How exciting! That sounds lovely!"

Apparently, the people in the retirement home loved her, especially since she had been programmed to be very polite, with a posh British accent. Some of the patients said that they felt as if they were living in Downton Abbey after she had arrived. William told me they sometimes seemed to forget that she was a robot and that he felt a bit heartbroken that they would have to take her back one day, since they were just doing a trial and robots were still cost-prohibitive for most retirement homes.

George looked very proud of his son. The story about robots taking care of the old and the sick, however, made him shake his head.

"I hope you won't send one of those robots over to take care of me if I get sick," he said. He was trying to joke, but I could tell from his voice that he wasn't. William gave George a loving nudge.

"Don't you worry, Papa. You won't get rid of me that easy!" George seemed pleased. "But there will be other old and sick people who don't have anyone to take care of them. And even though a human might be best, a robot that acts like a human is better than one that doesn't."

"The robots are great and all that," George said, "but why don't you tell Maya about your company, too, William." George turned and looked at me. "William's company is one of the most admired and fastest-growing companies in Silicon Valley."

"Really? That's amazing, William."

William looked a bit embarrassed. It was kind of adorable.

"So, what's the secret to your success?" I asked.

"It's pretty simple, really," William replied. "The success has come because people love working there."

I was surprised by his answer. I had expected something else—like skillful engineers, strong management, disruptive technology, innovative design, committed investors . . .

William didn't seem to notice my surprise.

"From day one, Ray and I agreed that we would create the kind of company that we ourselves would love working for. We have both had our fair share of miserable workplaces, and we have seen how bad work environments lead to bad outcomes for those companies."

I was intrigued.

"We knew the way we built our company, the people we hired, and the culture we built would be what set us apart."

William's face lit up as he talked about his company. I glanced over at George, who was beaming with pride, listening to his son speaking.

"We see our culture as the foundation of everything we do. Culture determines how people work together, solve problems, support each other, develop products, treat customers—and how they feel about their jobs. Get the culture right, and the rest will follow. That has been our mantra since day one."

He took a sip of his wine and smiled, almost apologetic. "Please tell me if I'm talking too much. I tend to get very passionate about this subject."

"No, please continue," I said. "This is really interesting!" Culture had not been on the agenda in any of the companies I'd worked for. I wanted to learn more.

"So, what is your company culture like?" I asked.

"Well, first of all, it is a place where great people who want to make a difference come together," he explained. "The people working for us are already brilliant, so our job is really to unleash their collective brilliance and inspire them to achieve things they didn't even know they were capable of themselves."

He leaned eagerly forward in his chair.

"Our culture is all about innovation, passion, and joy. To do the impossible. And to enable that, we need to create an environment where people feel they can be themselves, have fun, explore, experiment, and make mistakes—and know that it is safe to do so."

"And how do you create such an environment?" I asked, fascinated by the subject and the kind of work culture William described.

"Well, neither Ray nor I have a tradition of taking ourselves very seriously, which of course helps. Then, we spend a lot of time talking with our people, inspiring and supporting them, making sure they feel safe and trusted, loved and cared for. We also tell them that failing is a necessary part of learning and that if they make a mistake or mess up, we'll have their back."

I was astonished. William's company sounded like the diametric opposite of TechnoGuard. There, the only thing people did to each other's backs was stab them.

And trust, love, and care? Who even used those kinds of words in a company setting? Well, clearly William did. I was not so sure how those words would fly with executives back in New York though.

Still, I had to admit I would much rather work in a company like the one William described than the kinds of companies I was used to—and probably would end up working at when I returned to New York. I felt queasy just thinking about that.

"It sounds incredible, William," I smiled and took another sip of my wine. "But isn't your job, as the CEO, primarily to deliver growth, results, and profitability?"

"Of course," William replied. "But those are *outcomes*. When we invest in our people and our culture, and create an environment where people thrive and have fun with what they do, great results follow as a consequence."

I turned toward George with a smile. "I wish I could bring your son with me to New York. I can think of quite a few CEOs who would choke on their coffee if they heard him speak."

George chuckled. William laughed too.

"Be careful what you ask for, Maya," William teased.

I felt my face flush and desperately hoped the two men didn't notice.

Thankfully, I was saved by George getting up from his chair.

"I'm sorry to interrupt such an interesting discussion," he said. "But I think it's time for those of us over eighty to get to bed."

George walked around the table and gave me a warm hug. When William stood up, I prepared to leave as well.

"No, please. Don't go anywhere, Maya," William protested. "I'll be back soon."

I sat down again and watched William follow his father inside. I was nervous about being alone with William. Those butterflies in my stomach wouldn't leave me alone.

As I listened to the big waves hitting the shore, I took a deep breath. Inhale. Exhale. William is just a friend.

"Hey, want to go stargazing?"

William was back, carrying a bottle of wine and some big blankets under his arm.

"Sure." I smiled, trying to sound cool. Inside, however, I was anything but.

I picked up our wine glasses and walked with William down to the beach. We walked as close to the water as we could possibly get without getting wet. The sand felt cool under my feet, and I wondered whether the sand actually was that cold, or if it was just me, feeling very warm . . .

William arranged the blankets on the sand and waited for me to sit down before he joined me. He was close enough that I could reach out and touch his hand.

As he was uncorking the bottle, he said, "Maya, I want to thank you for what you have done for Dad."

"What do you mean?" The surprise in my voice was genuine.

He poured a glass of wine and handed it to me.

"When I left the island a month ago, I could feel that Dad was in low spirits. The light in his eyes was fading, as if he was slowly giving up on life. I felt powerless; I didn't know what to do."

William poured himself a glass and took a sip before continuing.

"I tried to be here as often as I could, but it never felt like enough, and I couldn't be away from the company more than I already was."

I nodded, still unsure what good, if any, I had done.

"But when I came back this time, Dad was a different man. He was energetic and happy. His eyes were shining. I hadn't been home for more than five minutes before he started talking about how he'd met you on the beach and how you loved the movie *South Pacific* as much as he does. His whole face lit up when he said he had been singing for you and that the two of you drank coffee together every day."

I felt warm in my heart just thinking of George. He probably didn't know this, but he had done as much for me as—apparently—I had for him.

"Your presence has breathed new life into the old man. He simply adores you."

I took a sip of my wine and said, "And I adore him. Your dad is a very special man, and I feel so lucky to have met him." And *you*, I thought, but didn't dare to say that out loud.

We were both quiet for a while, just sipping our wine and looking at the stars. I had never seen so many stars in my entire life. Looking up, there was more light than darkness.

After a while, William spoke softly. "When I was a little boy, Mom used to point to the biggest star and tell me that Grandma and Grandpa were up there, waving down at us."

I smiled in the dark. "How funny," I said. "That is exactly what my mom told me, too." I lifted my head toward the stars. "We used to wave to my grandparents every night before I went to bed." I smiled at the memory.

We sat quietly and listened to the waves for a while, then I asked: "Do you believe, like George does, that our loved ones are waiting for us among the stars?"

William was silent for a moment, then said, "Yes, I think I do."

He paused for another moment before he continued, "But I haven't always believed it. I used to *say* that I did, though, just to make Mom happy." I could hear him smile in the dark.

I easily imagined him as a young boy, standing on this beach, hand in hand with Aimee, waving to the stars, skeptical but too polite and kind to contradict her.

"I've always had a bit of an engineering brain," he continued. "I wanted everything to be proven and rationalized. But the older I've become, the more I've come to realize that there is so much in the world that simply cannot be explained. And that just because we can't explain it, doesn't mean it doesn't exist."

Again, I thought about Mom. She would have loved to be part of this conversation.

"Have you had any of those unexplainable experiences?" I asked, curious to hear more.

I noticed him nodding in the dark. "Ever since Mom died, I have had experiences that cannot be explained, but I still know they happened. And the more I have accepted what I can't explain, the more of these experiences I'm having. So, I've stopped questioning and rationalizing them and have just embraced the fact that life is way more amazing than our limited human brains are capable of understanding."

He was quiet for a while. He leaned back on his elbows and looked up at the stars. "I call it the beautiful unexplainable," he said.

"The beautiful unexplainable," I repeated, like tasting the words. "I like that."

I was silent for a moment, then asked, "What kind of experiences did you have after your mom died, if you don't mind me asking?"

"OK." William leaned on his arm as he looked at me. "With the risk of you thinking I am out of my mind, a lot of strange little things happened right after Mom died." He paused for a moment, looking for the right words. "It was as if she was trying to communicate with Dad and me. And you should know that neither Dad nor I really believed in those kinds of things before she died. We didn't say it straight out to her, but she knew, and I think it really frustrated her sometimes."

William pulled his hands through his hair. I sensed that he was a little bit uncomfortable sharing this, which made the fact that he did even more special. I gave him an encouraging nod.

He took a deep breath and continued, "Before Mom got sick, every morning at 8:00 a.m. she used to make Dad and herself smoothies. A few months before she died, she bought a new blender that she insisted Dad should learn to use. She even wrote down the recipes for all his favorite smoothies in a little book that she put next to it. She wasn't sick then, but maybe she had a feeling or some kind of premonition about her illness."

While William was speaking, I saw a star out of the corner of my eye. I wondered if it was the same star I had seen the night before, shining brighter than all the others.

William followed my eyes before continuing to tell his story.

"One morning she fainted on her way to the bathroom. Dad quickly got her to the hospital, while I hurried over on the first flight from San Francisco. At the hospital we were told that Mom had an undetected, rare heart disease—and that there was no cure for it. Only one week after she fainted on the bathroom floor, her heart stopped beating. And suddenly, she was gone."

William's voice broke a bit, and he fell silent. He took a sip of his wine and looked out over the ocean for a while. I sat silent with my knees toward my chin and watched the ocean and listened to his warm, deep voice.

"Dad and I were devastated. We never got to say goodbye. A world without Mom was something neither Dad nor I had ever wanted to imagine, so when it happened, we were in shock and didn't know what to do with ourselves. We forgot to eat, we hardly slept. We were both walking around like zombies the first few days after she died."

William refilled my wine glass. After we both took another sip of our wine, he continued.

"One morning, about a week after she died, we heard a noise in the kitchen. We ran in and found the blender running. We turned it off and looked at each other. We wanted to come up with a rational explanation for this, but we had none. Then suddenly Dad squeezed my arm and pointed to the clock on the kitchen wall. It was 8:00 a.m. We both laughed, then cried a bit, and then we looked in the recipe book Mom had left Dad and made ourselves a smoothie before we left the house that day."

I set my glass down in the sand. "What a story," I said. "No wonder George feels certain that she is there, waiting for him."

William nodded. "There were other things, too. Postcards that said 'I love you' fell down from shelves, Mom's favorite song, 'Happy Talk' from *South Pacific*, started playing in the most unlikely places around town, and this little red cardinal kept showing up every time we talked about her."

I smiled. I knew there had been something special about that little red-headed bird.

"And then there were the butterflies. So many butterflies."

William was quiet again. I could feel his eyes on me. My eyes welled up when he talked about the butterflies.

"It must have been really tough losing your mom at such a young age," he said, compassionately.

I nodded. I was glad George had told him my story, so I didn't have to.

"Did you ever feel her presence after she died?" William asked.

A memory came back to me of an orange butterfly that sat on the same spot in the garden every morning for a whole week, the week after Mom died. I had walked over to it and said hello. Sometimes, I'd tell it what I was thinking about. I felt it was Mom saying hi, that somehow she and I were still communicating. But when I told Dad, he got angry and told me, "Don't be silly. Your mother is gone and that is that."

I was overwhelmed by the memories.

"Yes, I think she was there," I said after a while. I didn't bother drying the tears I could feel running down my cheeks. "I think she sent me butterflies."

William's voice was filled with warmth and empathy. "Mom used to say that butterflies were hellos from the other side," he said. "She said they symbolized transformation from one way of being to another."

I nodded, still moved by the memories.

William was quiet for a little while. "But she also used to say that our true mission as human beings is to feel as happy and free as a butterfly while we're still on this earth."

I felt a sudden urge to cry. It was like Mom was speaking to me.

A big wave crashed onto the shore and the wind blew the hair away from my face.

We were both looking up at the sky when we suddenly saw two giant lights illuminate the sky, only to disappear without a trace.

I sat up, startled. "What was that?" I asked.

"I don't know," William said and shook his head. "But I have a feeling it was a sign." He paused and smiled. "Maybe it was our moms saying hi."

I liked that idea. Mom and Aimee, sisters in spirit, letting us know that they're still there, watching over us.

We continued watching the stars for a while. The giant lights didn't return.

Moved by the experience, I tucked the blanket closer around my body and turned toward William. "Do you believe there is a God?"

William leaned over to his side and looked at me. "Yes, I actually do." He sounded almost surprised by his own reply. "However, I don't believe in the God I learned about in Sunday school, the kind of God that judges us. The God I believe in lives inside our hearts. She only wants the best for us. She wants us to be happy, to live freely, and to enjoy our time on this earth."

I took a deep breath and contemplated what he had just said.

William added, "To me, God is pure love."

I almost wanted to cry, just listening to William speak.

"That is the most beautiful way I have ever heard God explained," I said.

William smiled and rolled onto his back and looked up at the stars.

"And it's interesting how you refer to God as a woman," I continued.

William spoke softly. "The source of everything, the one who gave birth to a world, who loves her children unconditionally. That sounds like a woman to me, or at least a predominately feminine energy."

After a while he turned his head toward me. "What about you, Maya? Do you believe there is a God?"

I was quiet as I pondered the question.

"The God you just explained, that is the kind of God I can believe in. I have a hard time accepting religion. Most people seem to think they have the one and only answer and anything that doesn't fit into that is considered wrong or a sin. I think the misinterpretation of religion has done so much harm in this world."

I looked over at William, unsure if I should continue. He nodded, and I took a deep breath and added, "I used to believe in a higher power, then I lost it for a while, but after I came here, it's like that is all coming back to me. I still struggle with the rational part of it, though. My dad never let me believe in anything, unless I could rationalize, explain, and defend it. But how do we rationalize love, feelings, faith, miracles . . . ?"

William nodded. "We can't." He paused before he continued, "I guess that's why I like to call it the beautiful unexplainable."

I nodded. I liked that there was a way to describe the unexplainable—by not explaining it.

It was getting chilly. I sat up and William wrapped another blanket around me. When he touched my shoulder, I shivered.

"I don't want you to get sick," he said, concerned.

"Thanks, I'm fine." I smiled. I didn't want to explain the shivers.

William poured the last of the bottle of wine into our glasses and we sipped quietly while watching the waves glisten under the stars.

I couldn't help thinking how different William was from any other man I'd ever met. I had to admit that I really liked him, and I had a feeling that he liked me, too. But I wasn't sure in what way. I was used to men trying to pick me up after the second drink, but he hadn't tried anything. The fact that he hadn't made any advances made me feel simultaneously relieved and insecure.

Maybe he just saw me as a friend. Maybe he was back together with that girl in San Francisco that George had mentioned he was taking a break from. I didn't know what to think or feel. All I knew was that I wished this moment would never end.

Suddenly, a sound came from George's house. William looked over at the house.

"I better go in and check in on Dad."

"Of course!" I said, feeling my heart sink. Reluctantly I said, "This has been so lovely, but maybe we should call it a night."

I didn't want to leave, but I didn't want to come across as too eager either.

"Oh, OK. Sure. Tomorrow is a new day," he said.

Was it just wishful thinking or had there actually been a hint of disappointment in his voice?

William rolled the blankets together and carried the empty bottle and wine glasses as we walked side by side up to the small hedge that separated the two houses.

We smiled at each other in the dark.

"Goodnight, sweet Maya," he said and gently kissed me on the cheek.

"Goodnight, William," I said, wanting to kiss him back, but instead I just waved goodbye and walked back to my house.

That night, it was not the ocean I dreamt about.

ISLAND LIFE

The next day I woke up to a knock on my veranda door.

"Hey, Maya, you still alive?"

It was William. Oh no, he mustn't see me like this. "Just a minute!" I shouted as I ran into the bathroom and splashed some water on my face, quickly applied moisturizer, some mascara and lip balm, and put my messy hair in a bun on top of my head.

I wrapped a sarong around me and walked out to meet him. As I passed the clock in the kitchen, I noticed it was 11:30 a.m. Crazy!

William was sitting on the steps and turned around when he heard the screen door open. He smiled brightly and handed me a white paper bag. "Good morning, sleepyhead. Care for some coffee and donuts?"

Last night over dinner I had told him and George about my typical New York breakfast. He promised that he would soon introduce me to the best donut on the island. Apparently that day was today.

"Good morning, you obnoxiously energetic neighbor," I said and held an arm up over my face, pretending to shield it from the sun while, in fact, I was trying to hide my newly awoken face.

"Dad said you were a morning bird, but he must have mixed you up with someone else," William teased.

I laughed and sat down on the steps beside him. The coffee smelled heavenly, and the donut was too tempting not to try. I took a bite.

"Yum!" I said and took a big sip of the coffee.

William smiled. "I was thinking. I know you mostly have been chilling in the garden and haven't properly been introduced to the island yet, so if you don't have any other plans today, I thought I'd take you sightseeing. What do you say?"

Sightseeing with William? I was thrilled.

"Sounds like a perfect way to spend the day," I said and took another bite of the donut, trying to play it cool. "When do we leave?"

"Whenever you're ready."

"Give me five minutes to get dressed," I said as I stood up and left him on the porch.

"My kind of gal!" He laughed. "I'll be in my car."

While I got dressed, images from last night's dream flashed through my mind. I blushed just by thinking of them.

"Careful, Maya," I said to my reflection as I got dressed.

Ten minutes later I walked out the door and headed toward William's car, wearing shorts, a T-shirt, and flip-flops, with my hair still in a messy bun.

I had quickly packed a beach bag with a towel, sunscreen, and my Aloha Baby bathing suit, which I silently prayed I wouldn't have to wear.

"You're looking cute," William said.

My heart skipped a beat, but then I reminded myself that's the kind of things friends say to each other. "Thanks! You're not looking too bad yourself," I said and jumped into the seat next to him. William laughed. He was wearing jeans, a white T-shirt, and pilot glasses. He looked ridiculously handsome, but I tried not to dwell on that.

A few minutes later we were heading south along the coast in his old open Jeep Wrangler. It was nice not having to drive for once and to be able to just admire the scenery. William clearly knew the road like the back of his hand and drove twice as fast as I would have dared.

"OK, we have three stops today," he said.

I was curious about what he had planned.

William looked over at me, pretending to hold a microphone with his left hand, speaking with a tour guide voice, "First we'll eat the best food on the island, then we'll take in the most breathtaking view, and finally we'll be going to the best beach on Kaua'i and have ourselves some serious fun."

For a split second, my mind went back to last night's dream, but I firmly pushed the memory away.

"Sounds absolutely perfect," I said and sent him a friendly smile. He smiled back. Yes, definitely friends.

The first thirty minutes we hardly spoke. I was enjoying the view, the wind in my hair, and the sight of his tanned, muscular arm and his hand resting on the steering wheel. He looked very relaxed and happy. William exhibited a different kind of chill than Josh, but he was definitely chill. I could feel his eyes on me sometimes, but when I looked back at him, he looked away.

When we passed Kealia Beach, I tried to see if I could spot Josh, but he was nowhere to be seen. Then William turned his face toward me and smiled, his messy brown curls flying in the wind, and I forgot all about Josh.

We drove through the town of Kapa'a, which took about two minutes, and stopped at a Mexican food truck that was parked on a dirt road alongside the main road.

"The best burritos on the island," William explained and jumped out of the car.

He seemed to be good friends with the man behind the counter. The two of them talked quickly in Spanish and laughed a lot. Ten minutes later, we were on the road again with burritos in hand.

"I hope you don't mind eating while driving. We have somewhere we need to be in thirty minutes," he said and took a big bite of his burrito.

I took a bite of mine too. It was delicious. I had to use a napkin to stop the sauce from running down my cheeks, but that didn't stop me from taking another big bite.

William looked at me and smiled. "I love a woman with an appetite!"

For a moment I stopped chewing and looked at him, trying to look offended. When I spoke, I still had food in my mouth. "Are you saying that I eat like a pig?"

William threw his head back and laughed. "Ha ha, no! But I am saying that you are not like any other woman I've ever met, Maya Williams." I suddenly saw a spark in his eyes that signaled something more than friendship. But just as my heart was about to make a big jump inside my chest, I reminded myself that he was probably just teasing. After all, I was his cute, funny, and clumsy friend.

After we both had finished our burritos, William reached into the glove compartment, pulled out his cell phone, and made a quick call. I didn't understand a word of what he said but guessed it was Hawaiian.

"Hawaiian, Spanish, English?" I commented dryly. "Any other languages I should know about?"

William grinned. "French. Tahitian. And a little bit of Italian, but only food-related words."

"So how come you speak so many languages?" I asked, embarrassed about only speaking English and a little bit of really bad high-school Spanish.

We were cruising farther south. It looked like we were heading toward Lihue Airport.

"As so much else in my life, I owe it to my mom," William said with that loving look in his eyes. "She always said that if only people could learn to communicate better with each other, a lot of conflicts would be avoided."

I enjoyed my daily doses of Aimee-wisdom.

"Mom was born and raised in Tahiti and already spoke fluent English, French, and Tahitian, but from the moment she set foot on this island, she decided to learn to speak Hawaiian like a local, out of respect for the natives."

We passed by a small community that looked like it was inhabited by native Hawaiians. The buildings were smaller and simpler than most of the other houses I'd seen on the island.

I noticed a group of children playing with a ball outside a small worn-down house. An elderly woman was hanging her sheets to dry.

"Mom was a quick learner, and her eagerness to not only learn the language but also the origin and deeper meaning of the words was one of the reasons she ended up winning the trust and respect of the Hawaiians. That, and how she built her company on the principles of the aloha spirit."

I looked over at William.

"This might sound like a silly question to you, but what exactly do you mean by the aloha spirit?" I asked. "I thought aloha meant hello and goodbye."

William smiled. "Yes, it means hello and goodbye—and a lot more. Aloha is a way of living and treating each other. Aloha stands for love, peace, compassion, and mercy. The word itself actually means *the breath of life*."

"The breath of life," I repeated. "That is beautiful."

William smiled and nodded. "The aloha spirit is ingrained in the Hawaiian people and its culture," he explained. "It is one of the reasons Hawaii is considered paradise on earth by so many. It's not only about the beauty surrounding us, but also about the friendliness and spirit of our people."

"This is so interesting. And you're saying that your mom was leading her companies with the aloha spirit?"

"Yes, of course," he replied. "But there is nothing unique with that here in Hawaii. Companies that don't live by the aloha spirit don't survive. People won't work in companies that don't treat others with kindness, love, and compassion. Customers won't buy from them, and other local companies won't do business with them. It's as simple as that, really."

I looked down at the bag I had bought at the souvenir shop after my shopping spree. "Live with Aloha," it said. It made more sense to me now.

We passed by the airport, and a few minutes later we turned into a parking lot, next to a large heliport. Several helicopters were standing on helipads, picking up new passengers while dropping off others.

William parked the car, turned off the engine, and turned toward me with a big smile.

"Ready for the next item on our list?"

I swallowed nervously. I had neither been in a helicopter before nor felt the urge to be in one, but William's enthusiasm was irresistible, and the sound of the propellers overwhelming, so I just smiled and shouted, "Are we actually doing this?"

William grinned and waved toward one of the helicopters.

The pilot waved back at us, and a few seconds later we dashed out of the car and ran, hunched over, toward the helicopter.

The pilot smiled cheerfully as we climbed in and quickly shook hands, and then he and William gave each other an affectionate hug.

Seated at the front, William in the middle with the pilot to his left and me to his right, we buckled up and put large headsets on.

One minute later the helicopter lifted softly, and suddenly we were high in the air. I didn't even have time to think about being nervous.

The pilot introduced himself as Kalani. William told me he was the son of the minister that had attended the ceremony on the beach the other day.

"Kalani is a Hawaiian name that means sky," William explained.

"Very fitting indeed," I smiled and nodded toward Kalani, who steered the helicopter effortlessly toward the northwest side of the island.

I looked at the landscape below.

William had not exaggerated when he spoke of the most breath-taking views of the island. Soon we flew over waterfalls and canyons, lush jungles, long white beaches, and steep cliffs.

There were mountain formations so perfectly formed that they looked unreal. Whales and dolphins were playing in the crystal blue water below.

I was overwhelmed, unable to speak.

When we flew up the Nā Pali coastline, with emerald-colored cliffs towering above the ocean and small beaches tucked in between the perfectly shaped stone formations, the song "Bali Ha'i" started playing in the headset. And soon after, the majestic mountain of Bali Ha'i appeared below us.

I had goosebumps all over. Overwhelmed with gratitude, I turned my head toward William and mouthed a "thank you."

William smiled warmly; he put his hand on mine and gave it a squeeze. Our eyes met, but the moment was interrupted by Kalani's eager voice in the headset. "Hey, look who's here!"

We were right above Tunnels Beach and could see George sitting in his beach chair. Kalani turned the helicopter toward him, hovered above him for a moment, and then moved the helicopter from side to side in a big hello.

George was on his feet, waving with both arms to us. I could imagine his happy face. He clearly had been in on William's plans.

We all waved, and I blew him a kiss, even though I knew he couldn't see it. But William did. I could feel his eyes on me, but I didn't dare to look back.

As we waved George goodbye and continued farther south on the island, Kalani explained that Kaua'i is the oldest of the Hawaiian Islands. In spite of being only approximately 550 square miles, Kaua'i's climate is different in the south than in the north.

"While the sun is mostly shining in the south, on the northern part of the island it rains a bit almost every day during the winter months," he explained. "Thanks to all this water, the island is exceptionally green and lush, and that is why it is called the Garden Island."

On our way back to the south, Kalani steered the helicopter toward the center of the island.

"Now we're heading toward a mountain called Mount Wai'ale'ale, which means 'overflowing water' in Hawaiian," Kalani explained. "It's a shield volcano, known as the wettest place on earth."

As we approached the gigantic green crater, he steered the helicopter into the middle of it. Suddenly we were surrounded by steep cliffs on three sides, like a cave without a ceiling.

"The mountain has an average annual rainfall of 460 inches. The island needs the water to keep its high energy level in balance," Kalani explained and pointed toward one side of the cave. Streams of water were running down the mountain walls.

"It is called the 'weeping wall,'" he said. The sight of it moved me. The mountain *did* look like it was crying.

The helicopter was hovering in the middle of the cave. The air was vibrating, and I could feel waves of energy surging through my body.

"Look!" William said. All of a sudden, right in front of us, a 360-degree rainbow appeared. It nearly took my breath away.

And then, in the briefest of moments, I was enveloped in something so powerful and beautiful that I can only describe it as an embrace by the divine, a kiss from God, and a deep knowing in my heart, that I was safe, that I was loved, and that everything would be fine. I wanted to cry, and I wanted to laugh, so I did a little bit of both. William took my hand again and squeezed it. I knew I wouldn't have to explain. It felt as if he somehow just knew.

As we slowly flew back to the airport, listening to a beautiful Hawaiian song on the headset, I was thinking how much this island was changing me. What a different person I had already become.

Whatever happened in the future, I knew I would look back at these days as the best and most magical days of my life. I glanced over at William. He was leaning over Kalani and pointing at something on the ground, and they both laughed. He was so full of life and joy.

I wondered what would happen between William and me, if anything at all.

A new song started playing in the headset. It was Doris Day who joyfully sang "Que Sera Sera"—what will be, will be. I smiled. OK, message received.

Back at the heliport, Kalani landed the helicopter softly on the ground. A group of tourists were eagerly awaiting their turn.

We thanked him for the trip and as we got out of the helicopter, William took my hand and held it tightly as we ran with hunched backs toward his car. I loved the feeling of my hand in his.

Inside the Jeep, we both leaned back in our seats with a happy sigh.

"Wow," I said. "That was the most amazing experience of my life. On so many levels."

William smiled. "I had a feeling you'd like it."

As we drove slowly out of the parking lot, he asked, "Are you ready for the last stop of the tour?"

"Oh, you mean the 'serious fun on the beach' part?"

"That's right!" William smiled and winked. "That is, if you think you can handle it."

I blushed. Thankfully, William didn't seem to notice.

After driving another hour and a half, thirty minutes of it on an extremely bumpy dirt road through Polihale State Park, we finally arrived at a gorgeous beach, almost empty, with big waves crashing against the shore.

"This is where Mom first introduced me to bodysurfing," William said as he looked over the beach and the deep blue ocean. "And today I thought I'd introduce it to you."

William had packed a cooler, a big blanket, and a beach umbrella. As soon as we put our things down on the beach, he threw off his T-shirt, shouted like Tarzan, and ran right into the water.

I tried to not look, but I couldn't help but notice how good he looked in his shorts. I changed into my hideous bathing suit, feeling a bit annoyed with myself for not getting a better one, but then I thought "screw it"—and ran after him. Life was too short to worry about silly bathing suits.

Out in the water William explained how to catch the perfect wave and just go with it, body straight, arms out, head up, and mouth closed.

On my first attempt, a huge wave pulled me under. I panicked and swallowed a gallon of ocean. Back up on my feet again, I smiled and pretended that I was enjoying it. I figured this wasn't the best time to tell him how much I hated having my head underwater.

The second and third attempts didn't go much better. Somehow, I always ended up inside the wave instead of on top of it. I was relieved when William suggested a little time-out.

"Maya, there is one thing you need to understand," he explained, with laughing eyes.

"OK, and what's that?"

"There's no way you can control the ocean. You just have to trust it. The ocean wants to play with you, not to be in a battle with you."

I had to laugh. Yes, I knew I had control issues and had never been good at trusting anyone—including the ocean, apparently.

William, however, was in complete surrender, surfing one wave after another, cheering with joy every time he managed to ride a wave all the way to the beach.

"Let go of control, just go with the flow, and have fun," he said.

And when I decided to do just that, the perfect wave came, and I shouted with joy as it carried me all the way to the shore. It almost felt like flying.

After the first successful wave, I was unstoppable; I wanted to do it again and again. I didn't get it right every time, but I noticed that the more I relaxed and trusted, the better it went.

After having played in the waves for hours, we were happy and exhausted. My throat was sore after all the laughing and howling, and all the saltwater I'd drunk.

We sat down on the blanket, still laughing. I thought William looked adorable with his hair wet and eyes red from all the saltwater. He served up some cold beer and sandwiches from the cooler and I told him they were the best things I'd ever tasted. And I meant it.

The sun set in the ocean like a giant red fireball. We watched as its light reflected in the wet sand. Everything—the sky, the ocean, and the sand—took on the color of gold.

We sat there quietly until the sun had set, and the first stars appeared in the sky.

I was overwhelmed by all the impressions of the day.

"Imagine if life were made up of days like these," I said with a sigh. William looked at me and smiled. "But it is."

We looked at each other, and this time no one looked away. My heart started racing, and my mouth felt dry. When William slowly leaned forward, a familiar inner voice shouted loudly, "Careful, Maya!" and I quickly looked away.

When I looked back at William again, he was looking over the ocean. The moment was gone. I felt like I should say something, but I was at a loss for words.

On the drive home we didn't speak much. It was a comfortable silence, like all silences with William were. But there was something in the air that hadn't been there before. Something had happened on the beach, but I wasn't sure what it was. I couldn't remember ever having felt like this before, and it both scared and excited me.

"Let go of control, go with the flow, and have fun," he had told me. "Don't fight the ocean." I had finally managed it with the waves. But I still didn't know how to let go of the need to control how I felt about him.

I must have fallen asleep on the drive back, because the next thing I knew the Jeep had stopped, and we were home.

William turned off the engine and sat still for a moment. He took in a deep breath, and I felt he was about to say something. One part of me was curious to know what it was. The other part of me desperately wanted to get out of the car and run.

The latter won.

"Thank you so much for an amazing day, William," I blurted out, before he got to say whatever he was planning to say.

"You are the best friend a girl could dream of. See you tomorrow. Please give George a big hug from me."

Before William could respond, I jumped out of the car and ran toward the beach house. When I got to the back door, I fumbled a bit with the key. Once inside I slammed the door behind me and sank down on the couch with my face in my hands.

I sighed. What the hell was wrong with me? Now I would never know what he wanted to say.

I got back on my feet, went into the bathroom, splashed some cold water on my face, and stared back at my own reflection. How come I looked like I was forty but felt—and behaved—like I was fourteen?

For a moment I thought about calling Lisa, but then I realized I wasn't ready for her well-intended advice just yet.

Instead I went to the kitchen, opened the fridge, took out a bottle of white wine, poured myself a glass, and went outside.

I sat heavily down on the couch, facing the ocean.

Deep breaths. Think clearly, Maya. William is just a friend.

I took a sip of my wine and looked at the dark, blue ocean and the crescent moon, hovering right above the horizon.

OK, I had to admit there had been some special moments between us today, but that could happen between friends too, right? Like, really good friends.

Maybe that was what William was going to tell me, just before I ran out of his car. That he only had friendly feelings for me?

Naturally, he would want to tell me as soon as possible to make sure I wouldn't get hurt. That was the sort of man William was: kind, honest, and compassionate. A man of the aloha spirit.

Phew. The more I thought about it, the happier I was that I'd said it first—and ran out of the car before he could tell me.

After I finished my glass of wine, I went back in and got ready for bed. I opened my bedroom window and breathed in the ocean air. I thought about how a glass of wine and some self-talk really *could* do wonders.

I felt just fine now.

I crawled into bed and rested my head on the soft pillow. While listening to the soothing sound of the waves and feeling the gentle breeze on my face, I slowly drifted away.

Then, in the short space just before I fell into a dreamless sleep, I heard a soft whisper, "But what if?"

And the last thing I remembered was an ache—deep inside my heart.

THE CHILDREN OF
THE RAINBOW

Most of the children had already gathered around the big bonfire on Ke'e Beach, overlooking Bali Ha'i. I had brought a blanket to sit on and a knit sweater. Even though the days were warm, I'd learned how cool it became once the sun went down. Some of the children were running around chasing each other. Others were laughing and rolling around in the sand.

"OK, dear ones, time to gather," Lani called out, and the children immediately stopped running and came and sat down by the fire. They looked like they had come from every corner of the world, and everyone was dressed in the different colors of the rainbow.

"Aloha, dear children of the rainbow," Lani said before she started welcoming every child.

"Aloha, Jenny, it is good to see you."

"Aloha, Keke. I am happy you are here."

"Aloha, Luke. I am glad to see your happy face."

She gave each and every child a personal welcome. The children replied with "Aloha, Lani."

I was glad I had learned the true meaning of "aloha."

When it was my turn, Lani looked at me and said, "Aloha, Maya. The children of the rainbow and I are happy you wanted to join us tonight."

"Aloha, Lani and the children of the rainbow," I replied. "Thank you for having me. I am honored to be here."

Lani smiled warmly at all the children.

"As children of the rainbow we know that our mission on earth is to be kind, compassionate, and loving. We live by the aloha spirit in everything we say and everything we do, and our mission is to bring more happiness into this world. As always, I would love to hear about some of the nice things you have done since we last met."

All the children but one eagerly raised their hands.

Lani smiled as each child shared what they had done that week.

"I gave Noah a hug when he hit his head yesterday," one kid said.

"I told Leyla that she is always so kind and helpful," another almost shouted out.

"I asked an old lady if I could carry her grocery bag," another kid said.

"I gave myself a hug and said I should be kind to myself," a small girl added.

"I told my grandma how much I love her," a tall boy said.

"I helped a dog find his owner," Liat shared.

"I told my mom that she doesn't need to be sad and that everything will be fine," a tiny boy with big brown curls and glasses too big for his face said softly.

Lani walked over and gave the little boy a hug. Something squeezed at my heart when I looked at him.

When everyone but one girl, who was sitting a bit outside the circle, had shared their stories, Lani leaned toward her.

"How has your week been, Molly?" Lani asked with a loving voice.

"Fine," the girl replied and looked down at her hands that were resting in her lap.

"Do you have a story to share?" Lani asked.

The girl shook her head.

"You are one of the kindest people I know, so I am sure you have a story, if you think really hard."

The girl continued looking down at her hands.

Lani smiled and waited, patiently.

When the girl finally spoke, her voice was trembling.

"You always say that aloha starts with loving ourselves so we can extend the love to others."

"Yes." Lani smiled warmly and nodded, encouraging her to continue.

"I don't love myself," Molly almost whispered.

Lani walked over and gave the timid, little girl a hug.

"Maybe just for a moment you have forgotten how loveable you are. So, let's remind you, dear Molly."

And then one child after the other started speaking.

"I love you, because I think you are one of the kindest people I know."

"I love you, because when you smile it is as if the sun starts shining."

"I love you, because you always like to make other people smile."

"I love you, because you always say nice things to me."

"I love you, because you are fun to play with."

All the children had something nice to say to Molly. Slowly, her face lit up from all the love she received from the other children.

"See?" Lani said. "You are loved by so many, sweetheart, and if you ever should forget how to love yourself again, remember the love that surrounds you at all times, and you can always borrow some of ours."

It was heartwarming to see the little girl's smile.

Then Lani picked up her guitar. "Let's sing 'Children of the Rainbow,' dear ones."

Their enthusiastic cheer told me that they clearly knew the song well.

When Lani started to play, the children started singing about the beautiful world of the rainbow children with star-filled heavens and deep blue seas, where we all are sisters and brothers and forever live in peace.

When they finished singing, they all clapped their hands, and then

Lani served them fruit from a big basket she had brought along. The basket was filled with pineapples, mangos, papayas, and coconuts. No wonder all these kids look so healthy and happy, I thought to myself. Imagine growing up in paradise.

While the children were busy serving themselves some fruit, I asked Lani about the song.

"It's a Norwegian children's song from the seventies," she told me.

"Norwegian? How did you come across that?"

She laughed. "I dated a Norwegian guy for a while when I lived in New York, and he sang it to me. I thought it was magical to learn that someone literally living on the other side of the planet from Hawaii had made a song about the children of the rainbow."

"That's amazing."

Lani nodded. "My friend helped me translate it into English and I've been singing the song ever since. It's such an important reminder of how small the world is, that we are one big family, and that we all arrive with one wish: to be happy and to live in peace."

When all the children had finished eating the fruit, one of the boys shouted eagerly, "Lani, tell us about the legend!"

"Yes, Lani, please," another voice chimed in.

Soon all the children were clapping their hands shouting, "Legend, legend, legend!"

I had no idea what legend they were talking about, but I joined the children clapping hands and shouting, "Legend, legend."

"OK, OK." Lani laughed and winked at me.

It was slowly getting dark, and the orange flames were lighting up the little faces sitting quietly and looking at Lani with great anticipation. For a little while, the only sounds were the crackles of the fire and the waves hitting the shore.

Noah, the little boy with the big glasses and dark curls, carefully sat down beside me. He looked up at me with a shy smile, and when Lani started talking, his little hand found mine and held on to it tightly.

"Once upon a time, there was a land called Mu," Lani began.

The light from the fire lit up her face, and she looked at the children as she spoke.

"Mu was called the Motherland of Man and Paradise on Earth, as the people living there were happy, loving, playful, and friendly. They knew not of war, since no one wanted to fight.

"They knew not of hunger, since nature abundantly supplied them with the sweetest of fruits and anything else they could desire. They knew not of jealousy or hate, since all they could feel was love. And they knew not of sadness or grief, as whenever they lost someone they loved, they just passed over to another dimension, their energies and love still alive and present with their loved ones."

Noah squeezed my hand. There was something very special about this shy little boy. I wanted to put my arms around him and hug him. Instead, I just carefully squeezed his little hand back.

"Then one day, tragedy hit. The land, once known as paradise on earth, started shaking, the ground ripped open, and gigantic waves caused the entire continent of Mu to sink deep down into the ocean. Only the highest mountaintops remained over the ocean, creating the islands we today know as Hawaii. Only the people who had lived on the hilltops of Mu survived. They called themselves the Children of the Rainbow and continued living lives of love, joy, and play, with people of all colors considered equals, alongside animals and Mother Earth."

I looked at the children sitting around the bonfire. They were all staring at Lani with big eyes, captivated by the story.

"There were no kings or rulers," Lani continued, "and no one controlled anyone else. Instead, all were connected, respected, and loved by their ohanas—their families—and the elders, bringing the wisdom of life, nature, and the universe to the young ones, guiding them and teaching them about the beauty of life. The children's favorite playground was the rainbow, which transported them to other places and dimensions. They could travel back and forth in time, and there were no limits to what the children could do, because they knew of no limitations. No one had ever told them things could not be done; therefore they could do them."

"Wow! Imagine!" a little girl with red curls shouted and clapped her hands.

Lani smiled at the little girl, then continued gravely, "Then one night, ships filled with guns and men of hate and greed invaded the Land of the Rainbow."

The little faces around the bonfire looked worried, and the little red-haired girl covered her ears with her hands. She seemed to know what came next.

Lani continued: "The Children of the Rainbow greeted the men as friends, but most of them were captured, and many were killed by the evil men. Of those who weren't killed, many died of sickness and diseases that were brought into the land of beauty and innocence."

Little Noah huddled closer. I could tell he didn't like this part of the legend. I carefully put my arm around him, and he leaned on me, seeking comfort in my embrace.

"However, a few people hid away on mountaintops and in caves. And one night, the wisest of them, represented by people of every color, came together on a beach, like this. The women and men who sat around the campfire listened to the gods and read in the stars that the age of the Rainbow Children was coming to an end. Their last deed as humans on this earth was to travel to every corner of the world to spread the wisdom of love and to speak the voice of Mother Earth and tell her stories."

The children listened with big round eyes.

"The stories they told were about the universe's plan to restore love and happiness on earth when humanity was ready and had learned what it needed to learn. The men and women called themselves

Rainbow Travelers, as they used the rainbow to take them to other worlds and dimensions, but also to move to faraway lands that would have taken years to travel to by ship."

Lani paused, and everyone was quiet, waiting for her to continue.

"Today, the descendants of the Children of the Rainbow can be found in all four corners of the world. They are the so-called indigenous people, the people of wisdom, who had to suffer for their wisdom as the evil people have greatly outnumbered them."

All the children's eyes were on Lani. Some of them were holding hands. A black girl with braids was holding her arms around a little blond-haired boy. An Asian boy was holding hands with a little red-haired boy on his left side and on his right side, a girl with brown hair, freckles, and a yellow dress was leaning toward his shoulder. Liat and some of the other children were sitting with their legs crossed, leaning their little chins in their hands, looking at Lani, hanging on to every word she said. Little Noah was still leaning on me as I kept my arm around his shoulder and his tiny hand in mine.

We were all entranced with the legend.

"And now, as we are entering a new age of wisdom, when evil will be fought with love, and harmony restored between nature and all people, the Children of the Rainbow are back on the earth plane, to show the world what happiness and love look like. And while their descendants are spread all over the world, Hawaii continues to be the home of their souls and the place where the Rainbow Children can always restore and recharge for their important mission in life."

Finally, she said, "Dear Children of the Rainbow, change starts with you and me. With happy thoughts and good deeds, we are making a difference. Let's make this world a happy place."

After she ended her story, the children remained quiet. Only the sound of wood burning and waves hitting the shore broke the silence. In the distance, parents stood by their cars, waiting to pick up their children.

Lani looked up, saw the parents, and realized it was time to wrap up.

"OK, dear ones, thank you all for coming today. We'll see each other again next month. Let's end today's fire chat the way we always end it." She picked up her guitar again and all the children, with their light voices, sang "Happy Talk" from *South Pacific*. Never had the song sounded lovelier.

When the singing finished, all the children got up and gave Lani a hug before they ran toward their parents—everyone but Liat and little Noah, who was still sitting quietly, looking down on the sand, firmly holding on to my hand. He seemed to know that no one was picking him up.

After she had waved all the other children goodbye, Lani said tenderly, "Do you want to come with us, Noah?" She took the little boy's hand.

He nodded and stood up, still looking down. Lani sat down on her knees and took his little face in her hands.

"Noah, please look at me," she said with a warm voice.

He lifted his head and looked into Lani's loving eyes, tears welling in his eyes.

"Noah, sometimes when your mom is not feeling well, she forgets things. It has nothing to do with you. I promise. She loves you very much. And Liat and I love you very much, too." She gave the little boy a hug and kissed him on the cheek.

"Now, let's go find out how she is doing, and if she isn't feeling well, you can stay with us tonight. OK?"

Noah nodded, and as he did, it felt like something burst inside of me. I turned away so he wouldn't see it. But Lani noticed. She squeezed my arm.

"We'll speak soon," she whispered.

I watched the three of them walking toward Lani's car, little Noah in the middle, holding hands with Lani on one side and Liat on the other.

Not until I saw them drive away did I allow myself to cry.

It was as if I could feel what the little boy felt, and it nearly broke my heart.

FINDING THE DREAM

One week after the fireside chat with the children, Lani and I met for a morning coffee in Hanalei. William and I had bumped into her a few days earlier at the farmers market. When William and George had insisted that I should join them for another dinner before William went to San Francisco for a few days, I offered to buy the ingredients. And since William was going to cook, he insisted on coming along. It had turned out to be a highly memorable shopping experience.

William knew almost everyone there. He talked and joked around with the farmers and their children, juggled coconuts so well that people around him started applauding, and then invited me to dance on the muddy lawn when two local musicians started playing their ukuleles.

Back at the house, William demonstrated his excellent cooking skills by turning a bag of vegetables, bread, and olive oil into one of the best meals I'd ever had. I chopped vegetables and George sat in his favorite chair and watched us while enjoying a glass of his favorite wine. He didn't seem to be able to stop smiling.

After our island tour there had been nothing but friend vibes between William and me. Things had been very relaxed and comfortable, there had been no more "moments," and I had accepted—and was totally fine with the fact—that William and I would never be more than friends.

I knew it was all for the best. After all, anything else would have been way too complicated. And scary.

The coffee house where I met Lani was a small white cottage with a little porch surrounding it, packed with people chatting and enjoying their morning coffee. Right outside on the lawn, tourists and locals were lounging and drinking coffee. Some were enjoying freshly baked goods served in colorful paper bags.

A few children were chasing each other around, and some young men with long shorts and colorful caps were lying on the grass discussing the early-morning waves. It was as different from a regular New York coffee shop as you could possibly get.

I thanked Lani for inviting me to the Children of the Rainbow fireside chat and told her what a special experience it had been for me. The legend had really gotten to me, and I asked whether she had invented it herself. It reminded me of something my mom would do when she made up fairy tales to tell me on the fly.

Lani laughed. "I wish I had enough imagination to come up with something as extraordinary as that, but no. My grandma told it to me, her grandma told it to her, and so on."

I was even more intrigued.

"It is one of the many legends that has been shared at fireside chats for thousands of years, the way wisdom is passed on from generation to generation," she said.

"But what feels extra special is that the distant future all the generations have been talking about is now. Rainbow Children are being born on this planet, millions of them all over the world. Their mission is to make this world a more kind, tolerant, and happy place and help heal Mother Earth, who is being abused and exploited by the people driven by greed and power."

I sighed. "It sure is needed."

I nodded toward the front page of a newspaper someone had left on the lawn. "It looks like the world has gone off its rails lately."

Lani smiled.

"Sometimes, things need to get worse before they get better," she said. "There is a global awakening right now that is way too positive to make it into the news."

Lani's optimistic view of the world gave me hope. In fact, just knowing that she was in it made me believe that a better world was possible.

I asked Lani about Noah. I hadn't been able to get the little boy out of my mind—the way he had smiled up at me when he took my hand and the despairing look on his face when he knew no one was picking him up.

Lani told me that Noah's mom at times struggled with taking care of both Noah and herself and that some days, she would just lie in bed with empty eyes and see no point of getting up.

No one knew who Noah's father was, so this seven-year-old boy was left to take care of his mother whenever she was having an episode. Lani said she checked in on them as often as she could and made sure there was always food in the house; she also helped clean when his mother wasn't feeling well.

Occasionally she took Noah home with her, but mostly he wanted to be with his mother. He was worried that if he went away, she would be even sadder.

"Poor little child," I said, my heart aching for him.

Lani nodded. "Yes. There has been talk about foster care for him, but as long as she has more good days than bad, she is allowed to keep him. And Noah knows he can always count on me, should his mother get really sick."

I shook my head and looked at her.

"How are you able to give so much to so many?" I asked. Lani didn't seem to have an egocentric bone in her body. Everything she did seemed to be serving some greater cause, making a difference in someone's life and bringing love and care to those who needed it. And as if she didn't do enough already, her friend Jesse had told me that Lani had established the Rainbow Children Foundation, primarily financed by herself, plus donations from friends and family, which provided monetary support to families struggling to make ends meet. I knew Noah and his mother were one of the families the foundation helped.

"I just do what I feel is the right thing to do," Lani replied to my question. "Liat and I are privileged. We have love in our lives, a roof over our heads, and constant access to fruits and vegetables from my parents' farm. We don't need a lot. After all, we live in paradise." She smiled. "To me, it feels much better to help others than to spend money on things I really don't need. I don't see it as a sacrifice. I do it because I *want* to; I do it because I *can*."

She leaned on her elbows and smiled at me. "Besides, my dad always said that the love you give, you get back. Multiplied. And I know that to be true."

Lani's dad certainly sounded very different from mine.

I lay back in the grass and stared up at the sky. I thought about how little time I had spent doing good for others. My focus had always been me, me, me. *My* job, *my* achievements, *my* goals, *my* promotions, *my* career, *my* success. Even before I finished asking myself the question of why I had become so self-absorbed and narrow-minded, I kind of knew the answer. It was the way I had been trained to think. It was the norm of our society and the design of our systems. Me, mine, and myself. Eat or be eaten. The winner takes it all. But I didn't want to be like that any longer. It didn't feel right. It wasn't me anymore.

I shared my frustration with Lani. "I wish I had met you sooner. Maybe I wouldn't have wasted the last fifteen years of my life doing meaningless crap." I tried to say it jokingly, but it was way too close to the truth to be funny.

Lani smiled as she lay back on the grass beside me.

"Maya, I've come to believe that everything we do, everything we experience, and everything we learn happens to us so we can use it for something meaningful. There's no point in beating yourself up for what you didn't know when you didn't know it."

We were both silent for a while, then Lani turned toward me and asked, "So what do you want, Maya?"

Her question threw me off guard. My mind started spinning. What *do* I want? That was a question I'd never really asked myself. I had always focused more on what was the "right" thing to do and what others expected of me instead of what *I* wanted. Whatever that was . . .

My lack of a meaningful response frustrated me.

When Lani noticed the pained expression in my face, she took my hand and asked me to sit up in the grass with her. "Let's do a little exercise," she said.

She asked me to sit cross-legged facing her. "Don't worry, it doesn't look as weird as it feels," she said.

I looked around to see if anyone was staring at us, but no one seemed to notice. This was Kaua'i.

"Now, close your eyes," she said.

I took a deep breath and closed my eyes.

"Good. Now see yourself at the bottom of a hill. It's a beautiful hill—green and lush, but very steep."

I was surprised at how easily I could see it.

"At the bottom of the hill there are plenty of things to do, things that will keep you busy and comfortable and give you what you need."

I nodded. I could see that, too. I saw my apartment, a job similar to the one I had, and my daily routines.

"Know you are always welcome to stay here," Lani said. "You can just continue doing things the way you used to, and life will continue exactly as it was."

My heart started beating faster. I could feel the stress building in my chest, the pain in my neck, the fear in my mind. My mouth dried out.

"No!" I whispered. "I don't want that."

"Deep breaths," Lani said. "Good. Then we have established what you don't want."

I nodded slowly.

"But know this: deciding not to stay means you are willing to climb."

I sighed. "I knew there was a catch."

Lani chuckled, then said, "OK, start walking up the hill. It's not going to be easy. You've never been here before. It will at times be fun and exciting, and other times you will feel insecure and lost. There will be hurdles and there will be challenges. People will try to stop you, and there will be times when you try to stop yourself. Are you ready to face these challenges and keep going?"

I nodded. "I am."

"OK," Lani said. "Now let's have a look to see what is on top of that hill. What do you want so much that you are willing to climb and do whatever it takes to get there?"

I took a deep breath. Something was growing in my chest.

"Now, for a brief moment, I'll give you a pair of wings. I just want you to fly up and see what is waiting for you on top of the hill."

I took another deep breath. "OK."

"You will find three large trees up there. Each of them symbolizes one thing worth climbing for."

I shook my head. "I can't really see anything. It's so light up here. I think I've got the sun in my eyes."

"That's OK," Lani said. "Just look around. Your eyes will adjust."

I could almost feel the soft ground under my feet. Slowly the white turned into green, and gradually the green turned into the shapes of trees.

"I see them now," I said.

"OK, take a close look at one of them. What do you see?"

I started laughing. One of the trees was made up of fluttering butterflies. "I see butterflies! Lots and lots of butterflies!"

"Nice! What does that tell you, Maya?"

I was quiet for a while. My heart swelled in my chest. "That I want to be free and happy like a butterfly?"

"Good," Lani said. "Now you can continue."

I could hear children laughing behind me, the sound of a car passing by. Still, it was like I wasn't there. I was on the top of that hill.

"I see the second tree now. Lots of people are gathered under it. I see myself, too, speaking with people, guiding and leading them. I feel like I'm making a difference in their lives."

"Nice," Lani said. "And the third tree?"

I saw it. It was filled with red flowers. When I went closer, I could see that the flowers were shaped like little hearts.

"Wow," I said and slowly walked toward it.

Lani sat quiet, still holding my hands.

"Such a lovely tree," I said and exhaled.

Suddenly the tree changed shape and color and turned into a person, a man. First, I could only see his back, but I knew instantly who he was. He turned around, his brown eyes were laughing at me, while his face was getting closer and closer.

"William!" I gasped and opened my eyes in shock.

I was confused. It felt like I had been away for hours, but I realized it had only been a few minutes. The same surfers were lying in the grass beside us, the same children running around laughing. Everything was the same, yet everything felt different.

Lani was still holding my hands firmly, looking into my eyes.

"Hey, welcome back," she said. "You came back a bit quicker than I had planned, but it seems like you had a good time on top of that hill."

I nodded and swallowed.

"It was an interesting exercise, but it freaked me out a bit." I shrugged, still in disbelief of what I had seen.

"What about it freaked you out?" She smiled and tilted her head to the side.

"William," I said. "I saw William."

Lani was quiet and just smiled, waiting for me to continue.

"But I have no idea what he was doing up there. He and I are only friends."

Lani laughed. "Right," she said, not sounding very convinced.

"What do you mean, right?" I asked, suspicious.

"My goodness, Maya. I've seen you together. The chemistry between the two of you lit up the entire farmers market the other day! You did not look like you were just friends!"

I stared at her dumbstruck.

Lani laughed.

"It's really quite adorable how you don't seem to see what is obvious to the rest of us," she said.

I shrugged, oblivious to what she was getting at.

"C'mon, admit it! You're crazy in love with William. And honestly, from what I have seen, he's crazy in love with you, too."

"We're just friends. There's nothing between us." I heard my own voice fade as I said those words out loud, because suddenly I realized they weren't true.

Lani laughed. "Frankly, and to be brutally honest with you, I think you are two middle-aged cowards in love. Neither of you daring to be the first one to say how you really feel, because you're scared the other one won't say it back."

I stared at Lani. She looked back at me, with a big grin on her face.

I realized she was right. I had pushed it away and suppressed it as much as I could, but there was no use denying it to myself anymore. I had fallen for William. Big time. And when I envisioned my happy future life, I struggled to see it without him in it.

Something Josh had said to me on the beach came back to me— that when we have two equally scary scenarios, we should choose the one we think will lead us to the life we want for ourselves.

I was terrified by the thought of being rejected if I told William how I felt. But I was equally terrified by the thought of never finding out whether he felt the same way.

And all of a sudden, I knew what I had to do.

AN UNEXPECTED VISITOR

Back at the house, I noticed that William's car wasn't there. When George and I had our coffee that morning, a tradition we had more or less kept intact since the first morning we met, he told me that William would be back from San Francisco later that afternoon.

I was honestly glad to get some extra time to mentally prepare for what I was going to say.

I had called Lisa from the car on my way back to the house. Her advice was pretty much the same as Lani's. "Stop being so afraid, Maya. Go after what you want. Tell him how you feel."

"What if it turns out he only sees me as a friend after all?" I could feel my courage slip the closer I got to the house.

"Well," Lisa said, "if it turns out he doesn't feel the same, you will survive that too, believe it or not." She laughed warmly. I was not sure I agreed, but I supposed she was right.

"You can do this, Maya. You are stronger and braver than you think. Call me later, OK?"

"OK," I said and hung up.

· · ·

The sun had just set when I slowly walked over to George's house. I was wearing the dress that Lani and William had convinced me to buy at the farmers market the other day—white with little green palm trees, quirky but cute, and it fit me perfectly. My newly washed hair was hanging softly over my shoulders and I was barefoot, my new favorite footwear.

I noticed William's car was parked outside. Music and warm laughter were coming from the house. Just the sound of his voice made me feel happy.

My heart was racing, and my mouth was dry, but I was determined that I would not chicken out.

"Scared, cowardly middle-aged people," Lani had called us.

"Fear is what holds people back from living the lives of their dreams," Josh had said.

I was done being scared. I finally knew what I wanted. And I would not let some silly insecurities or fear of rejection stop me.

George's veranda was empty. I slowly walked up the steps and was just about to knock on the door when it opened and William came out, carrying a bottle of wine and two glasses. He was laughing, as if someone had just said something really funny.

In his linen shirt and linen trousers, he looked like he could be a model for "casual island living" in a fashion magazine. He was so handsome it hurt. When he saw me, he stopped in his tracks and for a millisecond something came over his face that I couldn't quite read. Then he seemed to pull himself together and smiled. "Maya! Hi! What a nice surprise!"

The door opened again and a tall, gorgeous brunette, dressed in cutoff jean shorts and a tight white T-shirt, came out. She looked like a supermodel. She smiled a big white smile and reached out her hand.

"Oh, hi there. I'm Rebecca!"

Her handshake was firm, and she had the same air around her as William: confident, warm, friendly. I already hated her.

I shook her hand and made an effort to return the friendly smile, while trying to ignore the voice inside my head that had started trashing my self-confidence.

Honestly, what did you think? That William would be interested in you? How stupid can you be? Good for you that you were saved by the bell; talk about being close to making a total ass of yourself. Not that it would have been the first time.

I looked up and saw William's mouth moving and Rebecca laughing, but I couldn't hear a word. I had to concentrate on standing upright and forcing a smile, while desperately trying to find a way out of this embarrassing situation.

"Why don't you join us for a glass of wine?" Rebecca asked.

Did she have to be that nice? It would have been so much better if she had been a total bitch. And preferably ugly, too. But I guess that was too much to ask.

"I actually just came by to see how George was," I said, relieved to finally come up with an excuse for standing on their veranda like a fool.

"Dad is just taking a little nap. Have a glass of wine with us until he wakes up?" William suggested.

"Thank you, but I'm sorry I can't stay. I have something I need to do. So sorry, but I have to go."

I turned to head back down the steps.

"It was very nice meeting you, Maya," Rebecca said cheerfully.

I nodded and tried to smile, realizing that I probably failed at it. "You too, Rebecca."

I looked over at William. "Say hi to George from me," I blurted before I raced down the stairs, grateful that my legs still could hold me.

William looked puzzled. I knew I was acting weird.

But I had to get out of there.

I reeled as I walked back toward the beach house. What a fool I had been! How could I have believed that William would ever have been interested in me? Clearly, he preferred supermodels with legs up to their ears. I wanted to kick myself. That stupid hilltop. It had messed with my head, numbed my normal sensibility, and made me start believing in fairy tales.

A deep sadness and emptiness overcame me, as I realized this was the beginning of the end. With Rebecca there, everything would change. It had been George, William, and me, and now it would be the three of them. I wouldn't fit in anymore. I would go back to being the weird neighbor. Now they could tell funny stories about me and forget about me as soon as I leave the island.

I was angry with myself for letting my guard down and allowing William to sneak his way into my heart. And I was angry with Lani for planting the idea in my head that he had been interested in me. How much easier it would have been if I had still been fine with us being just friends—if I hadn't started asking myself what I wanted and if I hadn't allowed myself to dream.

I was so absorbed in my own misery that I didn't even notice the black Mercedes parked on my lawn until I nearly bumped into it. As I approached, a car window slowly opened, and I heard someone say my name.

"Maya Williams, is that you?"

I stopped and stared in disbelief at the face that looked back at me from the back seat of the car.

"Mr. Hatchett?" I asked, incredulous.

A man in a driver's uniform walked around the car and opened the door. Mr. Archibald Hatchett, the chairman of TechnoGuard, stepped out.

He was taller than I remembered, but that might have to do with me not having a habit of being barefoot at work. He was dressed in a dark three-piece suit. I had never seen anyone who fit less into his surroundings than Mr. Hatchett did at that moment.

I stared at him, expecting him to disappear into thin air at any second. Clearly, this was just a hallucination. It wasn't until he shook my hand and asked if he could come inside and talk for a minute that I realized he was for real.

I led him to the house and suggested he make himself comfortable on the veranda while I got us something to drink.

"Thank you. I wouldn't mind a whisky, if you have it," Mr. Hatchett said with his posh British accent, which made this whole picture even more absurd.

"Sorry, I only have wine," I said.

"That would be fine," he replied and sat down in a chair that faced the ocean. "My oh my. Quite a view, I must say."

As I was pouring us the wine in the kitchen, I watched Mr. Hatchett through the window. Last time I had seen Archibald Hatchett, he was on the cover of *Time* magazine.

I had only met him in person once, six months earlier, when I had been asked to give a presentation for TechnoGuard's board of directors. I remembered how he had challenged and tested me, and how I had been able to answer all his questions without wavering once.

Fail to prepare, prepare to fail. No one puts Maya Williams in a corner. He came and shook my hand afterward and told me he'd been impressed. Apparently, I was later told, that was not something that happened often.

"Thank you, it was actually quite refreshing to be asked so many intelligent questions, Mr. Hatchett," I had replied. After all, I wasn't exactly accustomed to that from the executive team.

At first, he seemed surprised, then he chuckled. "I look forward to following you, Maya Williams. Something tells me you will go far."

Well, he certainly had been right on that one, even though I doubted this was what he had in mind.

I walked out to him, still barefoot, carrying two glasses of white wine.

Mr. Hatchett turned around and smiled at me. He looked like a slightly older version of Pierce Brosnan, very elegant with a British sense of flair.

I handed him a glass and sat down on the chair opposite him. With no idea what to say, I just sat silently, waiting for him to speak.

Mr. Hatchett took a sip of his wine, looked down at the glass suspiciously, and then began.

"First of all, I am delighted to see you alive and healthy, Maya," he said. "When you didn't answer your phone or reply to my emails, I asked my secretary, Mrs. Avery, to investigate the matter further. When she told me that you were still on Kaua'i, I must admit I was quite surprised."

Mr. Hatchett leaned forward in his chair and put the glass of wine back on the table.

"Mrs. Avery was able to find someone at a car rental company in Poipu who had your name on record and was willing to share your address with us for some hush money." He chuckled, clearly amused by the whole situation. "Then, when we finally had your address, I decided I would pay you a visit myself. Thankfully, I was already in San Francisco, so I asked my pilot to pop over to Kaua'i for the day."

I stared back at him, nodding at the last sentence, as if I thought popping over to Kaua'i in a private jet was the most natural thing to do.

"I will be leaving again in a few hours, so let's get right to it, shall we?"

He picked up the glass and took another sip of wine. The face he made told me that he didn't particularly care for it, but it was all I had, so it was going to have to do. Before he continued, I took a large sip of my own, still unnerved by the visit.

"Last week we fired Alistair Parker."

I could feel my jaw drop. I had to make an effort to put it back in place and keep a neutral face.

Mr. Hatchett continued, as if there was nothing dramatic about that statement. "It turned out that he has been lying to the board for quite some time. After the conference you attended here, we did some digging and learned that he withheld crucial information from share-holders, falsified reports, inflated numbers, and methodically cheated on his travel expenses for years."

I shook my head. So, the rumors had been true. And Alistair had been behind it all.

"It took us some time to gather enough evidence against him and the CFO, but last week we were finally there, and now they are both out. They should be very grateful that we are not pressing charges."

I raised an eyebrow.

"At least not at this moment," Mr. Hatchett continued, with a tell-ing smile. "Right now we need to focus all our energy and resources on saving the company, instead of taking them to court."

I nodded. That made sense.

"TechnoGuard is a broken company. Some of our best engineers and sales reps have already left. Our stock has plummeted. We are losing clients to our competitors every day, and the board has agreed that our top priority now is to rebuild trust in the market and to stop the flood of people leaving the company. If this continues, pretty soon there will be no one left."

I suspected that I knew why he was here. He'd probably come to offer me my old job back. And I already knew what my answer would be. No thanks. Alistair Parker might be gone, but I knew the corpo-rate drill well enough to know he would simply be replaced by some other high-strung, self-absorbed, white male CEO-type. It would be the same old shit with a different wrapping. Like always.

Mr. Hatchett mustered the courage to take another sip of his wine. He tried not to pucker his lips, but I noticed he still hadn't changed his opinion of my ten-dollar bottle. He put the glass on the table, leaned forward in the chair, and looked directly at me.

"We need someone in charge who knows the business, the market, and the company. Someone who can deliver great performance and who has demonstrated real leadership in challenging times."

OK, great, but why was he telling me this?

"After careful consideration, I have decided you are the person for the job, Maya. I am here to offer you the position as the CEO of TechnoGuard."

I coughed, choking on the wine I'd just swallowed. If he'd said that he'd like to send me to the moon, I would have been less surprised. After all, this was the company that hadn't had a female executive for twenty years, and last time I checked, they were still struggling with that whole idea.

Mr. Hatchett studied the expression on my face and continued. "I was as appalled as anyone about what you did at the investor conference, but after I realized how rotten the leadership of TechnoGuard really was, I have come to realize that what you did was a true demonstration of integrity, courage, and leadership. Thanks to your presentation and all the positive media coverage you got afterward, we have been able to separate the unethical behavior of the few at the top from the company as a whole."

I was still struggling to take it all in.

"Had you lied onstage that day, our story would have been much worse. Honestly, I don't even know if the company would have survived it."

He paused and took another sip of his wine. "Now we need to demonstrate that the things you stood for onstage are the things we stand for as a company. And I can't imagine anyone who will do that better than you." He paused for a few seconds, then said, "We will, of course, compensate you generously."

My mind hadn't even gotten to that yet. I was still trying to figure out whether this was some sort of sick dream.

"You will, naturally, enjoy all the benefits that Alistair Parker had: a competitive salary, a generous stock option plan, a private driver, and, of course, the best corner office overlooking Central Park."

If he had expected a more enthusiastic response from me, he didn't show it.

"I know thirty-six hours is not a long time to consider such a big offer, but I am afraid that is all I can spare. If you decide not to accept, we will have to go with number two on the list. Which I hope we won't have to do. But the clock is ticking, and we really need to make a decision soon."

I nodded, acknowledging what he said, as he gave me a business card where he had written down his private cell number.

He set down his glass on the table before shaking my hand. "Call me."

I nodded.

And then he was gone.

For a while, I just sat there and stared into thin air. Then I walked back into the house, undressed, and lay down on my bed. I felt confused and exhausted and just wanted to sleep. I hoped that when I woke up again, I would be able to see things more clearly.

· · ·

I woke up again at 4:30 a.m. After another hour of tossing and turning, I finally got up, made myself some coffee, and walked out on the veranda. I sat in the chair where Mr. Hatchett had been sitting only a few hours earlier.

The whole thing felt like an absurd dream, but Mr. Hatchett's business card was still lying on the table in front of me, proof that he'd actually been here.

I was flattered by his offer. And had someone told me this would happen a month ago, I would have thought it was the best thing that could ever have happened to me. But now, I wasn't so sure.

Yesterday, with Lani, I thought I knew what I wanted. But today, everything seemed different. Questions were buzzing around in my head. Would I be happy doing this? Would I be free to do things the way I wanted to? Would I be able to make a difference? Or would I just be pulled into the same soul-sucking corporate misery, surrounded by gray cubicles, dead eyes, and empty faces? Did I really want to walk right back into backstabbing corporate politics and having to deal with the incompetent and sexist executive team?

The thought of it all made me feel a bit sick.

But for the first time I also felt miserable thinking about staying on the island, having to witness William and his girlfriend living their happy island life.

How quickly things had changed.

The sky was getting light. The sun was on its way up. I wrapped a towel around myself and walked toward the beach. George was already in his chair.

"Good morning, sunshine!" he called cheerfully.

I sat down heavily in my accustomed seat.

"Oh dear. You look like you have a lot on your mind today, my friend," George said as he handed me Aimee's cup with fresh coffee in it.

I nodded and told him about Mr. Hatchett's visit and the surprising offer.

"What a story!" George laughed. "That could have been a scene in a movie!" Then he saw my face, stopped laughing, and looked at me with warmth in his eyes. "Do you have any idea what you will do?"

I shook my head slowly and gazed over the ocean, as if the answer to his question could be found somewhere out there. Then, suddenly, I came to think of something Lani had said the day before, about how everything we do, experience, and learn happens to us so we can use it for something meaningful later. To make things better. To do good.

I'd been thinking that I might not be the right person for the job because I was no longer the same person as I was a month ago. But then I came to think that maybe that was exactly why I was right, and why I should do it.

I heaved a sigh.

"I have to admit that I feel a bit sick from the thought of going back to that company," I said and looked into George's kind eyes. "On the other hand," I continued after a brief pause, "I'm thinking that as a CEO, I will actually be in a position to change all the things I don't like."

It felt as if the cloud that had surrounded my mind the last twelve hours was finally clearing up.

"It will be an extremely challenging task, though," I said aloud—almost to myself.

George took my hand. "Maya, we don't do things because they are easy. We do them because they are important." He smiled and squeezed my hand. "If anyone can do that job, it's you. All you really need to decide is whether you *want* to do it or not."

I looked around at the beach, Bali Ha'i, and the Pacific Ocean. I thought about my friends and my life here, and what the last three weeks had taught me about myself, about life, and even about work and business. All of it, together, had made me into a different person. I saw the world, life—and myself—through a different lens now. And nothing could ever change that.

But I also knew I couldn't stay on Kaua'i forever. It was time for me to get back to reality, to go back to work. As much as I had loved living in paradise, I realized my time here was over and that the dream had come to an end.

Besides, it was an extraordinary offer that Mr. Hatchett had given me, and I knew I'd be a fool not to take it.

I gave George a big hug. "I will miss you so much, my dear, dear friend."

George hugged me back. "I'll see you soon, Maya. Now, go out and show 'em what you're made of!"

I nodded and fought my urge to cry.

George took my hand again and held it firmly for a moment.

"Please make sure to say goodbye to William. He will be sad to see you leave."

I bit my lip, and the tears that rolled down my cheeks weren't only because I hated to say goodbye to George.

"I'll see you soon, George," I said with a heavy heart and gave him another hug before I walked back to the beach house to give Mr. Hatchett my answer.

Back inside, I dug my laptop out of my bag and began to compose my response. I wanted to lay out the terms of my acceptance and felt it would be better to do so in writing.

From: m.williams@gmail.com
To: a.hatchett@technoguard.com
Subject: Job Offer

Dear Mr. Hatchett,

Thank you for your surprise visit and for offering me the
role as CEO of TechnoGuard Inc. After careful consideration, I would like to accept your job offer with the following conditions:

1. For a period of three years, I will have the
   freedom to make all the changes I deem
   necessary to get the company back on its feet.
   Unless there is a drastic decline in sales or
   share price during this period, this agreement
   will hold.

2. I will never again be told to lie on behalf of
   the company.

3. All the senior citizens who attended the investor conference in Kaua'i will receive an offer
   to buy ten thousand TechnoGuard shares for
   one dollar.

If you accept these terms, I am excited to accept the role
as CEO of TechnoGuard Inc.

Kindest regards,

Maya Williams

CREATE

I did then what I knew how to do.
Now that I know better, I do better.

MAYA ANGELOU

BACK IN THE CITY

The moment the wheels of the airplane hit the ground at JFK airport, a feeling of heaviness overwhelmed me. It felt as if I had been living inside a dream and had now landed back in reality, a reality I didn't quite know how to belong to anymore. I had slept most of the trip, trying to escape the emotional turmoil going on inside me. As the plane left Lihue Airport, I'd felt as if I were being torn in two, and only half of me was leaving the island.

My feet felt heavy as I walked the seemingly interminable distance from the plane to the exit. Coming out on the street, the chaos of people, cars, noise, and strange smells were a shock to my system. A large man in a chauffeur's uniform bumped into me and yelled, "Hey, watch where you're going!" and moved on. I was back in New York alright—and it sucked.

While waiting in the taxi line with about forty other people, I turned my phone back on. I hadn't checked it since I went through security at Lihue Airport. Something squeezed around my heart when I saw there were three missed calls and a text message from William: "I can't believe you left without saying goodbye! Please call me!"

I cringed. I felt embarrassed about how I had behaved when I met him and Rebecca the day before. And I was ashamed that I hadn't even tried looking for him when I left.

I texted back: "So sorry. Had to leave in a hurry. George can explain. Just landed at JFK, will call you later." But deep down I knew I probably wouldn't.

I sent a text to Lani, too: "Had to leave for NYC in a hurry. Will call you later and explain. Miss you already! xx Maya."

She replied instantly. "Oh no! I'll miss u too."

Another text immediately followed. "How did it go with William?"

I paused for a second, then texted her back. "It didn't. His girlfriend was there."

"Girlfriend???" she texted, followed by another: "So sorry! Are you OK?"

I wasn't really, but I replied: "I'm fine. Guess it's time to move on."

After thirty minutes in the taxi line, it was finally my turn. I tossed my carry-on in the trunk of the car, opened the door, gave the driver my address, and sank into the back seat. As we drove toward Manhattan, I looked out of the window. It was as if all the colors had been sucked out of the world, and it mirrored the way I felt.

When the cab stopped outside my building, Fred came out to greet me. It was a relief to see his friendly smile as he picked up my luggage and welcomed me home.

"I was starting to get worried, Maya. I thought you'd only be away for a few days," he said as he walked with me toward the elevator.

I smiled apologetically. I hadn't even thought about notifying Fred.

"I decided to take a little break, and it turned out to be a bit longer than first intended," I explained.

"Good for you!" He took a closer look at me. "And it seems to have done you a lot of good, if you don't mind me saying so."

"Thank you, Fred!"

As I caught a glimpse of myself in the large gold-framed mirror in the hallway, I noticed that I *did* look different. Tanned, a few pounds lighter, and more relaxed. Dressed in jeans, sneakers, and a sweater with Kaua'i printed all over it, my wardrobe had certainly taken an interesting turn.

"And how have you been, Fred?"

"Same old, same old," Fred said. "The missus is happy, and the kids are good, so no complaints."

An elderly couple stepped out of the elevator. The woman eyed me suspiciously.

"Hello, Mrs. Jankowich," I said. Then I nodded toward her husband, "Mr. Jankowich."

"Who is that?" the old woman asked her husband.

"It is Ms. Williams, dear," her husband explained. "The nice young woman who lives next door."

The old woman shook her head and squeezed her husband's arm harder.

"I have never seen her before," she said and threw me another suspicious look before they walked out the door onto busy Central Park West.

Fred and I winked at each other.

"Same old, same old." I grinned and pushed the button for the eleventh floor.

In the cab, I had hoped that things would feel better as soon as I got home, but as I opened the door and stepped into my airy, beautifully designed apartment with its large windows overlooking Central Park, I couldn't help thinking about how much I already missed the flowery curtains, the pineapple lamps, and the soothing sound of the ocean.

• • •

One hour later I walked through the doors at Tony's. Lisa was already there. I immediately noticed something had changed.

Lisa was leaning over the bar, her hand was touching Antonio's, and she was whispering something in his ear. He laughed softly, his eyes glowing.

"I go away for three weeks and look what happens," I teased.

Next thing I knew I had Lisa's arms around me and her voice in my ear: "Maaaya! I've missed you!"

She gave me a big warm hug. Then she realized what I was saying and started to laugh.

"Well, with you abandoning me, I had to have something to do."

Antonio pretended to look offended.

"What? Is that all I am to you? Something to do?"

Lisa laughed and leaned back over the bar counter and kissed him on the mouth. "Mi amore," she said softly. I found it incredibly endearing to see a grown man blush.

Then Lisa turned around again and took a proper look at me.

"Oh. My. God. You're like a different person!" She lovingly pulled my sun-bleached hair. "It's not only the way you look, it's what you radiate!"

She put her face close to mine; her eyes were shining with excitement as she whispered, "Does this mean you finally got laid?"

I burst out laughing and shook my head. Lisa had definitely not changed.

We sat down at our regular table, under the big picture of Sophia Loren eating spaghetti. The picture always made me hungry.

As if Lisa had read my mind, she shouted, "Antonio darling, can we have some pasta and wine, please?"

"Coming up!" He smiled cheerfully as he walked into the kitchen.

Lisa took my hands and leaned over the table. "Now, tell me everything. I want details!"

We managed to polish off both the pasta and the bottle of wine before I finished my story. There was a lot to tell, and, true to form, Lisa asked a lot of questions along the way.

When I was finished, Lisa was quiet for a while. I watched her as she sat with a puzzled expression on her face.

"There's something about this story that just doesn't feel right," she said.

"What?" I asked.

"This Rebecca character. She just doesn't fit in. It should have been you on that veranda. You and William. You sound perfect for each other. It just doesn't make sense."

I laughed dryly. "Well, if you'd seen her you might have thought it made all the sense in the world."

Lisa looked a bit annoyed at me.

"I have no idea where you got the notion that all men care about are looks. And even if they did, you'd still be first in line. What you and William had sounds special. It sounds deep and fun and real. It feels wrong that it ended that way."

I sighed and patted her hand.

"I guess some things just aren't meant to be." I could feel a tear in the corner of my eye but was determined not to cry.

"But you know what, Lisa?" I managed to smile. "I am happy to know I can feel that way for somebody at least. I guess that is something to celebrate, right?"

I raised my glass and downed what was left of my wine.

"Look at you, all wise and reflective." Lisa beamed as she leaned over the table to give me another hug.

"You'll be alright," she said and kissed me on my cheek.

I nodded and got ready to leave. "And now I've got an important job to do."

As I was putting my coat on, I told Lisa that I was meeting with Mr. Hatchett and a woman from the board the next morning.

"CEO Maya Williams," Lisa said proudly. "You go get 'em, girl."

"You bet!" I threw goodnight kisses to her and Antonio before I stepped into the chilly New York air.

Even at that late hour, the streets were packed with people and cars, everyone still in a rush. The city that never sleeps.

Not quite ready to go to bed yet, I crossed the street and walked slowly home alongside Central Park.

I wrapped my scarf and coat closely around me to protect me from the cold winds that always seemed extra strong along the avenues. I'd forgotten to wear gloves, so I put my hands deep into my pockets and watched the people around me to see if I was the only one feeling the cold. A middle-aged couple walked quickly through the park, their arms tucked into each other's. A young man was walking his Burberry-coat-wearing dog. And a woman in a neon-colored running vest and headlamp jogged past me. I could hear her heavy breathing and noticed the cloud of air coming out of her mouth.

I was getting close to my apartment building when I saw him. A man, wearing a parka and a big scarf. I could only see his back. It seemed like he was looking down at his phone. There was something familiar about the broad shoulders and the way he moved his head. My heart stopped.

"William?"

The man turned around and looked at me as if he had heard my thoughts. A stranger's face looked back at me.

Of course. I shrugged. What had I been thinking?

"Enough," I told myself before crossing the street.

It was time to get on with my life, and I was determined to do so.

DAY ONE

I took a deep breath before I walked into the main entrance of TechnoGuard's office building. Ruth had texted me to take the elevator right up to the thirty-seventh floor. She had already moved my things and given away my office to someone else. I had to smile. Ruth was indeed a woman of action.

As I stepped out of the elevator, she stood in front of me, dressed in a black-and-white Chanel-style dress, her hair tied back in a tight bun, glasses on her nose, and a professional, friendly smile.

"Welcome back, Maya," she said and shook my hand. I knew she was putting on an act in front of the other executives and their assistants.

I decided to play along and shook her hand back.

"Good to be back, Ruth," I said.

I went around the floor and greeted everyone who was there. The receptionist was new. I had guessed that the CFO would had taken Agnes with him. Most of the executive office doors were closed, their indicator lights glowing red.

I knew they weren't overly eager to welcome me, so I was not surprised by their absence.

Mr. Hatchett had given me a warning when I met with him the day before. "Let me put it like this," he said, "they all would have preferred themselves as the new CEO. There might be some hurt egos around, but nothing you can't handle—of that I am certain."

As I followed Ruth toward my new office I reminded myself of George's wise words: "We don't do things because they are easy. We do them because they are important." I wanted to do something that mattered, to make a difference, and now I knew I would.

• • •

Alistair Parker's old office was unrecognizable. The heavy old brown furniture was gone. In its place were a glass desk with a slim beige leather chair and an elegant white designer sofa next to a glass-and-steel coffee table. In the corner, where Alistair used to have his brown globe filled with bottles of liquor, there was now a stylish espresso machine with steel-colored cups resting on a glass shelf.

"Wow, Ruth. This is beautiful! But you've only known for a few days. How were you able to pull all this off?"

Ruth closed the door behind us. "All the furniture is borrowed from my friend Gerard's office design firm. He said you could test it for a few weeks, and if you like it, he will give us a really good price."

"You are amazing. Do you know that?"

"Anything for our new CEO!" She clapped her hands like an eager little girl and gave me the hug she had been holding back in front of the others. "You know, Maya, I always knew this would happen. Just not this way, or this fast!"

"Tell me about it!" I laughed and sat down on the fancy sofa. It was difficult to take it all in. The whole situation felt surreal. One moment I had been wearing flip-flops and living a chill island life on Kaua'i, and the next I was back in Manhattan in my high heels and corporate suit, in my corner office—as the CEO.

I looked around. My new office was everything I had ever dreamed of. I could see the tops of the surrounding skyscrapers on one side, Central Park on the other.

I wondered if I would get time to go for a walk later.

"So, where do we begin?" Ruth sat down on the edge of one of the beige leather chairs, her iPad in her lap. "I have never worked for a CEO before," she said.

I grinned. "And I've never been one, so I guess we'll just have to wing it."

After Ruth and I had finished planning our week, and she had gone back to her office, I walked over to the espresso machine in the corner. I inserted the coffee pod and pushed the button, and as I did, I felt a rush of longing for the espresso maker on the stove in the beach house, where I would stand barefoot on the wooden floor, dressed in a sarong, enjoying the scent of coffee mixed with the ocean breeze.

"No one leaves Kaua'i the same person they were when they came," Josh had told me. Now I knew that to be true.

I didn't think Mr. Hatchett and the board knew what they had signed up for, though. But they would soon find out.

After I finished my espresso, I left my office, smiled at the new receptionist, pushed the elevator button, and went down to the thirty-sixth floor to say hi to the team.

It would be a long day. And by the end of it, everyone in the company would know that there was a new kind of CEO in town.

• • •

"You suggest we do what?" John Cooper, TechnoGuard's chief information officer, stared at me as if I had just fallen from the sky. Then he looked at the other executives sitting around the large conference table on the thirty-seventh floor.

Only a few of them met his eyes.

I could feel the confusion in the room, and I didn't blame them. One month ago, I had been VP of sales and had only been allocated thirty minutes a month to speak to them. Now I was their boss. A boss with very different ideas than they were used to.

"I understand it may sound a bit drastic, but drastic is what we have to go for," I explained. "Hordes of talented employees are leaving us every week to go and work for our competitors. Their expertise and skills are walking out the door with them, making our competitors stronger and us weaker by the day."

I looked around the table to see whether the executives understood the gravity of the situation. They all stared blankly back at me—except for John Cooper, who seemed to be fuming with anger.

I continued. "I have been hired to turn things around. To win back the trust of the customers, investors, and the market. And to do that, we will first need to win back the trust of our employees."

I paused for a few seconds to make sure the words sank in.

"And I know this for a fact: we won't do that by sitting in an ivory tower far away from where the real action is."

"So, changing our offices into, what was it you called them—creative hubs, chill areas, and a coffee bar—and making us move down to the thirty-sixth floor, is your idea of the first smart, strategic move as our new CEO?" John Cooper spat out with contempt in his voice.

"To rescue this sinking ship and rebuild what has been lost, yes, that will be my first strategic move as your new CEO," I said, my voice sounding as sharp as I intended it to be.

Apparently, it worked. John looked away. Then I paused and softened my voice a bit.

"Listen," I said, "I know this may feel weird to you. It honestly feels pretty weird to me, too. But here's the thing: I intend to do everything I can to make this company healthy and thriving again. I have promised the board I will get our profitability and our share price up, and I have every intention to deliver on those promises."

The men around the table paid closer attention now, just as I knew they would.

"But to achieve this, we can't just continue with business as usual. We need to start doing things differently. And you might not like all of it." I paused. "The revamp of the offices will only be the first change we make," I continued as I poured myself a glass of water.

"We also need to make some significant changes to the way we work. To stay competitive in the marketplace, we need to build a collaborative, innovative, and fast-moving culture. And we need to make it attractive to work for us by creating an environment where people enjoy coming to work in the morning and are inspired to give their best."

The executives stared at me in disbelief. I had just used a number of words that probably never had been uttered in this meeting room before, at least not in that combination.

I reiterated my point with a smile, hoping to lighten things up a bit. "Happy employees lead to happy customers, which lead to better results. This, in turn, creates happy shareholders and a more sustainable company. It's simple math, really."

"Gosh." John laughed sarcastically. "Why don't we all just hold hands and sing 'Kumbaya'?" He looked at the other executives for back up. "I guess this is what you get when you have a woman as a CEO."

The room fell silent. I glared at him. "What did you just say, John?"

The other executives looked down at the table.

John suddenly seemed to realize the magnitude of what he'd said.

"C'mon, lighten up. I was just cracking a joke. Don't take it so personally."

I took a deep breath. Don't go there, Maya. "Fine. But that was the last ignorant, sexist comment I will allow from you or anyone else around this table. To make this work, treating each other with respect is the absolute minimum. Which means you can also lay off giving me nicknames."

The room went dead silent. I glanced at the men around the table, but no one dared to meet my eyes. Good. They were starting to realize I was well informed and wasn't going to put up with any of their nonsense.

After the meeting, I sat down with Ruth to explain the changes we were making.

"I don't get it, Maya." She didn't even try to hide the disappointment in her voice.

"This was your dream. The corner office, overlooking Central Park. You have it now. And now you're giving it up, just like that?" She snapped her fingers.

I knew this had been her dream, too.

"I'm sorry, Ruth. But I'm not giving anything up," I explained. "The dream has just changed."

Ruth stared at me, and when she spoke there was a sense of bewilderment in her voice. "What on earth happened to you in Kaua'i, Maya?"

I walked over to the floor-to-ceiling windows.

Far below me, little creatures were scurrying up and down on narrow streets, in and out of big black buildings. I felt chills running down my spine and looked over at Central Park. I really needed to take that walk soon.

I took a deep breath and turned toward Ruth.

"I guess I woke up," I said.

Ruth looked confused.

"It will take some time and a bottle of wine or two to explain it all, but for now, all I can say is this: I've changed, Ruth. And there's no going back."

YEAR ONE

T he first year, I hit the ground running with my proposed changes. The gray cubicles were removed, offices were rebuilt, and all the executives, including myself, moved down to the thirty-sixth floor to sit with the teams. As the thirty-sixth floor turned into a more inviting, collaborative working space with colorful furniture, the thirty-seventh floor re-emerged as a beautifully designed social area with creative meeting rooms, a customer experience center, a chill lounge, and a combined juice and coffee bar. The employees and customers loved it—the executives not so much—but after a while even they seemed to have settled into their new habitat.

Over the next few months I learned how to be a CEO, mostly through trial and error, and sometimes by being shown the ropes by Mr. Hatchett, with whom I had regular meetings. There was a lot to learn, but knowing the company, the market, the products, and the customers as well as I did certainly helped. It didn't take long until I was up and running on my own.

"You're a natural," Mr. Hatchett told me after my first presentation to the board, just three months into my new role.

It was true that I had always been well prepared, but now I realized that my biggest strength was my ability to combine the street savvy of having spent seven years close to the customers with the top-level perspective of a CEO. Just six months after I came back, we won a number of new deals and saw a steady increase in sales.

While being a "natural" in business, I was less of a natural when it came to the people side of things. It was humbling having to realize how fundamental the human aspect of our business was in order to make things work, and it was embarrassing to admit how little attention I had given this in my previous roles.

I knew I had a lot to learn, and I knew who could teach me: the employees themselves. So, from day one, I spent a lot of my time talking to people, in one-on-ones, team meetings, around the water cooler, and at the new coffee bar on the thirty-seventh floor. I took the time to learn about their jobs, their challenges, their likes and dislikes, and I asked for their advice on how we as leaders could best support them and make it easier for them to do a great job.

I carried a spiral notebook with me wherever I went and after just a month I had to get myself a new one.

At times I felt overwhelmed by all of the information I needed to process and all the new things I had to learn as well as the huge responsibilities and expectations that came with my new role.

So, when Mr. Hatchett suggested that I might want to get myself a mentor, I jumped at the chance. "Give Lucy a call," he suggested. "She's the most experienced and competent of everyone on the board. I think the two of you will get along really well."

Lucy and I had met the day after I returned from Kaua'i, and I was extremely impressed by her. In fact, I was starstruck by her mere presence.

Lucy Dellaware had held multiple executive and CEO roles in a number of Fortune 500 companies and was currently the chairwoman of two companies and a board member of three high-profile tech companies, in addition to TechnoGuard.

She had recently been featured in *Fast Company* magazine as "The Godmother of IT." Even the full-of-themselves kings of Silicon Valley went quiet when Lucy Dellaware opened her mouth.

"Soft eyes, strong grip," the *Fast Company* article had said of her. According to the article, Lucy had, in a recent board meeting, calmly told the young CEO of one of the world's quickest-growing social media platforms to stop his obnoxious behavior and start acting like the mature leader his organization needed him to be.

I was thrilled by the thought that she might mentor me.

"I don't know what Archie told you," she said when I finally had built up enough courage to call her. "But I don't do mentoring."

I stopped breathing. That was not the answer I'd been hoping for.

"It sounds so pretentious and boring," she continued, her voice deep and confident. "However, I would love to meet with you and chat."

I breathed out a sigh of relief.

"Why don't we have lunch next week," she said, "and if we both enjoy it, we can do it on a regular basis."

And with that, Lucy Dellaware, one of the most successful and accomplished businesswomen in the country, became my mentor, or monthly "lunch buddy," as she preferred to call it.

Lucy usually picked the time and place for our lunches, the venue as varied as the topics we discussed. One month we went to a three-star Michelin restaurant, the next we had hotdogs on a bench in Central Park, but most of the time we went to laid-back, low-key places with great food.

Regardless of the location, I loved our lunches, devouring every word Lucy said.

She asked a lot of questions, seemed genuinely interested in my perspectives, and was always very generous with her own insights and leadership experiences.

And one thing I could almost always count on was for Lucy to have a glass of wine with her food.

Once she commented on this habit. "I've lived too long in Southern Europe to enjoy a good meal with just a glass of water." She smiled at the waiter as he poured her a glass of Riesling.

During this particular lunch, we were sitting across from each other on tall bar stools at a sushi restaurant in Midtown. While waiting for our food, I wanted to find out what it had been like for her when she was just starting out, so she obliged me and talked about her early years as a CEO and what she considered her biggest mistakes.

I sat there with my notebook and a glass of water, intent on learning everything I could, and a little bit envious of her, drinking wine and not having to go back to an office.

"I was inexperienced and had no idea how to be a CEO, so I observed other CEOs and then tried to mimic their styles and behaviors." She took a sip of her wine. "*That* was a big mistake. I acted in a way that I *thought* a CEO should act, rather than doing what I felt was right and showing up as *myself*. Being a copycat didn't only make me a pretty lousy and ineffective CEO, it also left me feeling deflated, frustrated, and unhappy."

I noticed the strained expression on her face.

"I even tried to dress like the other CEOs. Considering that all of them were men, you can only imagine."

I laughed with her. I could easily relate.

Soon after, the food arrived, and I took a bite of my salmon sashimi. I glanced over at Lucy who was closing her eyes, slowly chewing and clearly appreciating her food.

Looking at her, it was hard to imagine her ever having been anyone but who she was today. Her thick gray hair tied loosely in a bun, dressed in a bright red blouse with black trousers, she had an air of confidence and strength. Yet she always wore a heartfelt smile. She quickly became a powerful role model for me.

"So how did you do it?" I asked. "How did you become an effective leader and CEO while staying true to yourself?"

Lucy sat quietly and reflected for a moment. "There really is not a simple answer to that question," she said after a while. "But I think it had to do with self-awareness. The moment I discovered my lack of self-awareness and understood better the reason behind my unconscious choices, that was the moment I could start making different ones."

"What do you mean by self-awareness exactly?" I asked.

Lucy had made it clear to me from the beginning that there was no such thing as a bad question, so I was never afraid to ask for clarification during our chats.

She took another sip of her wine before she continued.

"To me, self-awareness is about knowing myself. It's about understanding my own emotions and reactions, my weaknesses and strengths, my values and beliefs. Whether we want to admit it or not, our inner life is always reflected on the outside, and only when we understand ourselves better are we able to understand why we make the choices we do and how our actions and behaviors affect others."

I nodded at what Lucy said. It made a whole lot of sense and actually reminded me of something Josh could have said.

"In fact," Lucy continued after having given the topic some more thought, "I will go as far as saying that self-awareness is the foundation of all leadership."

She rested her elbows on the table and looked at me intently.

"If we don't understand ourselves, how can we possibly understand others? If we don't know how to lead ourselves, how can we even *think* that we can lead others? And there's no way we can *lead* ourselves unless we *understand* ourselves—who we truly are, deep inside." Lucy placed her hand on her heart.

Then she smiled brightly. "So, the answer to your question is definitely self-awareness." She took another sip of her wine and looked happy with her conclusion.

I was fascinated by our conversation.

"So what happened? When did you change?" I asked, but was interrupted by the waiter who came to collect our plates. We ordered coffees and a dessert to share, like we always did. When the waiter had left, I asked again, "How did you become more self-aware? Did something happen to trigger it?"

I was thinking about my own experience. "Who do you want to be?" the soft voice had whispered. And suddenly I had just known.

"Oh, I can thank my daughter for that," Lucy said and smiled affectionately.

I was surprised. I didn't know Lucy had a child.

"One morning Annabelle, who was only five at the time, asked me what it was like to be a grown-up. 'Do you ever have fun, Mommy?' she asked me."

I smiled. What a wise little girl.

"I remember looking down at her big brown eyes and chubby cheeks, not knowing what to say."

Lucy seemed to be lost in memories for a moment, before she continued. "And then suddenly, it was as if I was looking down at myself. I recalled asking my parents the exact same question when I was little. I didn't remember exactly what they said, but I do remember they said something that made me think I never wanted to grow up."

Lucy took a deep breath, as if she'd just returned from the past.

"And that is when I decided I needed to make a change. If for no other reason than so my daughter wouldn't grow up thinking that grown-up life was miserable, that work was a drain, and that she—God forbid—had to look and act like a man to succeed."

"Wow," I said. Her story gave me goosebumps.

Lucy smiled and leaned back in her chair, sipping her wine.

"And then something really funny happened," she said.

I leaned forward, drawn deeper into her story.

"The moment I decided to lay off this whole 'role-playing' thing, and started showing up as my authentic self, things started going better at work. I relaxed more and was happier. Pretty soon my employees started trusting me more, and I actually ended up being a much better leader than I had ever been."

Lucy leaned over the table and looked directly at me to make sure I took in this next part. "When I stopped pretending that I was someone or something I wasn't, when I dared to be myself, to show vulnerability and admit my shortcomings, my team started relating to me in an entirely different way and began supporting me instead of avoiding me, which I felt earlier had been the case." Lucy laughed and shook her head. "Not that I blame them. The old me wasn't exactly a charmer."

We both laughed. I loved her self-deprecating sense of humor.

"That's such an inspiring story," I said. "How old is Annabelle now?"

Lucy got a soft look in her eyes.

"Annabelle is twenty-five, happy and wise and pursuing a career in social media, which she loves. It's also an area I know very little about, which I think was one of the reasons she chose it."

Lucy beamed. She radiated so much love and pride when she talked about her daughter.

"In fact, we're meeting up for coffee after this, if you'd like to meet her."

Lucy gave the waiter a little wave, to signal that she would like the check. She still hadn't allowed me to pay for any of the lunches, despite my insisting on several occasions.

"Oh, I'd love to meet her, but maybe another time? I'm afraid I have to get back to the office for my 3:00 p.m. meeting."

Lucy nodded. Once she settled the bill, we put on our coats and said goodbye and agreed to check in again in a month's time, our usual schedule.

On my way back to the office, I thought how amazing it was to get to know the woman, the mom, and the human being behind the professional façade. I was particularly fascinated to learn that Lucy had also gone through a journey to become who she was today.

It was as if I could hear Josh's voice inside my head: "Nobody is born a butterfly, you know."

"No," I whispered to myself. "We need to be willing to give up being a caterpillar first."

God, I missed Josh. And everyone else on that island.

· · ·

A few weeks later, I decided to invite everyone to an all-hands meeting and share my vision for the company. I wanted to convey all of the things I had learned from my conversations with the employees as well as our common goals for the coming year.

In the meeting, I told them about some changes we were making, toward more flexible and shorter work hours and that everyone was welcome to work from home when needed, as long as they still were able to deliver on their commitments. The announcement resulted in spontaneous cheers and applause.

Through my many conversations with TechnoGuard employees, I had learned how exhausted they were. Few had a life outside of work, and parents of small children only saw their kids on the weekends, due to the long hours they put in at the office.

I felt guilty, knowing I had been one of the leaders who had set the precedent and expectations that people should work twelve to fourteen hours a day, not once thinking about how this affected their lives, their families, and even their health.

Not only were twelve-hour workdays inhumane, they were a recipe for burnout and depression. And according to research, longer workdays actually made people *less* effective than if they worked shorter days.

When I announced the changes, most people looked very happy, but quite a few looked puzzled and even confused. Perhaps because they remembered the old me, how I used to speak, and what I used to expect from them.

What had happened? I could see the questions in their eyes.

I hadn't planned to, but recalling Lucy's advice about the importance of showing up as oneself, I decided to tell them a bit about what
had happened to me. I told them about how stressed I used to be
and that I had been diagnosed with "shallow breathing syndrome." I
demonstrated what that looked like, which got a good laugh. When I
told them that I had asked for an oxygen pill, they laughed even more.

I also shared what had happened at the conference in Kaua'i. Of
course, they had heard and read about it in the news, but I wanted
them to hear my version of the story.

I told them I had realized that I had to make a choice about who
I wanted to be in that moment. And I added that during my stay in
Kaua'i, I had learned to chill and connect with the things that mat-
tered to me, and it was with those things in mind I had returned to
TechnoGuard, as their new CEO.

"I want to make a difference, to improve things," I told the team. "I
want to come to work every day and feel happy about what I do and
how I do it. And I would like everyone working in this company to
feel the same."

I looked over the crowd. Everyone was listening.

"So, I thought, why not try to make TechnoGuard the best company to work for in our industry, in America—or in the world?! Make
it a place we all look forward to coming to in the morning, where we
enjoy our work and are inspired to give our best—and do amazing
work as a consequence."

Many were smiling now. "But to do that I will need your help.
Together we need to figure out what that looks like and co-create the
kind of company culture that will make us the best—and the happiest—team that we possibly can imagine!"

I could tell by the eager looks on people's faces that they liked what
they were hearing.

I drew a deep breath and smiled.

"Are you up for the challenge, Technoguardians?"

The roar from the room, the applause, and the energy of the people jumping to their feet said everything I needed to know.

That day when I left the office, I felt better than I had in a long time. I knew I was making a difference, not only for the company, but also in people's lives.

As I walked through Central Park, smiling at a group of kids chasing each other in the grass, I picked up my phone and texted Lisa.

"There in 5. Order us a bottle of Prosecco. I feel like celebrating!"

• • •

Nine months after I embarked on my new role, TechnoGuard was starting to look and feel like a very different company. There was a new and positive energy in the office that could be seen and felt. Where people used to sit inside their cubicles with glazed eyes and hardly communicate, they were now talking, laughing, discussing, and working together as teams in the open collaboration spaces.

The employees were visibly happier, and the sales results were steadily growing. We still had a long way to go—after all, we had started way below zero—but things were definitely heading in the right direction.

Determined to walk the talk, I rarely arrived in the office before 8:30 a.m. and tried to leave around five or six in the afternoon. I also avoided sending emails in the evening and on weekends, unless they were time critical. I knew whatever example I set would be mirrored by others.

The first time I showed up at Lisa's yoga class, she looked like she was about to faint. But when I continued coming on a regular basis, she was beyond thrilled. After all, I had been her hopeless, unresolved case for so many years.

It felt good to practice with her. It kept my body in shape, but most importantly, it reminded me of the importance of breathing. And I loved the end of the classes, just lying still on the mat and going to our happy place. I always went back to Kaua'i, to the beach, overlooking the ocean and Bali Ha'i.

I had called George five or six times since my return to New York. It was always good to hear his voice. It was strange, though, thinking about him sitting in his beach chair every morning, drinking his morning coffee from the cups William had made him and Aimee. I wondered whether anyone else had been served coffee from Aimee's cup. I felt a sting in my heart every time I thought about those magical mornings. They felt so far away. Almost as if they had never really happened.

"Why don't you give William a call? I know he would love to speak with you," George said almost every time we spoke. I told George that I would, but somehow I could never bring myself to actually do it. Somewhere deep inside I knew I still wasn't ready to hear his voice.

William had texted me now and then, asking how I was doing and how I enjoyed my new job. I had been a bit slow with my replies but had eventually answered him in a nice and friendly way, but without inviting dialogue. After a while, the texts stopped coming.

Then one day, on my way home from work, I got a text from him.

"Hey, Maya. I'm in New York. I'd love to see you. Dinner tomorrow? William."

My heart started beating like crazy, and my hands were shaking as I called Lisa right in the cab and read her the text.

"What do you think it means?" she asked.

"I have no idea. He probably just wants to say hi and catch up. After all, we are friends. Or were. At least I think we were . . ."

"But the 'I'd love to see you over dinner' part kind of insinuates something else, doesn't it?" Lisa loved playing Nancy Drew. "Maybe he's finished with Ms. Supermodel and wants to be with the true love of his life," she suggested.

I was reluctant to entertain any of Lisa's theories. "I don't know what to say or do, Lisa. I don't want to be rude and say no, but I don't know if I can handle seeing him."

"But what if, Maya? What if he is free now? Maybe he wants you as much as you want him. Wouldn't you want to know?"

I didn't want to go there, but Lisa ignited a little spark of hope in my heart with those questions.

I was quiet, so Lisa added, "Listen, Maya. I know how painful this whole William thing has been for you." Her voice was filled with empathy. It was as if she could feel my pain and fear and frustration. She always had. "Give it a chance, Maya. Meet him. What have you got to lose?"

I let out a deep sigh. "OK, OK," I said. "I'll do it."

Lisa was thrilled, and before we hung up, I promised to fill her in on the details later.

As the cab made its way up Sixth Avenue, I texted William back: "Great! Dinner tomorrow sounds nice. When and where? Maya."

That night I hardly slept. I kept checking my phone, but there were no new texts from William. Memories of him and me flashed through my mind, memories I had fought so hard to keep away. The conversations we'd had, the laughter we'd shared, the gazing at the stars, the dancing at the farmers market, the bodysurfing lessons, the unsaid that always lingered between us, the feeling of possibilities, of something magical, yet to be explored.

The next morning at work I was unfocused and nervous. Ruth asked me what was up, but I didn't feel like going into any of this with her, so I just told her that I hadn't slept well, and she seemed content with that explanation. The truth is, I didn't know what to think, feel, or expect about an evening out with William. It felt strange being equally filled with hope and dread.

"Friends, Maya, friends," the familiar voice kept telling me. But beneath that voice, another one whispered softly, "But what if . . ."

Around lunchtime, the text I had been waiting for finally arrived. "Osteria La Locanda, Soho, 7:30?"

I smiled, remembering how much he loved Italian food.

"Perfetto!" I texted back. And suddenly the butterflies, which had been quiet for so long, started fluttering inside my belly again.

At seven, I was dressed and ready to leave the apartment. I had tried on five different outfits and landed on a simple but classy green dress with matching sandals. It was summer in New York, so why not dress like it? I smiled at my reflection in the mirror.

My phone beeped. My heart skipped a beat when I noticed it was a text from William.

"Hey, Maya! Rebecca is in town too. Hope you don't mind that she's joining us. Can't wait to see you. W."

I couldn't decide what was worse: the disappointment or the anger. I let anger win. How could I have been so stupid? Again, I'd listened to the well-intended but naïve advice of a friend and allowed hope to sneak back into my heart. When would I learn?

I kicked off my sandals and went back into the living room, carrying my phone with me. The sun was still shining on Central Park; couples walked hand in hand, children played in the grass. It was a beautiful evening, but I couldn't see it.

I plopped down on the couch and took a deep breath.

"Sorry, William," I texted. "Something important came up at work. Have to cancel. Say hello to Rebecca from me and enjoy your dinner. M."

I unzipped my dress and left it on the floor. I walked into my bedroom, pulled down the blinds, and crawled under the duvet.

And for the first time since the day I returned to New York, I allowed myself to cry.

YEAR TWO

Having spent my first year as CEO making some pretty significant changes, year two was all about creating stability and continuing a healthy growth cycle.

I had hired Adriana Gonzales to oversee the newly established People & Culture team and Josie Becker as our new CFO, both highly accomplished professionals with great personalities. We now had three women on the executive team and were gradually getting closer to my goal of equal representation.

Sales were looking good. Employees and customers were happy, and everything was going really well.

Lucy and I had managed to keep our lunch-buddy schedule intact, and on the one-year anniversary of our first lunch, Lucy invited me to her place.

I was a bit surprised to find out that she lived in a bohemian townhouse in West Village, with climbing roses and a big pink bicycle leaning against the wall. The front door was wide open, and Lucy shouted, "Just come right in, Maya!" when I knocked on the door.

I followed Lucy's voice and walked through a living room with colorful walls and somewhat quirky furniture pieces that looked like they had been bought in secondhand stores—though I guessed they probably had been carefully selected and cost a bundle.

On the walls were pictures of her daughter and late husband, who had died when Annabelle was a young girl. Lucy hadn't talked much about him, except that he was the love of her life—and she'd never been able to imagine another man after him.

Lucy gave me a welcoming hug and asked me to sit down by the kitchen table as she finished making our lunch. I was happy to accept the glass of rosé wine she handed me. For once, I had blocked my calendar the entire afternoon and told Ruth I probably wouldn't be back in the office.

As I watched Lucy prepare our lunch, I sipped my wine and looked out of the open veranda door that led out to a small backyard. The smell of wet earth and grass reminded me of my childhood garden.

"I hope you like quiche, it's my mom's recipe." Lucy smiled as she walked toward me with two plates in her hands, wearing an apron over her denim dress. I noticed she had flour in her hair and was leaving a messy kitchen in her wake.

I found it utterly refreshing.

The food was delicious and the wine even better. We talked about everyday things and caught up on some of the topics we had discussed the last time.

When we finished eating, Lucy poured me another glass of wine and asked me to capture my first year as CEO in a few words.

I had to think for a moment.

"Difficult. Inspiring. And, nothing like I expected," I said after a while.

Lucy leaned back in her seat and smiled. "Interesting. Tell me more."

I took a deep breath. "Well, first of all I hadn't expected change to be so hard. Making structural changes is one thing, like rebuilding the offices, making some policy changes, reorganizing the teams. But changing people's mindsets and behaviors—and the way they work together—is something entirely different. Changing culture is hard."

Lucy nodded. Obviously, she was familiar with the challenge.

"And," I continued, "it's one thing to ask others to change, but to change *myself* and my own old habits was also way more difficult than I'd expected."

A cool wind came in through the open veranda door. In the distance I could hear sirens. The sound of New York.

"So, what have you done, to change yourself and your old habits?" Lucy asked.

I smiled at her. "Well, talking to you has helped a lot," I said. "Most of the things we have talked about, I have gone right back and tried to put into practice. And by becoming more self-aware, I have been able to do quite a bit of self-correction along the way." I took another sip of my wine. I was definitely not going back to the office afterwards.

"Another thing that has helped me a lot is the open dialogue that I initiated early on with the employees, when I asked them to help me become a good leader and let me know when I wasn't."

"And have they?" Lucy asked.

I laughed. "Yes, absolutely. One day someone called me on it in an all-hands meeting and wondered whether I knew that the parental philosophy 'Do as I say, not as I do' actually doesn't work. They were referring to the new work-life balance practice I was encouraging, and how someone had caught me sneaking back into the office one evening when I thought everyone had left."

Lucy laughed. "What did you say then?"

"Well, I had to admit that I was a recovering workaholic, so I just needed some time to let go of my addiction and actually start getting a life. But I also said that *my* lack of a life outside of work shouldn't stop them from living theirs."

Lucy threw her head back and laughed. "I bet that gave them a good laugh!"

"Yes, but they're right, you know. I can't say one thing and do something else. It takes away the credibility and makes people feel insecure about whether I really mean what I say."

Lucy leaned forward and looked at me. "The fact that the employees openly challenge you is a demonstration of how much they trust you and feel safe around you. That is quite an accomplishment, you know."

"I suppose that's true," I said and nodded slowly. "And I want them to. I don't have all the answers and I still have a lot to learn. Like the other day, when I made a stupid CEO decision without consulting the people who knew the situation and the customer best; the sales guys quickly let me know. Without sugarcoating it, may I add." I laughed. "And that saved us from making a bad—and probably costly—decision." I smiled and finished what was left of my wine. I could definitely get used to this wine-for-lunch habit. I made a mental note to block the afternoon after next month's lunch-buddy meeting as well.

"So this is what I'm thinking, Maya," Lucy said as she picked up our plates and carried them to the sink. "If most CEOs did only half of the things you already do, the corporate world would be a much better place."

She put the kettle on and started preparing coffee, while she continued talking: "Imagine if leaders realized that their job was to make the people in their organizations flourish, thrive, and make good decisions, instead of trying to control and pester them into just doing what they're told. Which often isn't what is best for the company—or the customers—anyway."

Lucy brought over some coffee mugs and a bowl filled with heart-shaped dark chocolates and sat down again.

"You also said it has been inspiring?" she asked and smiled.

I nodded eagerly. "It's been amazing to see the effect of the changes we have made. It's this new energy in the office and a new light in people's eyes that I have never seen before," I said and took a bite of the chocolate.

"And the business results are following as a consequence," I continued. Lucy nodded knowingly. She was obviously very aware of the positive growth TechnoGuard had experienced in the past year.

Lucy stood up again and walked over to the stove and slowly poured the hot water into a French coffee press. The aroma filled the room.

"And what did you mean about your first year as CEO being nothing like you expected?" she asked as she sat down again, placing the coffee press on the table between us.

I was silent for a moment before I spoke. "I honestly didn't know what to expect. But somehow, earlier, I was thinking of CEOs as these superior people who are smarter or better than anyone else."

Lucy smiled and waited for me to continue.

"But now I've realized that being a CEO is just a job, like anyone else's, only with a different—and bigger—responsibility."

Lucy nodded and slowly pushed down the plunger of the French Press. After she had poured the brew into our mugs, I picked mine up, breathed in the heavenly scent, and took a sip. It tasted as good as it smelled.

We sat silently, just savoring the coffee moment for a while before I spoke again. "I have to say that I feel humble and in awe of all the people who give so much of themselves for our company. And I can't even begin to explain how honored I am to be their leader. But I also have to admit that I'm terrified of letting them down, of making bad decisions that will jeopardize the company and the employees' livelihoods, or simply just sucking at my job!"

Lucy laughed out loud.

"That's called healthy paranoia, Maya, and in my book, that's a really good thing. Complacency is the enemy of progress."

She paused for a moment before she continued. "The way I see it, the problem is that very few CEOs share your sentiment, and instead consider themselves to be untouchable godlike figures that can do whatever they please. Who look after themselves before they look after anyone else, including their employees and the company they are there to lead."

I nodded. We didn't need to look far to find an example of a CEO who had done exactly that.

"I've come to realize something," I reflected out loud. "There actually aren't that many examples or role models out there who demonstrate a different way of leading. I am *so* grateful for you showing me that there is an alternative to copy-pasting those bad old CEO behaviors."

"Including dressing like them," Lucy said, and we both laughed and clinked our coffee mugs in a "cheers."

As Lucy went out in the garden for a quick phone call, I thought about how she had even become an inspiration to my wardrobe. Even though I'd kept some of my classic corporate outfits, I'd acquired quite a few new items, and as "the new Maya," I was definitely more relaxed and colorful in the way I dressed at work. "Happy colors, happy people," the sweet old lady in the souvenir shop in Kaua'i had said. She definitely had a point. I still had no hanky-panky to show for it, though. I chuckled silently at the memory.

When Lucy had finished her phone call, she asked if I wanted to join her in the garden. I was surprised to see her fish a cigarette and a lighter from the pocket of her apron. "Max one per day, and only in good company." She winked at me and lit up.

"I'd like to hear more about what has surprised you this first year," she said and took a deep inhale.

"Do you know what my biggest revelation this last year has been?" I asked, not waiting for an answer. "That my title, the corner office, and the prestige of the job ultimately meant nothing to me. However, I have discovered how much I enjoy being able to influence and change things to make a difference with what I do. And I have noticed that being in this position has made that a whole lot easier."

Lucy nodded and blew smoke rings out in the air.

"There is a saying, that power corrupts," she said. "That when people get to powerful positions they change into these bad, mean, greedy people."

I nodded. I knew of plenty of those.

"But I've learned that it's not necessarily the case," Lucy said. "Instead, power reveals; it shows people who you really are. If you're bad, you'll get worse. If you're good, you'll get even better. You're in the latter category, Maya." She smiled. Then she put out her cigarette in an ashtray she had hidden under a bush. "Bad habit, but it gives me so much joy." She winked at me as we walked back into the house. "Don't tell Annabelle, though."

It was time for me to leave and I thanked Lucy for the lovely lunch and inspiring chat and picked up my phone to order a car.

"I heard you declined the offer to have a personal driver on the company's dime," Lucy smiled.

"Yes," I replied. "Honestly, I found it a bit ridiculous. What do I need a private driver for? The yearly cost of a driver was enough to pay for a big company party, so I decided to allocate that money there instead."

Lucy laughed. "Way to go, girl!"

Two minutes later my cab driver arrived, and we hugged goodbye.

In the back of the car I reflected on some of the things Lucy and I had talked about over lunch.

I hadn't mentioned my biggest surprise with being a CEO: my salary. When I first got my new contract, I had to look at it twice. Was it one zero too many? When I realized it was correct, I was shocked. How could it be that a CEO earned so much more than an average paid employee? Or even a VP. It was insane.

When I told Lisa, she almost got angry with me. "Most male CEOs would never even have thought that thought!" she said. "Much less said it out loud! Take the money and be happy. Tell yourself you've earned it, and that they'll get their money's worth. And if the money is more than you need, just go ahead and use it for something good." She grinned. "I wouldn't mind a pair of new yoga pants."

That gave me an idea. In fact, a couple of them.

A few months later, when Lisa and I met at Tony's, I brought her a new pair of yoga pants, a key, and a rental agreement for the yoga studio I knew she had been dreaming about for many years. It was a three-year lease, already paid for, only awaiting her signature.

First, she didn't believe her eyes, then she refused to accept it, then she cried tears of gratitude, and then she danced her happy dance. Antonio and I were watching and smiling through all her emotional stages. We had already discussed and anticipated her exact reactions, and she didn't disappoint. Clearly, we both knew her well and loved her dearly.

Lani was on the phone the same day I made the first donation to the Rainbow Children Foundation. The donation included a note that it was from an anonymous giver, who would deposit the same amount every single month for the next three years.

"I know it's you! Don't you even try denying it!" She laughed. I pretended I had no idea what she was talking about. "On behalf of the children and their families, thank you so much! I promise I will spend the money wisely, and you'll receive monthly reports so you can see what a difference this money will make in people's lives." She paused, waiting for me to say something; but I was quietly smiling on the other end of the phone.

"And, just so you know, the first thing I will do is get Noah and his mother a better place to live. The place they're staying in now is a dump." My hand went to my heart, just thinking of that sweet boy and his mother. I was so grateful to be able to help them.

"And secondly," Lani continued, "with the size of these donations, I will be able to help some of the children and families at my old school in Harlem as well." I heard her smile. "But, since you have nothing to do with any of this, I'm really just calling to ask whether you have a couch I can crash on now and then."

"You know that nothing would make me happier, Lani," I said, and we started making plans for when she could come.

· · ·

Eighteen months into my role as TechnoGuard's CEO, things were going better than ever, and I was starting to relax and feel confident that I was handling this whole CEO role pretty well. That was, until I learned that not everyone agreed . . .

I was attending a customer meeting on the thirty-seventh floor when Ruth came in and whispered that she needed a quick word with me. I knew she would never interrupt if it wasn't very important, so I excused myself and followed her.

"It's Mr. Hatchett," she whispered. "He is trying to get a hold of you. He needs you to attend a board meeting this afternoon. Apparently, there have been some complaints."

I was a little taken aback. "Complaints? Oh, OK. Please let him know I'll be there. I'll try to finish up this meeting quickly, and then I'll head over."

Two hours later, I entered the main entrance of an office building in Battery Park in Lower Manhattan. The friendly receptionist told me to take the elevator to the forty-ninth floor. When I arrived there, I felt a bit dizzy and sat down in a deep chair, facing the windows overlooking the Statue of Liberty. I was feeling nervous. Whatever kind of complaint it was, it had to be pretty serious to make it all the way to the board.

When I entered the conference room twenty minutes later, I was surprised to see three members of my executive team at the end of the table. I shook hands with the seven members of the board, including Mr. Hatchett and Lucy, and nodded at John Cooper, Gary Arlington, and Brad Miller, who all refused to look at, much less acknowledge, me.

After I took my seat, Mr. Hatchett began the meeting.

"Welcome, everyone. The reason for this meeting is that we have received a letter of complaint from three members of the executive team at TechnoGuard, and we consider it to be a serious matter."

Mr. Hatchett nodded toward the three men at the end of the table, who nodded back. "Gentlemen, would you mind explaining your complaints and why you consider them a threat to the future success of TechnoGuard?"

John cleared his throat and stood up. He looked at everyone around the table, except me. "We have expressed in our letter that we are concerned about Maya Williams' competence, skills, and ability to serve as the CEO of TechnoGuard, and we have plenty of evidence to back this up. Items one through ten," John said as he started clicking through a PowerPoint presentation with copies of emails I had sent, transcripts of speeches I had made, and pictures of me in various situations, looking very relaxed and informal in all.

On behalf of himself, Arlington, and Miller, he expressed concern over several policy changes I'd implemented, highlighting the flexible work practices and the unlimited vacation policy, for a start.

I had wanted to see whether these policies, that had become very popular among start-up companies, might work in a more traditional corporate setting like ours.

And they did.

Employees felt trusted by being given a bigger responsibility for their own work life and appreciated the focus on results and deliverables over hours spent in the office.

With the new experience of freedom, trust, and empowerment, their sense of responsibility for the results and overall performance of the company had increased. So far, no one had misused the trust given to them. And I didn't think anyone would.

But of course, it wasn't in John Cooper's, and his allies', interests to mention this.

"The third policy change Maya Williams has introduced this last year," John continued, "is a nine-month paid parental leave program for both moms—and dads." He almost spat out the last word, his contempt for the whole idea that even dads should be allowed parental leave becoming obvious to all. I was extra proud of this one. I had never thought about the emotional—and practical—challenge it must be for new parents to have to go back to work and leave their infants in child care just a few months after they were born. From my meetings and chats with the employees I had learned so much, and it opened my eyes to realities I previously knew nothing about. I had even asked Adriana, our Chief Culture Officer, to look into the possibility of renting a space on the thirty-eighth floor that could work as a nursery when the new parents returned from their leave. I was glad I hadn't told John and company about those plans yet.

John continued, saying that they found it problematic that several times, in all-hands meetings, I had encouraged people to make brave decisions (leaving out that I had added "as long as you think it is in TechnoGuard's best interest"), and that I shockingly had told employees that sometimes it is easier to ask for forgiveness than permission.

The morning yoga classes on the thirty-seventh floor and the fact that I spent way too much time speaking with employees were other things that worried the three executives.

"All in all," John Cooper said, "the main problem, the way we see it, is that Maya Williams doesn't act like a real CEO at all."

While John spoke, I started realizing how blind and naïve I had been. I, who used to be the queen of corporate politics, had totally missed what was going on right under my nose.

I knew the executive team hadn't been thrilled with me as their CEO to begin with, but I thought things were good now. They hadn't said anything in our monthly meetings, and they seemed fine with the changes we'd made. Now I understood why. They had been busy collecting evidence and building their case against me.

In one of the pictures that was shared with the board, I was dressed in a sarong, wearing a lei and flip-flops. It was from the opening of the refurbished thirty-seventh floor, when I had introduced the aloha spirit and launched the "aloha wall" to encourage people to recognize each other for being helpful and showing kindness, which was, of course, inspired by the Rainbow Children's fireside chat.

"As you can see, Maya Williams behaves as if she is leading a holiday retreat instead of a serious company," John said as he flipped to the next slide.

While I did understand the seriousness of the situation, I couldn't help but smile inside. Holiday retreat, now wouldn't that be something . . .

I had initially been so focused on the three men betraying me on the other side of the table that I hadn't really noticed the reaction of the members of the board as the executives were speaking. When I fixed my gaze their way, I was relieved. My mentor, Lucy, looked like she was about to burst into laughter at any moment. Next to her, Travis West, a man my age, grinned widely. In fact, the more slides the executives showed of me in different situations—whether I was wearing sarongs, jeans, or standing on a table giving a spontaneous speech to the team— which were all supposed to be incriminating and paint me as unprofessional, the more the members of the board seemed to smile and chuckle. I could tell it was not the reaction the executives had hoped for. Only one man looked a bit concerned. Mr. Brown, in his mid-seventies, did not seem particularly amused. However, I wasn't sure whether it was a reaction to the presentation or if it was just the way he looked.

As I listened to John speaking, I was fascinated by how the excecutives had turned all the positive things we had done in the last year into negatives: Empowerment and trust were translated as anarchy. Involvement and dialogue became socialism. Informality and fun were portrayed as unprofessional.

I realized that I had totally overestimated my own leadership skills and underestimated the wrath I had unleashed within the executive team. And I knew there was something important to be learned here.

The final piece of evidence they shared was a video, filmed in a karaoke bar, at the after-party of our last company event. It was of me dancing on a stage singing ABBA's "Mamma Mia" with Laura from HR and Bethany from sales. We all looked very happy.

This was the only part of the presentation that concerned me. Not so much the nature of it, but rather how they had obtained the so-called evidence.

John was collecting energy for his closing remarks.

"And with this we believe we have given you all the evidence you need to agree that Maya Williams is not competent in her role as TechnoGuard's CEO. Instead, she is putting the company at risk by turning TechnoGuard into the joke of the town."

John sat down. Not once had he or any of the other executives looked me in the eyes.

But I could see and feel their fear. These men were terrified. Maybe not of me personally, but of what I had come to symbolize: Change. Unpredictability. Feminine values. Female empowerment. Loss of traditional status and power.

And their fear was expressed in the only way they knew to express it: with anger, blame, and finger-pointing. At me.

These three men were fighting for their lives, or at least desperately clinging to the way their lives used to be. I felt a little sorry for them. They were fighting a fight they could never win. The fight against change is the fight we are all doomed to lose.

A deep sense of calm overcame me. I had stayed silent the entire time they had been speaking. After the men had finished their presentation, Mr. Hatchett turned around and looked at me. "Now, Maya. I think it is only fair that you tell your side of the story. If you don't mind?"

He was serious, but I could see the warmth in his eyes. I felt he was on my side, and I knew Lucy was too, but I still had five other board members to convince.

The fact that I saw them laughing at the pictures and the evidence the executive team shared didn't necessarily mean they considered me fit as the CEO of the billion-dollar Nasdaq-listed company they oversaw. But whatever the outcome would be, I knew I could only continue being myself.

I stood up and looked everyone steadily in the eyes, including the three men at the end of the table. They still failed to meet my gaze. In spite of this, I addressed them first.

"First off, I have to say that I had no idea that you felt so strongly against everything we have been doing in the last year, including the changes we have made and the way I have behaved. And, while I do wish that you had come to me first—and sooner, so we could have tried to work things out—here we are."

I paused and turned to address the members of the board.

"Yes, it is all true. Everything John Cooper has told you, every statement, every policy change, and every picture that has been shared with you here today. I've done and said all of those things." I paused and smiled. "And I'm proud of it."

I could tell I had the board's full attention. Even the executives looked up and acknowledged me now.

I turned toward Mr. Hatchett and addressed him directly. "When you came and found me in Kaua'i one and a half years ago, you said you wanted me to bring the qualities and values that I had demonstrated at the conference in Kaua'i to my new position. You said TechnoGuard needed a CEO that demonstrated values like honesty, authenticity, courage, and integrity."

He nodded at me. Was it just wishful thinking, or did he actually look a bit proud?

"Well, what you have been shown here today is what that looks like in practice." I smiled and then turned to address the rest of the board.

"So that you can have some perspective, allow me to remind you that this last year, transforming TechnoGuard into a company that people are happy and proud to work for has been one of my biggest priorities. I have chosen this as a strategy because it helps us attract and keep talent, inspires people to collaborate better, to innovate more, and to come up with greater solutions for our customers. And it leads to significantly higher performance and better results."

I looked around the table to make sure my points were being heard. The executives instinctively looked away, but the board members leaned in closer.

"Extensive research shows that highly-engaged employees deliver up to *50 percent* higher performance than those who are less engaged. And companies that have highly-engaged employees are on average *20 percent* more profitable, and over time they deliver significantly higher shareholder return."

I was emphasizing the business outcomes, knowing that at the end of the day, the board would judge me on the results I delivered, not on the level of happiness of our employees. However, it was my goal to make them realize the overwhelming evidence that the two were mutually inclusive.

"In spite of all the evidence that employees' level of engagement directly correlates with company performance—the higher the engagement, the better the results—the majority of US workers state that they are *not* engaged in their jobs." I looked intently at the members of the board, making sure they were all listening to what I had to say.

"Therefore, the big question is this," I continued. "How do we, as a company, go *against* this trend? How do we create a company culture where people feel happy and engaged and motivated—and deliver great performance as a consequence?" I stopped to pour myself a glass of water, primarily to give them time to reflect on my questions.

After a brief pause, I continued, "Many organizations and leaders make the mistake of thinking of the *disengaged employees* as the problem, as if people *choose* to be disgruntled and not care. The truth is that lack of engagement is rarely a choice, but rather a *symptom*, a *consequence*, of something else."

I was pleased to see that I still had everyone's undivided attention.

"The real problem, according to a number of studies, is the lack of *humane leadership* and *trust* that exists in most workplaces. When people don't feel safe, respected, and valued and are treated as 'resources' instead of human beings, they end up just showing up at work, doing the bare minimum, just waiting for the day to be over. Disengagement is to a large extent a *survival mechanism*, and it leads to bad outcomes for people, for companies—and ultimately for the shareholders."

A few were nodding to the last remark, and Travis was taking notes.

I walked over to the whiteboard.

"According to Gallup, the high level of disengaged employees cost US businesses alone more than *500 billion dollars* per year." I wrote the number on the whiteboard.

"In addition, you have the cost of burn-outs, stress-related health problems, and personal misery because of brutally long work days, minimal time for rest—and family time—and, in many places, a total absence of joy in the workplace."

I looked at the highly accomplished business people around the table.

"In short, and to be brutally honest with you," I said, "the corporate world has a huge *leadership* challenge. The old models are outdated and ineffective. Command and control doesn't work anymore. But trusting and engaging people do." I paused for a deep breath. "It's time for leaders, companies, and their boards to embrace a more humane leadership style and do what their shareholders are asking them to do: create financially healthy, sustainable, and thriving companies. And to do that, they need to start with caring about—and investing in—their *people* and their *culture*."

By now, I figured I had nothing to lose. I was determined to take it all the way, regardless of what the outcome might end up being for me personally.

I took a sip of water before I continued.

"Now, what does all this have to do with me not acting like a CEO *should*, as these gentlemen insinuate?" I nodded toward the three men. Lucy chuckled quietly.

"Leadership is not about what you say but about what you do. And trust is not something that can be demanded, it needs to be earned. Wanting to earn our employees' trust and to create an environment where people feel safe to be themselves, I needed to go first. And, that is precisely what I did."

I studied the executives at the end of the table. They avoided my gaze.

"What my colleagues have shown you today was evidence of me being Maya, who happens to have the role of CEO. Not a CEO who is played by a person called Maya. There is a huge difference and people can feel it."

Lucy nodded, and I gave her a little smile.

"The feedback I have gotten from our employees is that for the first time they feel valued, safe, and trusted at work. They give their best, dare to take risks, and constantly try to improve things, because they care—and they know they won't get fired when they ask a critical question or make a mistake. On the contrary, we let them know that we much prefer people try and fail than that they don't try at all."

Travis was still taking notes, and Mr. Brown looked like he was about to fall asleep.

"In this new environment of trust, employees and teams collaborate better, innovate more, and are more effective in solving problems and meeting customers' demands than they have ever been before. And they are having fun while doing it. Now isn't that something?" I smiled.

The majority of the board members smiled back at me now.

"Also, I'd like to mention that after we implemented the new flexible work and vacation policies and a more generous parental leave, people have become more productive with less time in the office, and report back that they feel a lot happier—with both their work and their lives. Not one single person has left the company in the past six months, and some of the people who left one and a half years ago are now asking to come back."

I walked across the room, picked up a marker, and drew two arrows pointing upward on the whiteboard.

"So, what have been the business outcomes of these changes thus far?" I pointed at the arrows. "For one, the level of employee engagement has spiked and so has our customer satisfaction score." I added a big "30 percent" to the whiteboard with a thick green marker. "And this is the increase in revenue since the same time last year."

I set the marker down and walked back to my place at the conference table.

"And as I am sure you all are aware of, the share price is gradually climbing back up to where it belongs." I took a deep breath and smiled. "So yes, I am proud."

Then I paused and looked over to John, Gary, and Brad.

"But there is one thing I am not so proud of."

The three men looked away. I could tell they were highly uncomfortable with the way things were unfolding.

"And that is that I have not done a good enough job working with and involving the executive team in all the changes we've made. I think I have done a decent job with the majority of the employees. But I clearly still have a lot to learn about how to lead, collaborate with, and win the trust of my own team. And that is something I would like to do something about. That is, if you decide that I have your continuous support." I looked around the table, meeting the eyes of every member of the board, before I sat back down in my chair.

I noticed that the air in the room felt lighter.

"Thank you, Maya. Thank you, gentlemen," Mr. Hatchett said as he nodded toward the end of the table. The executives gathered up their things and awaited their cue to leave.

Mr. Hatchett stood up as he gestured to the door. "Thank you, you are free to go now."

I nodded and stood up as the other executives filed out of the room.

"Maya, can I please ask you to wait outside for a few minutes?"

I felt a little nervous in the waiting area, but when Mr. Hatchett came out, I could tell he had good news. "The board members were impressed with you, Maya. They think you are a breath of fresh air and are demonstrating the values we want TechnoGuard to stand for. And of course, the results speak for themselves." He paused and smiled. "You have the board's continuous support."

I let out a sigh of relief .

Mr. Hatchett sat down on the sofa beside me. "However, the support does come with one condition. It sounds to us that you have been running a one-woman-band since you came back, and big kudos to you for having done so with great success. But real leadership is about building strong teams and an organization that can live on without you. And to do that, you need to have a strong leadership team that shares your vision, supports you, and is willing to go through fire with you."

Mr. Hatchett smiled warmly before continuing.

"And it sounded like you came to the exact same conclusion in there," he said as he looked toward the meeting room.

I nodded. "Yes, I did. And I definitely intend to take that responsibility seriously."

"Good," Mr. Hatchett said as he stood up. "Maya, I want you to know that I respect you tremendously for standing up for your own beliefs. There are not a lot of people of your caliber in the corporate world."

"Yet," I said.

"Excuse me?"

"There are not a lot of people like me in the corporate world yet. Times are changing, Mr. Hatchett. They will come."

"Yes, I hear you say that. But may I, as one of the old dinosaurs who believes in what you are trying to do, give you a bit of advice?"

"Of course. I would very much appreciate that."

His voice was serious, but his eyes were still smiling. "Sometimes, it is good to meet people where they are. You may have understood something that most of us haven't yet, but when you are stretching the band too far, people will get scared and resist, instead of supporting it. I think that is what might have happened with your executive team. Challenging people to step a bit outside their comfort zone is good, but asking them to travel to a different planet with you, when they haven't even heard about that planet before, might be a bit too much."

I laughed out loud. "Thank you. I will remember that."

After shaking hands with Mr. Hatchett, I got back into the elevator and headed down to the lobby. As I walked out of the building, I looked for a nearby café. There was a phone call I needed to make, and I wasn't looking forward to it.

After ordering my coffee, I sat down at a table by the window, fished my phone out of my bag, and made the call.

"Hi, Ruth. Maya here."

"Hello, Maya," Ruth replied as she always did, but her voice sounded tenser than normal.

"I just came from a meeting with the board. Apparently, there had been some complaints, so I had to explain myself a bit, but don't worry, all is well. I still have a job."

I could sense her simultaneous tension and relief.

"Thank goodness," she sighed.

"I have a question, though. How did John get his hands on the video you filmed of me at the karaoke bar that night? Didn't we agree that you wouldn't share it with anyone?"

Ruth's voice tightened. "I never wanted them to hurt you, Maya. I promise. I just wanted things to go back to normal."

"What?" For a moment I froze. I had been hurt by the executives' betrayal, but this one felt much worse. "Did you give it to them with the knowledge they would use it against me?"

"John never said he would show it to the board." Ruth sounded like she was about to cry. "He just said he needed it to give you a wake-up call, to get things back to normal. There have been too many changes, Maya. I just wanted things to be more like they used to be."

"Why didn't you come to me, Ruth? Why didn't you tell me?"

I had never heard Ruth cry before. "I don't know," she sobbed. "You're just so different. I sometimes miss the old Maya. But I never meant to hurt you."

"I know you didn't, Ruth," I replied. "But I can't go back to who I was. And I don't want to."

"But why not?"

I realized it wasn't only the executive team I hadn't paid enough attention to lately.

I sighed silently before I spoke. "Sorry it's taken so long Ruth. Let's have that dinner and bottle of wine we talked about. I will try to explain everything then."

Ruth said she would like that and we agreed to go somewhere after work the next day.

After we hung up, I collected my coffee from the counter and plopped back down in the chair, stared out the window, and exhaled.

I clearly still had a lot to learn.

YEAR THREE

M idway into my third year as the CEO, TechnoGuard was thriving. Revenue was up 50 percent from the year before, making us one of the fastest-growing companies in our industry. We had even made it to the list of the ten most attractive places to work in the country, and my relationship with the executive team had hugely improved. Suffice it to say, I was feeling pretty good about things.

A few weeks after the infamous board meeting, I suggested that the executive team go away together on a two-day offsite retreat. To my surprise, everyone agreed. A few weeks later, we all arrived in the Hamptons to stay in Mr. Hatchett's ten-bedroom mansion.

The house was gorgeous and practically on the beach, and all the furniture and decorations were navy blue and white, which immediately made me think of George. Ruth had stocked up the fridge with food, beer, and wine. She even prepared a bonfire for us on the beach. I invited her to stay, but she declined.

"I know too much about them," she whispered to me with a wink, and left.

I was glad I had decided—and managed—to push aside what I also knew and start with a clean slate. Lucy had once shared one of her mottos with me, "Begin again," which was about letting go of the past and seeing every moment as an opportunity for a new beginning. I had taken that advice to heart and it had helped me tremendously in my relationship with the executives.

When we first arrived, we explored the mansion, chose our bedrooms, and got familiar with the property. The atmosphere was a bit nervous and awkward to begin with; we were all clearly out of our comfort zones. But then Adriana put some Latin rhythms on the stereo and Gary popped open a bottle of champagne, and things started to loosen up.

Later, we sat on the large blue and white sofas on the oceanfront deck, had drinks, chatted, and ate the divine mushroom risotto John had cooked for us. I had no idea he'd been a chef in his younger days.

With the sound of waves hitting the shore in the background, the atmosphere was much more light-hearted and friendly than I had dared to dream it would be, and I finally started to relax.

After dinner, we took our glasses and blankets down to the beach, lit the bonfire, and listened to the waves while looking into the flames. After a while Oliver, our newly promoted chief marketing officer, picked up his guitar and started singing "Bridge over Troubled Water." As people started to sing along, I allowed myself to drift away for a moment.

I was pulled back in time, to a different place, sitting by a bonfire with the two men I adored, feeling enveloped in their love, their joy, their laughter. The sound of the burning wood and soothing waves; the smell of the Pacific Ocean, so fresh, so invigorating, so . . .

"Sweet Home Alabama," the team sang cheerfully. I shook off the memories and sang along.

The next day, after breakfast, we sat outside on the deck and had the open and honest conversations we had agreed were the most important reason for the trip. We talked about how things were at TechnoGuard and went over what worked and what didn't work, and how we envisioned the road ahead.

There were many things I hadn't understood, one of them being how extremely unhappy and offended they still were about having lost their executive offices. The office situation was what had started the whole campaign against me, John admitted. He said it wasn't only the decision itself, but the way I had just bulldozed over them, leaving no room for discussion. They said they would have accepted smaller offices, but having no office at all made their jobs more difficult.

I thought about Lucy's story and realized I had fallen into the trap of acting in a way I *thought* a CEO should act back then. I had been more focused on being decisive, getting things done, and demonstrating power than on taking a moment to reflect on what would have been the wisest thing to do. Had I done that, I would probably have involved them along the way instead of just running them over with my decisions.

We agreed that reinstalling the old offices was not an option. In fact, the executives admitted that they had come to really like what we had done to the thirty-seventh floor. Over a plate of crawfish for lunch, we agreed to build a number of smaller offices on the thirty-sixth floor. "But no indicator lights, right?" I joked. I was happy to see we were already able to laugh about those. I promised to communicate and involve them more with my ideas and plans moving forward, and they, in turn, promised to tell me when there were things they didn't understand or like.

Over a couple of beers after a game of beach volleyball, we decided to rename the executive team the leadership team and agreed that everyone would work on communicating more frequently with their own teams to improve relations throughout the company. We agreed to strive to maintain a company that was open and transparent so we could build trust not just within the company but also with our clients and shareholders—and that this would be everyone's responsibility.

The leadership team would later come to define TechoGuard's history as before and after the Hamptons retreat. That is how much things changed between us after those two days together on the beach. It was a simple yet effective approach to mending fences. By spending time together in a relaxed and informal setting, and taking time to listen to each other and try to understand each other's perspectives, we had established a level of respect and trust that I never thought we would have been able to achieve.

Back at the office, I started delegating more of my responsibilities to the members of my team, which freed up a lot of my time and allowed me to spend more time with customers and business partners and even attend networking events and conferences, something I hadn't prioritized in my first years as a CEO.

As our new dynamic unfolded, a sentence kept popping up in my head. It was something Mr. Hatchett had said to me after last year's board meeting: "Real leadership is about building strong teams and an organization that can live on without you."

In a strange way, that sentence kept resonating with me on a deep level.

. . .

One day, I was just back at the office after having attended a three-day cybersecurity conference in Orlando; I sat down at my desk to catch up on three days of unread emails. I was the only one from the leadership team who was still sitting in the open landscape, simply because I liked being there, and the employees seemed to appreciate having me around.

I was halfway through my unread emails when I heard a strange sound coming from the kitchen. Was someone singing? Suddenly people from every department came marching down the hallway carrying flags and balloons, clapping their hands, and cheering. Was it someone's birthday? I looked around to see what the fuss was about and found that everyone was looking at me, grinning.

Ruth was walking in front, carrying a big, rectangular cake. When she approached me, she carefully put it down on my desk. The cake was beautifully decorated, and someone had written *Forbes* all over it.

"What's going on?" I was confused.

"Congratulations! You have been nominated for the Business Woman of the Year award by *Forbes* magazine!" Ruth beamed, looking as proud as if she'd been my mom.

"I what?"

"They called while you were at the conference. We've been dying to tell you, but we wanted to do it properly."

"We?" I laughed and looked at the people standing around me. "You all knew?"

Apparently, Ruth had yelled her excitement when they phoned her, since they hadn't been able to get a hold of me.

I laughed and stood up from my seat. When I looked at all the people surrounding me, I was deeply moved by their proud faces.

"Whatever made them choose me for this, it's really a testament to the awesome job you guys are doing. This nomination is for all of us."

I noticed Ruth drying a tear.

"Well, what are you all standing around for? Let's eat!"

After we had finished the cake and people started heading back to their work spaces, I sat back down at my desk and continued to comb through my emails.

I noticed I had received an email from the Young Professional Women's Network again, whose invitation to speak I had turned down a few years earlier.

They wanted me to do a keynote and attend a panel debate on how to succeed in the male-dominated corporate world. This time I decided to accept.

I had a lot to say.

. . .

A few months later, on the day of the conference, I walked into the large convention center downtown. It was crowded with women and men dressed in corporate attire, wearing colorful conference badges around their necks.

I was wearing a long-sleeved, knee-length blue silk dress and a pair of ankle boots, making an effort to look presentable for the stage while not being too corporate.

Outside the conference room, there was a banner with a big picture of me.

"Maya Williams, Business Woman of the Year" it said. It still felt unreal. Only a month after I learned about the nomination, I'd received a call from *Forbes*'s editor-in-chief, letting me know that I'd won.

He said they wanted to run a piece on me, but instead of interviewing me, they wanted to interview the people working with me, and asked if I was OK with that. I thought it was a fun angle and said yes, and over a period of two weeks, a journalist hung out at the office and talked to a variety of people.

"You know you won't be able to control what the journalist ends up writing about you, right?" Ruth said suspiciously one day.

"I know." I smiled at her.

I was tired of all those glossy profiles, people talking about themselves, making themselves sound so perfect, when we all knew that the reality usually was anything but. I used to live my life trying to live up to other people's expectations and definition of what perfect looked like, but now that I'd stopped, I'd never felt better about myself, my life, or my achievements.

If I could be an example for others—showing that you can challenge the predesigned "boxes" and simply be yourself and do your own thing, and that happiness and success will follow from that—nothing would make me happier.

If a disgruntled employee or someone else who hated my guts finally got the opportunity to complain about me to the world, well, that was something that came with the territory of being open and transparent. I was willing to take that risk.

When the magazine came out, I must, however, admit that I was relieved to see the article had turned out well.

On the front page, there was a picture of me, sitting in the chill area of the thirty-seventh floor, chatting with some of my TechnoGuard colleagues, wearing my green dress and matching sandals. The heading read: *"Maya Williams, Business Woman of the Year, Doing It Her Own Way."*

In the article, the journalist had written a piece about the company, our culture, and the changes we'd made over the last three years, especially the ones that had to do with employee well-being and happiness and how that had a direct effect on sales results and the bottom line of the company.

Then, the rest of the article focused on my role in it all. With a little bit of digging, the journalist had been able to collect testimonials from people who'd been working with me years ago, someone who'd been at the conference in Kaua'i, and from a number of my current colleagues at TechnoGuard.

Some of the testimonials the journalist had dug up from the "old days" were:

> *"She was a bit like a machine."*
>
> *"I was terrified of her."*
>
> *"She didn't seem like a happy person."*

People who'd attended the conference in Kaua'i said things like:

> *"I'd never been so shocked by a corporate presentation."*
>
> *"I was convinced that what she had done was career suicide."*

"If it hadn't been for her, our lives might not be as good as they are today." That last statement came from a senior citizen who'd attended the conference.

The rest of the interviews were with employees who had experienced the transformation that happened after I returned as the company CEO.

"She returned to TechnoGuard like a different person."

"She's a kick-butt businesswoman with a CEO's perspective and a warm and caring heart."

"She doesn't take no for an answer. It's a bit exhausting sometimes."

"She's all in. Her passion is contagious."

"For the first time in my entire career, I actually look forward to coming to work in the morning."

"She dresses, acts, laughs, and speaks like no executive I've ever met."

"She really cares about people. I've never felt so valued for the work I do."

"She can be a bit too much. I sometimes warn my clients before bringing them into the office to meet with her. But, somehow, they all end up loving her."

"She has made us better by unleashing the energy and potential of our team. We'd go through fire for her."

I think the last comment was the one that moved me the most. I had no idea John Cooper felt like that now.

Finally, they had interviewed Lucy Dellaware and Mr. Hatchett.

"She's changing the corporate world and what it means to be in it," Lucy had said.

Mr. Hatchett's testimonial made me smile. *"There's no one like*

Maya Williams. She has 'IT,' in the double sense of the word. CEOs around the world, listen and learn—and you just might find yourself on a way more successful path."

The *Forbes* Business Woman of the Year issue was now out on the newsstands, and for the first time in my life, I was being stopped on the street and asked whether I was *the* Maya Williams. It was a surreal feeling.

It was also weird seeing my own picture blown up on a banner in the lobby of the convention center, so I turned my gaze to the pictures of the other panelists instead—and froze.

Seeing his self-satisfied smirk again made me sick to my stomach. Had I known he would be there, I would never have come.

Suddenly, I was thrown back in time, overwhelmed by memories I had tried so hard to push away. I was lying on the bathroom floor, crying, feeling dirty, humiliated, scared, and ashamed. I had crawled into the shower, desperately trying to wash away the feeling of his filthy hands all over my body, but I couldn't. Ten years later I could still feel the wet, disgusting tongue in my ear, the brutal hand that forced itself between my legs while the other hand covered my mouth when I tried to scream.

"I will destroy you," he had yelled after me when I managed to kick my knee between his legs and escape.

He almost had.

And now we would be speaking on the same stage.

I felt close to panic and desperately scanned my brain for an excuse to leave.

And then I saw him, my former boss and assailant, Robert Henderson, senior partner at Bernstein & Company, one of New York's leading management consultancies.

He was on his way into the conference hall, dressed in a shiny gray suit. His dark hair, turning gray, was slicked back with half a tube of gel, making him look just as sleazy as I knew he was. He was throwing long looks after one of the young girls walking in front of him, like a shark looking for his next victim.

Suddenly something new kicked in—ten years of overdue rage combined with a motherly instinct to protect these young women from having to go through what I had.

I walked quickly toward the conference hall. It was packed with people, mostly women. Robert Henderson was now standing at the front, near the stage, talking to a young blonde. I walked quickly and decisively up to him and tapped him on the shoulder.

"Excuse me," I nodded apologetically to the young woman, "but I have to borrow Mr. Henderson for a minute."

"Well, if it isn't the woman of the year," Robert said with a smug grin.

I squeezed his arm hard and led him toward a corner of the room where everyone could observe us without overhearing a word of our conversation.

"Listen, you little piece of shit," I said through clenched teeth, while forcing a smile in case others were watching. "You and I are going to be on that stage together, and when we are there you have one job and one job only, and that is to make sure that none of the women in this room ever has to experience anything like what you did to me."

He tried to laugh and shake off my hand, but I kept a firm grip on his arm.

"What on earth are you talking about?" he said.

"Don't play dumb with me. You know exactly what I'm talking about. And unless you want everyone else to know, including your colleagues at Bernstein & Co.—*and* the police—this is what you're going to do."

Sweat was running down his forehead now.

"C'mon, Maya. That was just a joke. I never meant to hurt you."

"Tell that to the cops," I said, my voice filled with contempt.

His eyes widened when he realized that my threats were serious.

"What do you want me to do?" His gaze was flickering, like he hoped someone would come to his rescue.

I continued smiling while speaking in a low and controlled voice. "Later, when we are having a discussion onstage, you are going to tell these girls that they need to stand up for themselves and never fall for dirty tricks, like being asked by their boss to come and look at documents in a hotel room after midnight." I nearly spat out that last sentence, concentrating hard to keep the smile on my face.

Robert pulled back, alarmed.

"I can't say that," he said.

"Yes, you can, and you will," I shot back at him with clenched teeth, still smiling, and squeezing his arm even harder. "Then, you will tell them that if they are ever assaulted or threatened by scumbags—like yourself—they should immediately report it to the police. God knows I wish I had," I growled.

Robert Henderson was nearly paralyzed now. He desperately tried to avoid my gaze. Streams of sweat were pouring down his forehead.

I flashed a false smile and said, "Then, from stage, you will tell Cynthia Jones, the founder of the Young Professional Women's Network, that you will donate 500,000 dollars from your *own* pocket to their Female Empowerment Initiative, which supports women who have been victims of sexual assault in the workplace."

Robert's face was covered in sweat despite his attempt to maintain composure.

"But . . . ," he said.

"No buts. Do it or I'll see you in court."

I stared into his eyes one last time, leaving no room for interpretation. Then I let go of his arm, turned my back to him, and walked over to the technician who was waiting for me in front of the stage with a microphone in his hands.

From the corner of my eye, I could see how Robert nervously dried the sweat off his face with a white handkerchief and hesitantly walked over to his designated seat. He looked small and insignificant, his face as gray as his suit.

When my name was announced over the speaker, I confidently walked up onstage and into the spotlight.

"Hello, ladies," I said. "I am Maya Williams, and I'm here to tell you a secret or two about being a woman in the male-dominated corporate world."

I paused and looked over the crowd.

"The biggest secret being this: the dominance won't last for much longer."

And as five hundred women jumped on their feet and clapped their hands and cheered, a familiar voice inside my head whispered softly: "Go fly, butterfly girl."

I smiled, nodded, and continued to speak.

SURRENDER

*We must let go of the life we have
planned, so as to accept the one
that is waiting for us.*

JOSEPH CAMPBELL

CHRISTMAS IN NEW YORK

It was almost Christmas, one of my favorite seasons to be in New York. I was walking down Fifth Avenue. The streets were packed with people admiring the lights and decorations that transformed the city into a colorful, magical world. A Salvation Army officer was ringing a bell, a big man dressed like Santa Claus was on a street corner shouting, "Ho-ho-ho!" every five seconds, and by Rockefeller Center the giant Christmas tree covered in colorful lights was shining on all the people skating on the ice rink to classic Christmas songs.

I was on my way to meet Mr. Hatchett at the Waldorf Astoria for an early dinner, to celebrate that TechnoGuard was in better shape than ever and that our share price was at an all-time high.

As I walked through the entrance of the iconic hotel, I smiled at the uniformed doormen and continued toward the restaurant, located in the heart of the main lobby. The dining area was beautifully decorated and packed with people. Archibald Hatchett, or Archie, as he now insisted I should call him, was already there. He stood up and waved as I entered the room. When I arrived at the table, I noticed a bottle of champagne in an ice bucket on a stand waiting for us. Archie, whom I still preferred to think of as Mr. Hatchett, was wearing a dark suit with a red handkerchief decorated with white snowflakes sticking out of the breast pocket.

"Elegant," I said.

"Thanks to my wife." He laughed.

As the waiter popped open the bottle of champagne, I sat down and looked around the crowded room with all the dressed-up people and the cheerful atmosphere. Apparently, we were not the only ones with something to celebrate.

After the waiter had filled up our glasses and left with a polite bow, Mr. Hatchett raised his glass, and I followed his example.

"Cheers to you, Maya," he said and smiled. "Three years ago, I suspected you would be great, but you have indeed exceeded all of my expectations."

"Thank you—and the very same to you!" I said.

It was a lovely dinner. We covered the gamut, discussing business, philosophy, politics, culture, and life itself. However, every time Mr. Hatchett started talking about the long-term plans for TechnoGuard, I felt strange. For some reason I struggled with being excited about it—or even seeing myself as part of it.

When I had accepted the offer to become CEO of TechnoGuard, I thought of it as a three-year plan. I had never been able to see beyond that. And now, when we had passed the three-year mark, I had a strange sense of completion. Even though I knew there was still a lot to be done, I wasn't sure whether it should be me doing it. I hadn't said anything about this to Mr. Hatchett, of course. I didn't even know what to say or where these thoughts and feelings came from.

Of course, it didn't make sense. Things were going well. I enjoyed my job. I was content with my life and proud of the things I had achieved. Business woman of the year—who would have guessed?

Still, I couldn't let go of the feeling that there was something else I was supposed to do now.

When we had finished our dinner and were waiting for our coffees, Mr. Hatchett looked at me solemnly.

"Maya, TechnoGuard would never have been the company it is

today if it hadn't been for your leadership and your somewhat . . . ," he paused and smiled, "*untraditional* approach to things."

I smiled back at him.

"I want you to know that I really hope you will commit to a new three-year period. But I have a feeling that you're not quite convinced yourself, are you?"

I realized Mr. Hatchett had picked up more than he let on. And that my poker face wasn't what it used to be.

"I'd be happy to offer you a higher salary and more shares to convince you to stay," he continued, "but something tells me that when you have decided what you want, none of that will matter anyway."

I was flattered. But he was right. I didn't care about the money or the shares. I'd already earned more than I could spend. I knew I would only continue if my heart was in it, and I wasn't sure it was anymore.

"Thank you, Archie, I appreciate your generosity," I said. "But you're right. Money is not what will determine my next move. And honestly, I'd be careful with hiring anyone who is primarily driven by that."

Mr. Hatchett grinned. "Look who's teaching who now," he said and winked.

I laughed, then turned serious again.

"I've had the most amazing three years, I've learned *so* much and am really proud of what we have achieved. But I owe it to you, the company, and myself to take some time to reflect before I commit to a new period. So if it's OK with you, I'd like to think it over during the holidays."

"Of course! Anything you say," Mr. Hatchett replied, then after a brief pause he continued. "I know you have groomed a few people on your team for an interim CEO role, and I appreciate that. But none of them are Maya Williams."

The coffee arrived and I was glad for the distraction. I didn't quite know how to respond.

After we'd both sipped our coffees, Mr. Hatchett went on. "But should you decide *not* to continue as CEO, I hope you will consider a role on TechnoGuard's board of directors instead. I know I have the board's full support for such an offer."

Again, I was flattered.

"Thank you, Archie. I really appreciate your generosity and belief in me. I will definitely consider everything you've said." I felt overwhelmed by Mr. Hatchett's unconditional support.

As he asked for the check, I thought about what a strange situation I was in: having already achieved everything I once thought mattered to me, I was offered even more. Yet, none of it excited me.

When the waiter brought our coats over, we stood up and I turned toward Mr. Hatchett with a heartfelt smile.

"Thank you for a lovely meal and the champagne—and for everything else!" I gave him a hug. "Merry Christmas, Archie!"

"Happy holidays, Maya," he said and gave me a warm hug back. "Enjoy your well-deserved break! See you next year."

We walked through the lobby and as we left the hotel, I noticed that Mr. Hatchett gave the doormen money, wishing them and their families a happy holiday.

Once outside, we smiled at each other, waved goodbye—then headed in opposite directions.

As I slowly walked north toward Central Park, I wondered what on earth was happening to me. Something was changing, again, and I didn't understand what it was.

Maybe I just needed a break, get some time to think and chill a bit. Thankfully I would have plenty of time for that.

The leadership team and I had decided to give everyone in the company two weeks of paid vacation over the holidays. Business was slow anyway, and people had been working so hard throughout the year and overdelivered on every target we'd set for ourselves, so they deserved it.

We all did.

When I approached Central Park, I decided to stroll through the Christmas market by Columbus Circle. It smelled of roasted chestnuts and mulled wine. Young Christmas carolers were singing a jazzy version of "Rudolph the Red-Nosed Reindeer," and people stopped to listen.

I made a stop at a small bookstand, thinking I might buy myself a couple of new books to read over the holiday.

My eyes fell on one that looked vaguely familiar. Where had I seen this before? Then I remembered. It was one of the books that always resided on Mom's bedside table. I remembered this one as a collection of poems and quotes.

I picked up the book and opened it to a random page. There was a picture of a dark blue sky covered with sparkling stars and a quote by Joseph Campbell, saying that we must let go of the life we have planned, so as to accept the one that is waiting for us. Reading this gave me goosebumps, and it suddenly felt like my blood started flowing more quickly through my veins.

I paid the lady at the bookstand for the book and went into the park. Christmas lights illuminated my path. Above me, snowflakes were in the air, and I watched how the last red leaves slowly fell off the trees and landed softly on the ground.

Suddenly, something tickled my nose. I thought it was a falling leaf and carefully brushed it away, but when it came back again, I followed it with my eyes, and that is when I realized what it was. It was a butterfly. A beautiful orange butterfly. It danced around me, as if it wanted my attention. A butterfly in New York in December? What were the odds?

I stopped walking, and suddenly I just *knew* what I was supposed to do.

I had to go back to Kaua'i. And there was no time to lose.

IN TRANSIT

I was sitting in a deep leather chair at a coffee shop at the San Francisco International Airport, waiting for my connecting flight. The airport was packed with people, but I had found a comfortably quiet spot in a corner, with classic Christmas songs playing lightly in the background.

It was December twenty-second, and holiday travelers were running in and out of the shops, buying last-minute gifts. I'd never been big on Christmas. At least not after my mom died. I had vague memories of happy mornings with Christmas presents under the tree, but those mornings ended, just like a lot of things ended, when Mom died. My dad used to say that Christmas was a ridiculous concept invented to make people spend lots of money on things they didn't need.

I had just taken the first sip of my coffee when I heard a voice I recognized.

"Maya! It *is* you!" The ever-gorgeous Rebecca was suddenly standing in front of me, dressed in a beige wrap dress and brown cashmere shawl casually thrown around her shoulders. "Oh, my goodness. I can't believe it. William and I were *just* talking about you!" She gave me a warm hug, as if we were the closest of friends.

Great. It's you, I thought, slightly annoyed that she hadn't changed one bit. She still looked like a supermodel.

"How are you? You look lovely!" she said and beamed.

"You too, Rebecca. It's so nice to see you again." And as strange as it seemed, I meant it.

"Has he called you yet?" Rebecca asked, her face suddenly turning serious.

"Who?" I asked, startled by her question.

"William. He said he would call you today."

I hadn't heard from William since I canceled our dinner. Why should he call me, and today, of all days? And why was Rebecca looking so serious all of a sudden?

Something squeezed my heart.

"Is something wrong?" I could hear the fear in my own voice.

"It's George," Rebecca said, her eyes welling up with tears. "The cancer is back, and this time they say there is nothing they can do. It has already spread, and they don't think he has much time left."

I felt paralyzed by the shock. I hadn't even known about George's first cancer.

"How is he doing?" I was finally able to ask. "Is he in pain?" My voice cracked, and I felt myself on the verge of tears. Oh, George. Sweet, sweet George.

"William says he is doing good, under the circumstances," she said. "But George has been asking about you lately. He wanted William to let you know. I think he really wants to see you. You know how fond he became of you." She gently touched my shoulder with her hand and looked warmly at me.

"I feel terrible," I said, wiping the tears that had started running down my cheeks with the sleeve of my cardigan. "I didn't know any of this. I haven't been back on the island in three years. I guess I haven't been a very good friend."

"You can't blame yourself for what you didn't know, Maya," Rebecca said sympathetically. "But maybe you could call him?"

"I'll do better than that. I'm actually on my way to Kaua'i and will go and visit him this afternoon." I gratefully accepted the tissue Rebecca handed me.

"What about you?" I asked. "Are you on your way to Kaua'i, too?"

"No, regretfully not," Rebecca said. "We're on our way to celebrate Christmas with my in-laws in Connecticut."

Wait. In-laws? "Your what?"

Just then, Rebecca looked over my shoulder. "There you are! Come and say hi to Maya!"

I held my breath and slowly turned around. A tall, broad-shouldered man with a chiseled jaw and kind eyes reached out his hand.

"Hi. Nice to meet you." He looked like a model, too. Beside him were two small children, dressed in matching coats and hats. They shyly looked up at me.

"Tom and Tara, this is my and Uncle William's friend, Maya."

Tom bowed politely and Tara curtsied. They were adorable.

"Maya, these are my twins, and this is my husband, Hank."

I couldn't speak. My head was spinning, trying to process it all.

"Ray, sweetheart, our flight is boarding," Hank said.

My jaw dropped.

"Ray? Are *you* Ray?"

My confusion must have been splashed all over my face. Rebecca first stared at me, and then she stopped in her tracks.

"Oh no, Maya." Her hand went up to her face. "You didn't think William and I were together, did you?"

I could only nod.

She shook her head.

"But we told you? When we first met? That we were friends from college and business partners?"

"I never caught the business partner thing," I said quietly, feeling incredibly stupid. "Besides, I thought Ray was a man."

"Ah, that silly name," she sighed. "I always call myself Rebecca, but all my friends insist on calling me Ray just because I've always been such a tomboy at heart."

You just don't look like one, I thought. I guess that is what had made me jump to conclusions. I felt ashamed about how I so quickly had judged her by her looks.

"It does explain a lot," she said. "The way you left abruptly that night and the fact that you have avoided William for years."

"Has he said that?" I asked.

"Yes!" She nodded. "So, all these years you had no idea that William had fallen in love with you?" Her voice was vibrating with emotions.

The ground below me started to shake. This was all too much. All I could do was shrug.

"Well, then there are two men on the island who will be happy to see you," she said and took my hand. "Just remember that one of them is very hurt. So, you might have to give him some time."

Rebecca's husband placed his hand gently on her shoulder.

"Ray, we have to go."

"Give him some time, OK?" Rebecca gave me a hug.

I nodded and hugged her back.

"Nice meeting you, Maya." Hank started walking toward the gate holding the twins' hands.

"Merry Christmas," Tom and Tara waved as they walked away.

"Nice meeting you all, and Merry Christmas," I waved back and managed a smile. Rebecca placed her hands on my shoulders and looked me straight in the eyes.

"Give both George and William a big, big hug from me. And don't you dare break William's heart again."

"You have my word."

Rebecca smiled and then turned to catch up with her family.

The next hour I just sat in the chair and stared at the empty air in front of me. I couldn't believe how stupid I had been. When I heard my name announced over the loudspeaker, I was jolted back into the moment and hurried toward my gate.

"Twenty more seconds, and we wouldn't have let you board," the woman at the gate said snippily.

I thanked her, scanned my ticket, and boarded the plane.

"Please fly fast," I whispered to the plane as I sat down in my seat and closed my eyes.

It felt like every second counted, and I couldn't be too late. I just couldn't.

BACK ON THE ISLAND

"Mele Kalikimaka" streamed out of the loudspeakers at Lihue Airport. It was comforting to be welcomed back by Bing Crosby and the Andrews Sisters, singing one of my favorite holiday classics.

As I waited for my luggage, the doors facing the street were open, and the warm, humid Kaua'i air filled the small arrival area. Three hens were walking between the newly arrived visitors, minding their own business, and in the doorway, Hawaiian-shirted taxi drivers waited for their passengers. Everything was just as chill as I remembered it. As the luggage spilled onto the small conveyor belt, I thought about when I had arrived here three years ago, dressed in my corporate suit, on my way to the conference that would change my life.

How different I had been then. How different life had felt.

A familiar voice made its way to me through all the other airport noise.

"Engelbert, Engelbert, look who's here!"

I turned around and saw Betsy, my flight mate from three years ago, dressed in a pink dress covered with yellow flowers. She had a lei around her neck and a big white hat on her head. She opened her arms and walked toward me.

"Come here, Maya doll. Let me give you a big hug!"

A few seconds later I almost drowned in Betsy's big soft arms.

"Imagine seeing you again!" Betsy said with a big happy sigh, while I carefully released myself from her embrace.

"What a nice coincidence," I said. "Funny I didn't see you on the plane."

"Oh no, we weren't on the plane," Betsy said.

I smiled, a little confused.

"We're just here to pick up some friends that are coming for a visit. We live here now. Thanks to you!"

"Oh, that's amazing!"

Betsy smiled and described how she and Engelbert had received an offer to buy 10,000 TechnoGuard shares for one dollar each.

"Apparently someone was looking out for us," Betsy said. Thanks to the money they earned selling the shares, they had managed to buy themselves a condo with an ocean view in Princeville, on the North Shore. "Our biggest dream, to move to Hawaii, has come true, and it's all thanks to you." Betsy had tears in her eyes and reached for some tissues in her purse, and soon she had to hand me one, too.

"I am so happy for you," I said and smiled warmly into Betsy's round, cheerful face.

Engelbert appeared with two large suitcases. He was followed by an elderly couple.

"Well, lookie here," he said with his deep, rumbling voice. "I'm so glad we can thank you in person. Had it not been for you, our lives would have looked very different today."

They were so happy. It warmed my heart to hear how everything had turned out so well for them.

"And by the way, we're not the only ones that are thankful to you. Many of our friends who attended that conference have done the same, and now we are a big happy family out here," Betsy said. She hugged me again and invited me to join them for dinner one evening.

My luggage finally arrived, so I thanked them for the invitation and put the piece of paper Betsy had given me with her phone number in my purse. I waved goodbye and promised to call, then hurried over to the rental company to get my car. I had no time to lose.

• • •

This time, the house I rented was a bit farther down the beach from George's place. I had wanted to rent the house I stayed in last time, but it wasn't available. I was lucky to have found a vacation rental over the holidays on such short notice. Just like last time, the owner had received a last-minute cancellation, and again it felt like it was meant to be.

I had booked the beach house for two weeks, with the possibility of extending my stay. I had no idea how things would play out. Before I left New York, I let Mr. Hatchett know that I might take an extended vacation and that the leadership team would be able to look after things while I was gone. I promised to check my phone now and then should he or anyone else need to get a hold of me.

"Or you might find me back on your veranda again," Mr. Hatchett had said with a smile. "But for God's sake, woman, make sure to have something better to serve me next time!"

We both laughed.

"Done deal, Archie!"

The house was cute, smaller than the one I rented last time, but with the same nice Hawaiian vibe. Once I unpacked, I opened the veranda door and admired the beach and crystal blue ocean below. Oh, how I had missed the Pacific Ocean. I took a deep breath. "Yes, I could get used to this again." The memory of this island had been stored in my heart. It smelled like home.

A large veranda surrounded the house and the big sofa in the corner looked perfect for some serious chill time. But first I had something else to do.

I walked into the bedroom closet and studied my Kaua'i wardrobe. I'd added a few items since my last trip: some new dresses and, of course, a new swimsuit. The Aloha Baby one had turned out to be really good for cleaning the sink and wasn't really wearable anymore. Thank goodness.

After a quick shower, I put on a casual summer dress and a little bit of makeup, brushed my hair, and smiled at myself in the mirror. "You can do this, Maya," I said and walked down to the beach and toward George's house.

The house I was renting was at a crescent-shaped beach, next to the one George lived on, so I couldn't see Bali Ha'i properly until I rounded its corner.

Even though this time I was mentally prepared to see Bali Ha'i, my reaction was just as strong as the first time. Overwhelmed by emotion, I sat down in the sand and stared at the majestic mountain in front of me. Waves of peace and happiness went straight to my heart, and somehow, at that moment, I just *knew* that everything was going to be OK.

I saw George's house in the middle of the beach. "Please give me strength," I whispered and continued walking. When I got closer, I saw a pair of skinny legs sticking out from a familiar beach chair.

"I knew you'd be back," George said before I could even say hello.

His voice was weak, almost a whisper.

"Hello, dear friend," I said and took his hand as I sat down in the sand beside him. His hands were only skin and bone; he seemed to be half the size of when I saw him last time. His eyes, however, were the same: warm, kind—and happy to see me.

"Welcome home, dear Maya." He squeezed my hand.

I stared back at him, fighting back my tears.

"I am sorry it has taken me so long. I've really missed you."

"I've missed you, too," he said.

I smiled at him. Don't cry, Maya. Be strong for George.

George lifted his hand to touch my face.

"Let me look at you," he said. "Just as beautiful as I remember."

He shivered a bit and tried to pull the blanket that was on his lap up toward his chin, but he was only able to move it a few inches.

I stood up and softly tucked the blanket around him and gave his shoulder a loving squeeze before I sat back down on the beach again.

I struggled to keep the tears back. "I was so sad to hear that you were sick, George. I had no idea. I am so sorry."

"Don't be," George whispered and patted my hand. "You're here now. That's all that matters."

We sat and watched the waves for a while, just like we used to.

"I never get tired of this view," George said after a while.

"Me neither," I said with a sigh. "I have missed it so much. I have missed all of this so much." I softly squeezed his hand.

The lulling sound of the waves was suddenly broken by intense banging sounds coming from the house next door, the house I had rented a few years ago.

"It's William," George said softly.

William? At the beach house? I looked over toward the house as George explained.

"When I was first diagnosed with cancer, about a year after you left, William moved back to Kaua'i and bought the house next door."

"Really?"

George nodded and smiled.

"Since he and Rebecca sold their company six months ago, he's been pouring all his energy into remodeling that house. That is, when he's not bothering me." George grinned.

I was glad to see George still had his sense of humor.

"You should go and say hi." George nodded toward the beach house. I had a feeling he knew exactly what was going on.

I looked toward the house where I used to stay. I could see William standing with his back toward us, wearing a pair of jeans covered with paint stains. He was hammering away on the veranda steps.

"OK. Maybe just a quick hello."

George winked and patted my hand as I stood up.

"I'll be back in a bit to check on you."

George smiled and motioned for me to go ahead.

"Yes, sir," I laughed, as I stood up and walked toward the house.

I held my breath as I took in William's back, shoulders, and hair. Just seeing him sent shivers through my body. I looked around. I could hardly recognize the house I had stayed in three years ago.

"Hi, William," I said. It came out as a whisper. I cleared my throat. "Hi, William," I said a bit louder.

He stopped hammering and turned around to look at me. He was just as handsome as I remembered. He still looked younger than his age but had more gray hair than last time, and there was a sadness in his eyes that I hadn't seen before.

"Hi, Maya. Welcome back," he said. I felt a coolness coming from him. "Ray texted me that you were coming. I'm sure Dad is really glad to see you."

I nodded. I didn't blame him for acting cold toward me, but it still hurt. I missed the warm smiles he used to give me. Maybe Rebecca had been wrong about his feelings for me. Or maybe he just didn't feel that way anymore. Standing in front of him, I knew my feelings for him had never gone away. I'd just become really good at suppressing them.

"How is he?" I nodded back at George.

"He's in the last stages of cancer. He's resisted any kind of treatment, except morphine for unbearable pain. The doctor thinks he might only have a few months, or weeks, left."

My eyes welled up. "I'm so sorry, William."

He nodded and gave me a sad smile. "Thank you, Maya."

I looked over at where George sat. "He seems to be in good spirits, though."

"Yes, that man is a wonderful nutcase. He still sings *South Pacific* songs with his scratchy voice and looks forward to meeting Mom again. So, it could be worse. But it's breaking my heart to see him in so much pain, and not being able to do anything to help, except just being here for him." Now William started to tear up.

I wanted to walk over to him and kiss the tears away. Instead I said, "He is so lucky to have you, William. Is there anything I can do to help?"

"Thanks, Maya. I'll let you know," William said as he picked up his hammer, signaling that the chat was over.

"The house looks great, by the way," I said.

He pulled his hand through his hair and smiled. "Thanks. It keeps me busy and helps get my mind off things."

For a second, I saw a glimpse of the William I remembered, the one with the boyish smile, but then that guy disappeared as quickly as he'd come.

"We'll catch up later," he said and turned toward the steps. He resumed hammering as if his life depended on it.

"OK." I tried to ignore the pain of rejection. I walked back to where George was sitting. He had fallen asleep in his chair.

The sun had set, and a deep sadness came over me. I adjusted George's blanket so his feet were covered and then walked back to the rental house. This was not how I had envisioned the evening unfolding.

When I got back to the house, I put on a pair of sweatpants and a cashmere sweater and made myself some tea. I brought the tea and a blanket out to the large sofa on the veranda. While drinking my tea, I watched the ocean and sky slowly turn dark. I was back in paradise, but my heart was heavy. I leaned back on the sofa and looked up at the sky. For a long time I just lay there, watching one star after another light up the dark sky. And when there were millions of them shining down on me, I folded my hands and whispered, "Please show me the way."

And then I fell into a deep sleep.

· · ·

As the morning light brightened the sky, I woke up, still on the sofa, under the open sky. Birds were singing and a rooster was crowing, but the sound of the powerful ocean waves drowned almost every other sound.

I took a deep breath and stretched my arms toward the sky.

"Good morning, Kaua'i," I said out loud and smiled. "Today will be a beautiful day."

I refused to let what had happened yesterday bring me down. I needed to put my personal feelings aside and muster all the positive energy I could for George.

A red cardinal, the little bird with the red Mohawk, landed on the white fence, surrounding the veranda. The way it tilted its head and looked at me, I wondered whether it was my old friend from three years back.

"Hello, little friend. I've missed you," I said.

The little bird flew around and then came back, looking at me as if to say, "C'mon. Get moving."

I laughed and went inside. I took a warm shower and put on a pair of jeans and a T-shirt and started to head over to George's house.

George was in his chair, covered with a thick blanket to protect him from the wind. His white sailor hat was pulled over his ears. For a moment I thought he looked more like a little boy than an old man.

"Good morning, my friend!" I gave him a warm hug and sat down in the chair beside him.

He nodded toward the beach bag between the chairs. "Can I offer you some coffee, my dear?"

"Always," I said and reached down into the bag and picked up the thermos. I recognized the two cups, one of which was Aimee's.

"May I?"

George smiled. "Of course. Aimee would have wanted for you to have it."

I swallowed and felt a lump in my throat as I poured us each a cup of coffee.

I carefully placed his cup in his lap between his hands and watched him lift the cup to his mouth to take a sip.

For a while we sat in silence, drinking our coffee, looking out over the ocean and Bali Ha'i.

"It's so good to be back," I said after a while.

"It's so good to have you here," George said.

Then we were quiet again. Somehow words seemed unnecessary.

William came by to look after his father, but when he saw us sitting there together, he just nodded and went back to the house to work.

After a while, I noticed George was about to fall asleep. I carefully took his cup from his lap, put it down in the sand, and gently put my hand over his. I held it and stroked it gently as I watched him fall asleep.

He seemed so peaceful. In spite of the pain and the inevitable outcome, he seemed to fully embrace and accept what was happening to him. It was almost as if he was already between worlds. I was honored and grateful to keep him company on his journey.

After sitting beside him in silence for a while, I squeezed his hand and stood up. I leaned over, gave him a hug, and I whispered that I would come back later.

"It's Christmas Eve tomorrow," he said. "Will you join us for dinner?"

"I would love to, George," I said and held his hand. "I'll bring dessert."

On my walk back to the house I wondered how William would react to the fact that George had invited me to join them for Christmas Eve. It felt a bit awkward, considering his rather cold welcome back.

Large waves hit the shore. I thought of something Ava once had said in yoga class—that when we change the way we look at things, the things we look at change.

This would be George's last Christmas, and he wanted me to be there. Everything else was irrelevant. Nothing else mattered.

William would just have to deal with it. And so would I.

THE HIKE

The next morning, Lani and I met for coffee and a hike to one of the waterfalls.

"Have you seen William yet?" We were walking side by side up a steep hill, surrounded by a lush, tropical landscape. As I struggled to keep up, I realized that Lani was in much better shape than I was.

"Yes, but he wasn't exactly thrilled to see me." I told her everything, including the meeting with Rebecca at the airport and how I realized how stupid I had been. "But from what I can tell, William doesn't have any feelings for me. He doesn't even seem to want to be my friend anymore."

I leaned forward and motioned to Lani that I needed to stop for a rest. It was exhausting trying to climb and talk at the same time.

Lani stopped and looked at me. She didn't even seem affected by the hard climb. "Listen, Maya. If someone had left you without saying goodbye, not answered your calls, ignored your texts, and canceled your dinner date, how would you have felt?"

I looked down at the ground, embarrassed. "I haven't really thought about it that way," I said, and looked into Lani's smiling eyes.

"William is probably just trying to protect his heart," she said. "Just like you have been doing all this time."

I nodded and remembered what Rebecca had said, about giving him time.

We started walking again.

"What do you think I should do?" A small seed of hope was planted in me.

"I think you should tell him how you feel. Tell him you are sorry. Dare to be vulnerable. I think that is the only way to find out how he really feels about you."

The thought of sharing all of that with William had me near panic. Telling him how I felt was just as scary now as it had been back then.

"You know what I always tell Liat?" Lani asked softly.

I shook my head.

"That when something really scares her, it's probably a sign that she should do it. Because when we are scared to do something, it usually means it's something that's really important to us."

I smiled. Lani was so full of wisdom. Liat was lucky to have her as a mom, and I was lucky to have her as a friend.

Lani took my arm, and together we walked up that last bit of the hill. Suddenly, right in front of us was a breathtakingly beautiful waterfall, rushing down the hillside to the ground far below.

"Yay, we made it!" Lani said and clapped her hands. We sat down on a large rock to drink some water and rest for a bit, while admiring the view in silence.

It felt good to be back together with my dear friend. We had become close over the last three years, as she had stayed with me in New York every time she went to visit her friends in Harlem, and as I had become more involved in her Rainbow Children Foundation. She and Lisa had also become close friends, which I always knew would happen.

On our way back down the hill, Lani asked when I was planning to talk to William and reminded me to not fall into the same trap as last time.

"Someone has to say it first, Maya. And I suggest that someone is you."

I nodded and promised to do it. But the idea still scared the living daylight out of me.

• • •

When we got back to our cars, I thanked Lani for a great hike and drove back to the beach house. The hike had made me sweaty, so I decided to cool off with a swim. I changed into a bathing suit, grabbed a towel, and went down to the beach. The waves were still big, so it wasn't ideal for swimming. Instead, I tried to do some body surfing.

It had been a while. The first wave that came pulled me under and I panicked a little. The second wave didn't work out much better.

Then I remembered William's advice: let go of control, just go with the flow, and have fun. And with that, I was able to surf on the third wave, all the way back to the shore.

Afterward, I dried off and lay down in the warm sand. I took some deep breaths and felt the softness under my body. It felt like the sand embraced me, as if it was welcoming me back. Oh, how I had missed this! The feeling of total relaxation.

As I was lying on my back, the waves put me in a dreamlike state. Suddenly, I heard a voice I would have recognized anywhere.

"Wow, girl. You've come a long way."

I shot up and turned around.

"Josh?"

I looked around, but no one was there.

I stood up and brushed myself off. I needed to go and find Josh. I had to tell him about everything that had happened since the last time we spoke. And I had to thank him. There was so much to thank him for.

A PLACE WITH A VIEW

The waves at Kealia Beach were some of the biggest I'd ever seen. The ocean was packed with surfers, lying on their boards outside the break, waiting for the perfect moment. I watched, fascinated, as one surfer after another caught a giant wave.

I looked around, but I didn't see Josh. I was hoping someone out there might know him, so I sat down on the beach and waited patiently for one of them to take a break.

I had waited for more than an hour by the time a young surfer followed a wave all the way to shore. I watched him jump off his board and walk up to the beach. He was soon followed by another young man. I gave them a few minutes to dry off and drink some water before I got up and walked over to them.

"Wow, guys," I said, sounding a bit cooler than I actually felt. "Nice surfing out there!"

They looked at me, smiling. "Thanks!"

"Hey listen," I said. "I'm looking for a surfer named Josh. You don't happen to know him, do you?"

The boys started laughing.

"There are lots of surfers named Josh," one of them replied.

"Ah, I should have known," I said and laughed with them.

"What does he look like?" one of the boys asked.

"He's in his early thirties and has shoulder-length blond hair and very blue eyes." I felt a bit embarrassed about how little I knew about him.

"Actually," I added, "he doesn't surf anymore. He had a bad accident a few years ago. But he still very much looks like a surfer." I smiled. "And he used to hang out on this beach all the time, watching others surf."

The boys got quiet and looked at each other. I could sense they were uncomfortable.

"Do you know him?" I asked, confused by the looks they gave each other.

The oldest boy scratched his head a bit.

"Do you mean the dude who died?" he asked.

"Died?" I said.

For a moment my heart stopped beating. The waves didn't make a sound.

Then another voice suddenly broke the silence.

"Whoa, what an awesome day, guys!"

A tanned, fit man came running toward us, carrying a surfboard under his arm.

The boys turned around and called for him.

"Dad, she's asking about a dude called Josh, who had an accident a few years ago. Wasn't he the one you told us about? Who died?"

The man put down his surfboard in the sand, looked at me, and nodded solemnly. "Yes." He paused, noticing my face. "You didn't know?"

I shook my head, in shock.

"I'm very sorry. It's been a while since it happened." He came over and shook my hand. "The name's Jez. With a 'z.' Josh and I were surf buddies."

"I'm Maya." I hardly recognized the sound of my own voice.

"He was the finest man I knew," Jez said. "The only comfort I have is that he died happy, among the waves." He pointed toward the big waves that kept crashing toward the shore.

"No one else was there when it happened. He went out on a day most wouldn't even dream of surfing. He was a bit crazy that way." Jez gave a little smile, then looked over at me.

I just stared back at him, unable to speak at first. Then I shook my head.

"But that doesn't make sense," I said, with a sudden glimmer of hope. "The Josh I'm talking about stopped surfing years ago, after a serious accident."

Maybe it was all just a big misunderstanding.

"He used to sit here and watch others surf," I continued. "He had blond hair down to his shoulders and very blue eyes."

"And an orange butterfly tattoo?" Jez asked and looked sympathetically at me.

I nodded slowly.

"Sorry, Maya, that's him."

A big wave crashed toward the shore. It looked like it was moving in slow motion.

"Josh would rather have died than stopped surfing," Jez said after a while. "Surfing was his entire life. It was like he and the ocean were having a passionate love affair. Regretfully, it turned out to be a lethal one."

I felt a deep ache in my heart, and fought the urge to cry in front of Jez and the boys. Jez nodded toward somewhere behind us.

"He's resting in the cemetary right across the street, if you want to pay him a visit."

I followed his gaze.

"When you think about it, it's the perfect resting place for someone who loved the ocean as much as he did." Jez smiled gently. "Now he can watch the waves and see us surfing from up there all day."

I nodded and tried to smile. "I think I'll walk over there now," I said. "Thank you for letting me know."

"I'm sorry you had to find out this way," Jez said as I waved him and the boys goodbye.

I took a deep breath and headed across the street. The slope, leading up to the cemetary, was covered with wildflowers. I decided to pick a few. I didn't want to come empty handed to Josh.

When I entered the quaint and serene cemetary, with colorful flowers next to each headstone, my heart was heavy.

I came too late for you, Josh.

Maybe I'd come too late for everything. I wiped my tears, as I walked around, looking for his headstone.

The newest ones were in the front, but Josh's name was not on any of them. I hadn't asked Jez *when* Josh had died, but after I'd looked at all the headstones of people buried in the last three years, I realized that Josh wasn't there.

Again, I felt a small glimmer of hope.

Then, suddenly, an orange butterfly came flying toward me. I watched as it danced around me before it flew toward the back of the cemetary and landed on something that looked like a plank sticking up from the ground.

When I got closer, I saw that the plank was in the shape of a surf-board. My heart started beating faster. Someone had painted "Josh the Surfer" on it, and below his name it read, "At One with the Sea."

I sat down beside it and carefully touched the small board. "Josh, dearest Josh. I am so sorry. I came too late," I whispered, tears streaming down my cheeks.

The grave was a bit unkempt, so I started removing the weeds that were hiding the lower part of the board. And that is when I saw the rest of the epitaph: "Born August 1, 1989. Died October 3, 2016."

I froze. I met Josh in October of 2017. How was that possible?

I put the flowers on the ground in front of the small surfboard and sat there for a while. My mind was spinning. I tried to make sense of it, but I couldn't.

Maybe someone had gotten the year wrong?

Yet somehow, deep inside, I knew that wasn't the case.

The butterfly was still sitting on the surfboard. I felt as if it was watching me.

I thought about Josh's warm smile, blue eyes, and infinite wisdom.

"It's all about how we choose to see life," he had said. "It can be serious and rationalized, or it can be playful and full of miracles. And whatever we choose to believe ends up becoming our reality."

I took a deep breath and was suddenly overwhelmed with a deep knowing in my heart. The kind that could not be explained but only felt.

I gazed over the ocean, then back at the small surfboard and stroked it softly with the tip of my finger.

"I choose to believe in miracles," I whispered. "I choose the beautiful unexplainable."

I smiled at the butterfly that circled over my head, then looked back over the ocean.

"Nice view," I said.

"You bet," Josh replied.

I smiled. Tears were rolling down my cheeks as I watched the butterfly slowly dance its way out of the cemetary.

"Thank you, Josh," I whispered. "You were there when I needed you. I will never forget you."

I sat by his grave for a little while longer, then got back up on my feet and slowly walked back toward my car.

On my way, I passed by an elderly woman, sitting on a bench, facing the ocean. With her eyes closed, she lifted her face toward the gentle ocean breeze.

"Do you feel it?" she asked as I passed her.

I stopped and looked at her.

She opened her eyes and smiled warmly at me. "It's the winds of change," she said. "I think great things are about to happen."

I smiled back at her. "I think they've already started," I replied, waved goodbye to her, and left the cemetary.

When I arrived at my car, it felt as if the orange butterfly was waiting for me on the windshield. Then, it lifted gently and danced around me a couple of times before it slowly flew toward the beach and out over the ocean.

I stood still and watched it until it eventually disappeared.

CHRISTMAS EVE

I had stopped in Hanalei on my way home from Kealia Beach to do some grocery shopping and buy ingredients for the dessert I was bringing to the Christmas dinner. I'd decided to make rice pudding with cherry sauce, the way my mom used to make it. The dessert was one of the few memories I had from my childhood Christmases. Mom once told me that *her* grandma, her dad's mom, first had taught her how to make it. Apparently it was a Scandinavian Christmas tradition.

Hanalei was decorated with Christmas lights and a Santa here and there, but nothing over-the-top. Here, even Christmas was chill.

On my drive home, I started to get a little nervous about the dinner again. I hoped it wouldn't be too awkward between William and me. I *would* speak to him at some point, but I didn't think tonight was the night. Tonight was George's night.

Back at the beach house, I put the groceries away, Googled "Scandinavian rice pudding," and began making the dessert. Thank you, internet.

While the dessert was cooling, I went to the bathroom to get ready. I put on a pretty red dress, freshened up my face, and had a little self-talk session with the mirror. "You can do this, Maya. There's nothing to be afraid of. You've got this."

I took a deep breath and let the air out, nodded, and smiled at my own reflection.

Back in the kitchen, I packed up the rice pudding and sauce and placed them in a basket, along with a bottle of wine and a few Christmas presents I'd picked up on the way home.

I had bought William a tool belt, as I had noticed he hadn't been wearing one. George was getting a new blanket, Navy style, to match his favorite T-shirt and hat.

Satisfied with the basket, I headed down the beach toward George's house. I arrived a bit early, thinking George and I could sit and chat and look at the ocean together, but he was fast asleep in his chair when I arrived. I sat down carefully in the sand, not wanting to disturb him. Not that it would have mattered much, as William was hammering away on the house next door.

I watched George's peaceful face. He was sleeping heavily, but now and then, a little smile came over his face, like he was dreaming about something nice. Maybe he was already on his way toward that place he had talked about—the place that looked like this beach, times ten, and with Aimee in it.

The hammering stopped, and I turned my head and looked over at William's house.

I took a deep breath and slowly stood up. My heart started beating quickly in my chest as I decided that this was the time.

I walked slowly—barefoot—over the lawn that I had walked so many times before. The hammock was still there, but it didn't look like someone had used it for a long time. It was dirty and filled with dead leaves. The house looked beautiful, though. William had put in larger windows and expanded the veranda. Everything looked newer and more modern, but it still had that Hawaiian charm.

When I approached the house, William was still working on the steps. I just stood there and looked at him, hoping he would notice me.

When he finally did, he looked startled and dropped the hammer on the ground. Then he stood up, ran his fingers through his hair, and brushed off some dust from his T-shirt.

"Hi, Maya," he said. Less cool today, but still tentative.

"William, can I speak with you about something?"

My voice was trembling and my heart pounded heavily in my chest. He nodded but stood still as he looked at me.

"I want to apologize for the way I behaved when I left the island last time. I left without saying goodbye, and later I didn't always return your calls or texts. I even canceled our dinner in New York, not because I didn't want to go, but because I didn't think I could handle seeing you and Rebecca together again, because of the feelings I had for you."

William looked confused by the last sentence. I swallowed and continued.

"The days I got to spend with you those three years ago were the best days of my life. I didn't know men like you even existed. But I got scared and convinced myself that we should just be friends."

I took a deep breath. It was now or never.

"But then I realized I had fallen for you, and that I had to stop being scared. When I went to tell you how I felt, Rebecca was there, and I thought she was your girlfriend, and I just freaked out and ran away. All the way back to New York. And never looked back. Or at least, I tried not to."

I paused and looked down at the grass, feeling nervous, vulnerable, and embarrassed. When I looked up, William had a bewildered look on his face.

I took a deep breath and added, "I am so sorry, William. I wish I had handled everything better. I just wanted you to know that."

I was just about to turn around and walk away, when he finally spoke. "But I don't get it. I told you that Rebecca and I were friends and business partners."

"Yes, I know that now, but at the time I didn't hear it. I was too shocked, confused, and embarrassed to really listen to anything. And

George had told me you were taking a break from some girl in San Francisco, so I just assumed that was Rebecca and that you were back together again."

"Oh, I see," William nodded. His boyish smile came back in glimpses.

"Well, no, Rebecca was never my girlfriend. And the girlfriend Dad told you about was Ellen. We decided to take a break six months before I met you, but we had an agreement that before we got involved with anyone else, we would tell each other and permanently end things between us."

He sat down in the grass now. I walked slowly over to him and sat down beside him, waiting for him to continue.

"Do you remember the night after our island tour?"

I nodded and looked down. I remembered it all too well.

"I wanted to tell you I would be going to San Francisco to meet with Ellen and tell her I had fallen in love with someone. With you."

Our eyes met. I held my breath and fought to keep my tears back.

"I wanted to respect Ellen and our agreement. But I still wanted you to know that I thought you were the most adorable, interesting, intelligent, fun, and beautiful woman I had ever met."

I wasn't able to keep my tears back anymore.

"But then you ran out of the car and called me 'the best friend a girl could have,' so I thought you just didn't feel the same way about me. But I still loved being around you, so I tried to push away my feelings and just be your friend."

I put my face in my hands. How could I have been so blind? Why had I been so afraid?

When I removed my hands from my face again, William looked at me with a soft smile before he continued.

"The night when you met Rebecca, I had just returned from San Francisco where Ellen and I had said our proper goodbyes. Rebecca came with me. She and Hank were looking to buy a house on the island, and I was going to show her around.

"After you came by our house that night, I told Rebecca how I felt about you, and she told me to stop being a coward and tell you how I really felt."

The memories kept flashing through my mind. How different the story I had been telling myself was from the one William now shared.

"The next day, when I'd finally mustered enough courage to tell you, Dad told me you had left. I tried calling and even went after you to the airport, but your flight had just taken off when I got there."

This was almost too painful to hear.

"And well, after that, you made it pretty clear that you wanted nothing more to do with me, so after a while I just gave up and tried to forget about you."

I felt ashamed for all the pain and confusion I had caused William.

"So that dinner in New York, with Rebecca?" I asked, not sure what I was asking about really.

"Yes, that was silly of me, I guess. I wanted to meet you one more time to see if I had a chance with you. But I freaked out a few hours earlier, so I asked if Rebecca could come along, as moral support."

I looked up at him. He looked just as embarrassed as I did.

"I'm so sorry I canceled our dinner. I really wish I had gone."

"Now, I can understand why you did," William said and looked down at his hands. "But at the time I was pretty devastated and decided I needed to cut you out of my life, because it simply hurt too much to keep hoping for something that seemed like a lost cause."

We were sitting beside each other in the grass, both of us a bit lost and confused. We had both misunderstood the situation and been too afraid to investigate it any further. Now, when we knew all the facts, neither one of us seemed to know what to make out of it.

I looked over at William. I wanted to take his hand and run my fingers through his messy hair and kiss him, but something was holding me back. There was still a distance between us, and when he spoke next, I understood why.

"I know you didn't mean to hurt me, Maya, but my heart was broken. And it's taken a long time to heal. I'm finally in a good place now, and Dad really needs me. So, maybe it's best that we go back to being friends."

"Of course," I said. I was a little devastated, but I also understood where he was coming from. Most of all, I wanted William back in my life. If he only wanted to be friends, I could live with that. It was better than nothing.

William smiled as he stood up and dusted himself off. "Well then, let's go and have ourselves a proper Christmas Eve."

I stood up. It was good to see William smile again. But I saw the sadness return when he said, "It's Dad's last Christmas. Let's make it a beautiful one."

I took his hand and squeezed it, and he held on to it as we walked over the lawn toward his father. George was awake, and when he saw us walking hand in hand, I thought I could see a tear glimmer in the corner of his eye.

"Hey, old man, you ready for a party?" William asked as he helped his father stand up.

"You bet," George replied. I watched as William helped George into the house, carefully sat him down in his favorite chair, and lovingly put the blanket around his thin body.

"I'm really glad it is you and not Agatha, the human robot, who is looking after me," George joked.

"Well, I did try to tempt her with a first-class ticket to Kaua'i and a life under the sun, but she preferred to stay and play bridge with her friends at the retirement home. So, old man, I'm afraid you're stuck with me."

George chuckled as his son lovingly patted his back. But when William turned his face away, I saw him drying a tear with the back of his hand.

That night with George and William turned out to be the most wonderful Christmas Eve of my life. William had made a delicious "Christmas pasta," and we shared the bottle of wine I brought. George hardly touched his food, though, and only had a few sips of wine.

When I asked him why he wasn't eating much, he said, "Nothing really tastes good anymore, but I use my memory of it to try and enjoy it anyway. But it's not important. The company is what I enjoy the most."

It was heartbreaking to see him so thin, but he still had that strong light in his eyes. I knew he didn't have long before he would pass over and reunite with his beloved Aimee. And I knew I would be there, right by his side, to the very end.

In spite of the cloud hanging over our heads, it was wonderful to spend the night laughing and catching up. George and William enjoyed hearing about all the changes I'd made at TechnoGuard and laughed when I told them about how I had introduced the aloha spirit to the company.

"Inspired by Aimee," I said, and smiled warmly at the two men.

George's eyes welled up as he reached his thin hand toward me. I pulled my chair closer and took his hand in mine.

I noticed William's eyes water, too, before he put on a cheerful smile. "And business woman of the year," he whistled. "When I saw you on the cover of *Forbes* magazine, I was so happy and proud of you."

"Yes," George said and beamed, "and then he bought ten copies and spread them all over the house, just to make sure I didn't miss it."

We all laughed.

"Well, it all started here," I said and looked around before my eyes landed on William. "But I have to admit that, at first, your talk about culture, inspired employees, and fun at work sounded like a crazy dream to me."

"And then you just went out and made it happen—times ten," William grinned. "Well done you!" He lifted his glass toward me.

George nodded and raised his glass too. "I remember once hearing Walt Disney say, 'If you can dream it, you can do it.'"

Then he looked both William and me deeply in the eyes. "Here's to having the courage to follow *all* of your dreams!"

"Cheers!" We clinked our glasses, and William and I looked first at George and then at each other and smiled.

After we finished the rice pudding, which actually turned out to be quite tasty, we just sat there, sipping our wine and looking out at the dark ocean. Only the sound of the waves broke the silence. When I looked back at my two favorite men in the whole world, I felt like the luckiest woman alive.

After a while, George said he was tired and should get ready for bed.

"Maya, would you mind coming in and giving me a goodnight kiss after William helps me change into my pajamas?" George asked when William helped his father up.

"You incurable flirt," William teased as he walked his dad to his room.

I smiled and said, "Of course, George. I'll be there when you're ready."

After I had cleared the table, I went back out on the veranda, sat down on the couch, and looked up at the starry sky. "Merry Christmas, up there," I whispered.

I wondered if Grandma, Grandpa, Mom, Aimee—and Josh— could hear me.

Soon after, William came out and placed a warm hand on my shoulder. "Dad would like his goodnight kiss now," he said and gently squeezed my hand as I passed by him.

When I walked into George's room, he'd already fallen asleep.

He woke up when I sat down and carefully took his hand in mine. His hand felt just like Mom's hand had felt toward the end. Frail. Like a little bird. And when he looked at me, even his eyes reminded me of Mom's.

Instead of their lights slowly fading away, it was as if their inner lights were turned on. Shining brighter than ever.

"How are you feeling, George?" I asked, stroking his hand softly.

"Happy, tired, and excited," he said.

I smiled lovingly down at him.

"Happy you and William are here, tired of being sick, and excited to soon be with my Aimee."

I leaned over and gave him a hug.

"I love you, George," I said.

"I love you, too, Maya."

We held hands and looked at each other, with tears in our eyes.

"Maya."

"Yes, George?"

"Do you remember the first time we spoke, and I told you that I wondered why God still kept me on earth? That I believed I still had a purpose to fulfill?"

"Yes, George. I remember."

"I know what it is now," he whispered.

I tilted my head, curious.

"It was you, Maya. You were my unfilled purpose."

My eyes welled up.

"And now you are back, and I can go in peace."

I couldn't hold back the tears, but I was still able to smile as they raced down my cheeks.

"William loves you very much, Maya. But he is a sensitive soul. You have to give him some time," he said, his voice growing weak.

I nodded and kissed his hand as I sat down beside him on the bed.

"I have all the time in the world. I will wait for him. I promise."

George smiled, and I could tell he was drifting off to sleep.

William entered the room and sat down on the other side of George's bed. We each held one of George's hands and looked down at him. His eyes were closed. It looked like he had fallen asleep, but then he suddenly whispered, "Will you sing for me, William?"

"Of course I will, Dad."

William started singing "Some Enchanted Evening" with a soft voice. Now and then his voice cracked, as if he was starting to cry. But he'd take a deep breath and keep on.

His voice was deep and warm, and I could see George slowly drift away, still smiling at the sound of his son's voice.

I closed my eyes as tears kept running down my cheeks, and when I opened them again, I saw that William was looking directly at me. My eyes met his, and while he finished the last line of the song: *"Once you have found her, never let her go,"* we were both crying, still looking into each other's eyes.

George had fallen into a deep sleep and we walked quietly out of the room and went down to the beach.

As we sat down on the soft sand, William took my hand and kissed it.

"I was wondering about something," he said and looked into my eyes. "Would it be OK with you if we kind of speed through that 'just friends' phase and move onto the next?"

I didn't need to answer. My eyes said it all.

And as I leaned over to kiss William for the very first time, it felt like two butterflies were dancing around us, only to ascend and disappear into the heavens.

BON VOYAGE, GEORGE

T he same people who had attended Aimee's ten-year remembrance ceremony three years earlier gathered around the bonfire to bid farewell to George.

George's beach chair was in its usual place, facing the ocean. A small, silver urn had been placed on its seat.

Everyone was talking and enjoying their food and drinks. The atmosphere was lighthearted and warm, just like George would have wanted.

The tall minister with the ponytail said a prayer in Hawaiian, and when he finished, everyone walked slowly down to the shore, where an outrigger canoe, decorated with leis in every color of the rainbow, was waiting.

Two young Hawaiian men, shirtless and with leis around their necks, gracefully launched the canoe in the water and everyone watched as William carefully climbed into it, holding the urn in his hands.

Soft ukulele music was playing in the background.

Each guest took their turn placing a lei in the boat together with a personal greeting. "Safe travels, old friend," "Ka Huaka'i Maika'i, George," "Bon Voyage, George."

When it was my turn, I softly placed my lei down and whispered,

"Thank you for everything, my dear, dear friend." William's eyes met mine and for a moment it felt as if George was there, too.

There was so much love.

When everyone had said their goodbyes, the two young men slowly paddled the canoe out to sea. William was sitting in the middle of them, cradling the urn with his father's ashes in his arms.

When the boat was far enough out, the men stopped paddling.

We all stood in silence as we watched William lean over the edge of the canoe and gently pour George's ashes into the Pacific Ocean.

After a few minutes of silence, the canoe slowly made its way back to the shore, and the ukulele player started playing "Some Enchanted Evening."

My eyes welled up as I listened to the music. I turned my head toward Bali Ha'i and whispered a silent thank you. Thank you for calling for me, thank you for leading me here.

My eyesight was a bit blurry from all the tears, but farther down on the beach I could swear I saw a young couple dancing.

The man was wearing an old-fashioned sailor's uniform, the woman's white dress was ripped and dirty, but even from a distance, I could see their happy smiles and how they simply couldn't keep their eyes off each other.

FLYING

There is freedom waiting for you,
On the breezes of the sky.

ERIN HANSON

A NEW DAY

I woke up to the happy song from the red-crested cardinal, my bird friend, who reminded me that a new day had begun.

I put on my bikini and went for my morning swim. I was all alone on the beach, which I usually was at this time of the day. I sank my body down in the crystal blue water and swam with long strokes toward beautiful Mount Makana, our beloved Bali Ha'i.

"Good morning, gorgeous." I smiled at her, while floating on my back, letting the underwater streams carry me farther down the beach. After a quick walk back up the beach, I returned to the house. Covered only in a towel, I put the coffee on the stove and stood there, watching it percolate, barefoot on the wooden floor, inhaling the scent of coffee mixed with ocean air, welcoming the new day.

After a quick shower, I put on a light summer dress and carefully kissed my two sleepyheads—the smaller, curly head resting on the arm of the bigger one. They didn't move, so I snuck out of the house, got into the Jeep, and drove into Hanalei for my morning meeting with Lani.

Over acai bowls from the food truck parked right outside of town we went through the checklist together.

"I can't believe this is actually happening!" I said to Lani, shaking my head. "If someone had told me we'd be doing this only two years ago, I would've said they were out of their minds."

Lani grinned. "Yes, and had we not been a bit out of our minds, I don't think we would have managed to pull this off."

"You're so right." I lifted my coffee to toast. "Here's to being out of our minds." We laughed and continued eating our breakfast as we went through all the things we needed to do before the grand opening the next day.

After breakfast, we hopped in our cars and started driving down the road. I smiled to myself; I couldn't believe this was my life now.

After about twenty minutes south on the main road, I turned onto a small side street that led up to a field. Lani was right behind me. After we parked, we just stood outside our cars and stared at the building in front of us.

"Kaua'i Chill, Connect, Create Retreat," the large sign over the entrance said.

The building was floating into the landscape, as if nature itself had designed it, with its natural materials and soft edges. Large floor-to-ceiling windows opened up toward the ocean on one side and showcased the waterfall-covered mountains on the other. It was perfect. It looked like something out of a dream.

I pinched my arm and laughed. "I'm not dreaming this, am I?"

"If you can dream it, you can do it. Isn't that what George said?" Lani smiled.

I nodded and swallowed. I missed him so much. I wish he had been here to see this. But then again, he probably was.

Lani and I looked at each other, took a deep breath, and held hands as we walked into the main building. The large room was filled with air and light, and the windows that pointed toward the ocean and the mountains gave the feeling that we were in nature, even when we were inside.

The way it all happened was like a dream itself. It was only a week after George had passed. William and I had been out driving, heading to one of the waterfalls, when I noticed the field. It was big, green, and lush, perfectly located between the ocean and the mountains. There were flowers everywhere and more butterflies than I'd seen in my entire life. I had a vision, and suddenly I knew what I wanted to do. It was all part of the life that was waiting for me.

The land had been for sale for quite some time. I made an offer and promised the seller that I would honor the land and the nature surrounding it. Soon after, I met with a local architect to start drawing the center, and a week later I went back to New York to wrap things up at TechnoGuard and sell my apartment.

I put most of my savings and the money I got from the sale of my apartment into the project and figured I would still be able to finance our activities for the first couple of years. I knew it took some time to build a new business.

I had agreed with Mr. Hatchett that I would hold on to my TechnoGuard shares, to not start any rumors or disrupt the great momentum of the company. I'd said yes to join the board for a two-year period and to become the next CEO's "Lucy" for her first year. *Our* lunches, however, would have to be over videoconference. I was so grateful for the technology that gave me the freedom to work from where I wanted: from my place in paradise.

As soon as I'd signed the contract for the land, I invited Lani to become my business partner at the retreat. I hadn't even finished asking before she shouted, "Yes!"

Not everyone had been as enthusiastic as Lani, though.

Dad was convinced that I'd gone insane. Again.

"Quitting your job as a CEO? Selling your apartment? Starting a retreat in Kaua'i?"

"Yes."

"What if you fail?" he asked.

"What if I don't?" I replied.

This was what I wanted to do. What other people, including my dad, thought about it didn't matter to me.

This was my dream, this was my life, and I was going to live it!

The retreat would be a place where leaders from all around the world could come to meet, learn, be inspired, discuss around the bonfire, and wake up to a new way of being and leading.

I knew that the leaders who came here would be transformed by the time they left. We would be arranging meetings and workshops at the retreat, and in addition, I knew the island would be working her magic on them. Just as she had done on me.

Lani and I had decided to open the retreat to locals as well. On weekends the place would serve as a community center, where people from all walks of life could meet. It was our way of giving back to the island and its people.

Inside the main building, there were lounge areas, a library, a juice bar, and several community tables, where people could sit and work or read or meet. The right wall was covered with a giant rainbow painted by the Rainbow Children themselves. And the left wall was decorated with butterflies. A particularly beautiful orange butterfly stood out a bit from the rest, and below it one could read:

"I do not know whether I was then a man dreaming I was a butterfly, or whether I am now a butterfly, dreaming I am a man."
—*Zhuang Zhou & Josh the Surfer*

At the opposite side of the entrance, between two large windows showcasing the green mountains, a glass door led out to a lush field with four smaller buildings, all constructed in the same style and material as the main one. These were the Chill, Connect, and Create houses. And then we had the Cinema, which had been my personal project.

While Lani went over to inspect the bedrooms in the Chill building, I took a deep breath and walked into the cinema.

Inside, there were four rows of big, comfortable red velvet chairs, and in between them small tables with tiny, old-fashioned lamps and—of course—a popcorn machine in the corner. It was a smaller version of my childhood cinema. Mom and Giorgio were there, too. The photo showed Mom wearing her 1950s dress, smiling with red lips, and Giorgio looking back at her with admiration.

I had sent Dad a letter, telling him about our project.

A week later he wrote back and included the photo, saying he might come and visit me on Kaua'i one day.

"I know how much those visits to the cinema meant to the two of you," he wrote. I was surprised. Maybe he'd understood more than I'd given him credit for all these years.

The walls in the cinema were covered with behind-the-scenes pictures and official movie posters from *South Pacific*. George had told me about the boxes filled with old photos and posters he had saved all these years, and how he would have loved to make an exhibition of them one day. I had done more than that. Now the entire cinema was a tribute to one of the most wonderful movies ever made as well as a legacy to George and Aimee's magical love story.

My favorite picture was the one of George and Aimee, taken right after he proposed to her on the beach. They both looked so incredibly happy. I thought this is probably what they still looked like, wherever they were.

I took another look around the room before I closed the door behind me and walked back to the main building. Once there, I heaved a sigh of relief.

What an incredible feeling it was, seeing my dream come to life, my visions being manifested, and knowing we were creating something that would bring happiness and joy into so many people's lives.

Lani was on the couch with her laptop, her feet propped up on the table, drinking a kombucha. What a wonderfully chill colleague I've got, I thought as I joined her.

"Look here," Lani said.

She was going through the list of executives who would arrive in a few days.

"There's an Archibald Hatchett in the group. Is that who I think it is?"

I grinned. I'd known it was a long shot, but I'd still sent him the invitation a few months ago and had been surprised when he'd signed up.

If Mr. Hatchett was open to the experiences of chill, connect, and create, he might inspire other "dinosaurs" to do the same, which gave me a lot of hope for the future.

Ruth had also accepted my invitation and would be arriving on the same plane as Mr. Hatchett. Even Lucy had said she would come, but only after I promised that we would be serving wine for both lunch and dinner.

And Lisa. My dear Lisa. She had visited a few months ago, and after just one day on the island she blurted out, "OK. This is home. I'm staying."

A week later she went back to New York to rent out her apartment and to convince Antonio to join her. I wasn't worried. I knew he would follow her anywhere. He was now looking at opening his own pizza place in Hanalei. I couldn't wait for easy access to those delicious pizzas again—and the generous glasses of wine!

Lisa would teach yoga classes and help out with the daily chores at the retreat. And since Ava was moving back to California, Lisa was offered the opportunity to take over the sunset beach yoga classes as well. Everything was falling into place so perfectly.

I couldn't wait to see Mr. Hatchett doing downward dog in the sand, learning about perspectives and illusions, and discussing life and the future of business around the bonfire on the beach.

A corporate spring was definitely coming.

It was starting to get dark when Lani and I walked slowly, arm in arm, toward our cars.

"I met Noah's teacher yesterday," Lani said. "She told me how well things are going with him and how amazed she is at how well he has handled everything. She said he looks calmer and happier and that he has even started speaking up in class."

"I know. I was so happy to hear that. He's such a brave little boy. I am so proud of him."

"Me too," Lani nodded. "So, have you told him yet?"

I shook my head and smiled. "We got the papers in the mail yesterday. We are telling him tonight."

Lani had tears in her eyes. "He will be so happy. He loves you guys so much."

"And we love him more than I ever thought possible. Thank you for bringing him to us that night. From the moment he walked in our door, I knew I wanted him to stay forever."

I gave Lani a big hug. We both cried a little. Happy tears.

"What are you hanging around here for?" Lani laughed through her tears. "Go home to those adorable boys of yours and give them both a hug for me."

I smiled and blew her a kiss before I jumped in my car and drove home.

I parked the Jeep on the lawn behind our house, the same place I had parked the first time I came to the North Shore five years ago. William and little Noah were in the kitchen with their backs toward me, stirring something on the stove. Noah was looking up at William as they talked and laughed.

Soft music was playing in the background. The large French doors facing the ocean were wide open. It was the most beautiful thing, the sound of the waves mixed with the music and the soft voices of the two loves of my life.

The house was almost unrecognizable from the first time I stayed there, but I had insisted that we keep the wooden floors, the stove, and the pineapple-shaped lamps.

After George's passing, William had sold George's house to Ray and Hank, who used it as their vacation home. Noah had already become best friends with Tom and Tara and couldn't wait for them to come back.

"Hey, what's for dinner, guys?" I said, and they both turned around and ran toward me. The next thing I knew, I was covered in kisses.

After dinner, we went down to the beach, as we did every night, to wave goodnight to all our friends among the stars.

Noah told his mom about his day and said that he missed her, but that she needn't worry, because he was safe and loved being here with us.

The three of us were lying on a blanket on the beach. My head was resting on William's arm, Noah was tucked in between us, and we were all holding hands.

A shooting star suddenly lit up the sky, and I whispered to Noah, "Make a wish. Make a wish."

I silently wished him happiness, freedom, and a beautiful life beyond his wildest dreams.

"I wish I could fly like a butterfly!" Noah exclaimed.

I squeezed his little hand. "Oh, but you can, my darling."

"How?" he asked.

I smiled in the dark and turned my head toward him.

"All you need to do is to spread your wings," I whispered in his ear.

"But how?" he asked and turned his little head toward me.

"Like this!" I said and jumped up on my feet and started running around on the beach, my arms out, shouting, "I'm a butterfly! I'm a butterfly!"

Soon Noah and William joined me.

And as we danced and jumped around in the sand, with the millions of shining stars smiling down on us, we lifted our little butterfly boy high up in the air, so he could feel what it was like, to be free to fly.

THANK YOU

W riting this book has been such an inspired, emotional, challenging, but most of all joyful experience. If you have enjoyed reading it nearly half as much as I have enjoyed writing it, my hopes and dreams for this book have already come true. Thank you, dear reader, for reading.

The book has taken some time to write, and like many other writers, I have struggled with self-doubt, procrastination, and lack of focus from time to time. I can't emphasize enough how much other people's confidence in me and my book idea has impacted the final outcome. In fact, without that support, I doubt there would have been a book for me to give thanks for.

Thank you for your support, "loving criticism", and unwavering belief in me, Gunn Haglund, Kathrine Aspaas, Liz Dadanian, Patricia Stang Auseth, Tove M. Helgaker, Trude H. Shelby, and my brother, Gisle Rød. You have all been invaluable to me in this process, and you are all invaluable to me in my life.

Thank you Anita Krohn Traaseth, Brad Keimach, Christina Tracy, Dawn Brown, El Herrington, Erika Ilves, Estere Mezzetti, Jason Angelus, Maria Tibblin, Mikael Hansson, Per H. Kogstad, Sarah Stennett, Sigridur Hannesdottir, Sinisha Buzunovic, Snorre Kjesbu, and Jacquie Lee who in ways you may know, or not even be aware of, have inspired the book.

Thank you to my Corporate Spring team and everyone else who tirelessly works to make the corporate world a better place, and for those who provide research and studies that show the benefits of it.

A special big thanks to Adam Grant, who not only inspires through his work but also through his incredible generosity of spirit.

I also want to send thanks to everyone who, in one way or another, has inspired the stories and the characters in this book. While it certainly is fiction, it is no secret that it has been inspired by many true events and people. However, any similarities with real-life people or situations (except from a few, who have given me their permission) are purely coincidental. Promise.

Thank you to the Greenleaf Publishing team for helping me turn my first draft into a real book; Daniel Sandoval for finding and believing in me; Diana Ceres, April Murphy, Jessica Choi, and Elizabeth Brown for their excellent editing; Daniel Pederson for skillfully managing the project; and Neil Gonzales for the awesome cover art.

Thank you Kaua'i, Bali Ha'i, and the creators of *South Pacific* for inspiring the story, and thank you, Mom and Dad, for cheering me on from your place among the stars. Thank you for all the butterflies too.

Finally, my deepest gratitude goes to my most favorite person in the whole wide world—my source of unconditional love and inspiration, my joy, my light, my sparring partner, and biggest supporter. The wise, brave, and beautiful soul who is traveling on this journey with me and who already is spreading her own wings, getting ready to fly.

My daughter, my best friend, my own Butterfly Girl.

Matilde, this book is for you.

ABOUT THE AUTHOR

As a young girl growing up in Norway, Annicken R. Day fell in love with old Hollywood movies, especially the musical *South Pacific* from 1958. When she visited the Hawaiian island of Kaua'i thirty years later, she learned by coincidence that South Pacific had been filmed there and that the mystical island of Bali Ha'i indeed existed. That was when the idea for the story about Maya Williams first came to her, a story inspired by Annicken's own life and experiences, and by people—and butterflies—she has met on her journey.

After fifteen years as a leader and executive in the IT industry, Annicken jumped off the corporate treadmill in 2012 to start her own company, Corporate Spring, with a mission to make the corporate world a happier place. Since then she and her team have helped and trained thousands of leaders around the world on how to build thriving corporate cultures, high performing teams, and successful businesses.

Annicken is the founder and CEO of Corporate Spring, co-author of the book *Creative Superpowers*, public speaker, executive advisor, and a passionate maverick for new ways of thinking, working, and leading in the new world of work.

Annicken spends the majority of her time between Oslo, London, and Los Angeles, where also her singer-songwriter daughter Matilde Redbridge lives.

Fly, Butterfly is Annicken R. Day's first novel.

Learn more about the author at www.annickenday.com.

Printed in Great
Britain
by Amazon

32250768R00203